Peng

WOMAN IN

Born in the industrial Midlands of England in 1923, Elizabeth Jolley was brought up in a German-speaking household – her father having met her mother, the daughter of an Austrian general, when engaged on famine relief in Vienna in 1919. She was educated at home and at a Quaker boarding school. She later trained as an SRN and nursed during the Second World War.

In 1959 she moved to Western Australia with her husband and three children. She worked in a variety of jobs, as a nurse, a door-to-door salesperson and as a flying domestic among other things, and now cultivates a small orchard and a goose farm. She conducts writing workshops in prisons and community centres and is a part-time lecturer at Fremantle Arts Centre and the Curtin University of Technology in Perth.

Elizabeth Jolley is the author of two other collections of short stories, *Five Acre Virgin* and *The Travelling Entertainer*, which have also been published together in one volume entitled *Stories* (1984). Her novels include *Mr Scobie's Riddle*, *The Newspaper of Claremont Street*, *Miss Peabody's Inheritance*, *Foxbaby*, *The Well* and *Milk and Honey*, all published in Penguin. Her work has been acclaimed in America as well as Australia and the UK, and the *Washington Post* called her style 'effortlessly comic' and her characters 'battily original'. The *Daily Telegraph* has written, 'Elizabeth Jolley's novels contain more of Australia than is to be found in many of those that simply echo its size' while Patricia Craig, writing in *The Times Literary Supplement*, said, 'Elizabeth Jolley's fiction is notable for the sharpness with which its incidents are envisaged and assembled . . . She knows how to make things hum.' Susan Hill has called Elizabeth Jolley 'a new, true original'.

ELIZABETH JOLLEY

WOMAN IN A LAMPSHADE

Elizabeth Jolley
22nd February 1989

PENGUIN BOOKS

Published with the assistance of
the Literature Board of the Australia Council

PENGUIN BOOKS

Published by the Penguin Group
27 Wrights Lane, London W8 5TZ, England
Viking Penguin Inc., 40 West 23rd Street, New York, New York 10010, USA
Penguin Books Australia Ltd, Ringwood, Victoria, Australia
Penguin Books Canada Ltd, 2801 John Street, Markham, Ontario, Canada L3R 1B4
Penguin Books (NZ) Ltd, 182–190 Wairau Road, Auckland 10, New Zealand

Penguin Books Ltd, Registered Offices: Harmondsworth, Middlesex, England

This selection first published by Penguin Books in Australia 1983
Published in Penguin Books in Great Britain 1986
Reprinted 1987, 1988

Copyright © Elizabeth Jolley, 1972, 1976, 1978, 1979, 1981, 1982
All rights reserved

Printed and bound in Great Britain by
Cox & Wyman Ltd, Reading
Set in Illumna

Except in the United States of America, this book is sold subject
to the condition that it shall not, by way of trade or otherwise, be lent,
re-sold, hired out, or otherwise circulated without the
publisher's prior consent in any form of binding or cover other than
that in which it is published and without a similar condition
including this condition being imposed on the subsequent purchaser

For Leonard Jolley
'Du bist die Ruh'

Acknowledgements

Grateful acknowledgement is made to the magazines and anthologies in which these stories first appeared:

'Adam's Bride' (formerly entitled 'The Bench') in *Meanjin*, 1979

'Hilda's Wedding' in *Looselicks*, 1976

'Two Men Running' in *The Bulletin*, 1981, and the anthology *Decade*, edited by B. R. Coffey, Fremantle Arts Centre Press, 1982

'Uncle Bernard's Proposal' in *Landfall*, 1973, and the Anthology *New Country*, edited by Bruce Bennett, Fremantle Arts Centre Press, 1976

'The Play Reading' in *Australian Good Housekeeping*, 1981

'One Christmas Knitting' in *Memories of Childhood*, edited by Lee White, Fremantle Arts Centre Press, 1978

'Woman in a Lampshade' in *Westerly*, 1979

'Wednesdays and Fridays' in *Quadrant*, 1981

'Dingle the Fool' in *Quadrant*, 1972, and the anthology, *New Country*, edited by Bruce Bennett, Fremantle Arts Centre Press, 1976

'The Shed' in the anthology *New Country*, edited by Bruce Bennett, Fremantle Arts Centre Press, 1976.

Contents

Pear Tree Dance

No one knew where the Newspaper of Claremont Street went in her spare time.

Newspaper or Weekly as she was called by those who knew her, earned her living by cleaning other people's houses. There was something she wanted to do more than anything else, and for this she needed money. For a long time she had been saving, putting money aside in little amounts. Every morning, when she woke up, she thought about her money. The growing sum danced before her, growing a little more. She calculated what she would be able to put in the bank. She was not very quick at arithmetic. As she lay in bed she used the sky as a blackboard, and in her mind, wrote the figures on the clouds. The total sum came out somewhere half way down her window.

While she was working in the different houses she sang, *'the bells of hell go ting a ling a ling for you and not for me'*. She liked hymns best.

'Well 'ow are we?' she called out when she went in in the mornings. 'Ow's everybody today?' And she would throw open windows and start pulling the stove to pieces. She knew everything about all the people she cleaned for and she never missed anything that was going on.

'I think that word should be clay–C.L.A.Y.' She helped old Mr Kingston with his crossword puzzle.

'Chattam's girl's engaged at long larst,' she reported to the Kingstons. 'Two rooms full of presents, yo' should just see!'

'Kingston's boy's 'ad 'orrible accident,' she described the

1

details to the Chathams. 'Lorst 'is job first, pore boy! Pore
Mrs Kingston!' Weekly sadly shook the table cloth over the
floor and carried out some dead roses carefully as if to keep
them for the next funeral.

'*I could not do without Thee Thou Saviour of the Lorst,*'
she sang at the Butterworths.

She cleaned in all sorts of houses. Her body was hard like
a board and withered with so much work she seemed to have
stopped looking like a woman.

On her way home from work she always went in the little
shop at the end of Claremont Street and bought a few
things, taking her time and seeing who was there and watching what they bought.

'Here's the Newspaper of Claremont Street,' the two shop
girls nudged each other.

'Any pigs been eating babies lately Newspaper?' one of
them called out.

'What happened to the man who sawed off all his fingers
at the timber mill?' the other girl called. 'You never finished
telling us.'

No one needed to read anything, the Newspaper of Claremont Street told them all the news.

One Tuesday afternoon when she had finished her work,
she went to look at the valley for the first time. All the morning she was thinking about the long drive. She wondered
which would be the shortest way to get to this place hidden
behind the pastures and foothills along the South West
Highway. It was a strain thinking about it and talking gossip
at the same time, especially as she kept thinking too that
she had no right really to go looking at land.

All land is somebody's land. For Weekly the thought of
possessing some seemed more of an impertinence than a
possibility. Perhaps this was because she had spent her childhood in a slaty backyard where nothing would grow except
thin carrots and a few sunflowers. All round the place where
she lived the slag heaps smouldered and hot cinders fell on
the paths. The children gathered to play in a little thicket
of stunted thornbushes and elderberry trees. There were
patches of coltsfoot and they picked the yellow flowers

eagerly till none was left. Back home in the Black Country where it was all coal mines and brick kilns and iron foundries her family had never had a house or a garden. Weekly had nothing behind her not even the place where she was born. It no longer existed. As soon as she was old enough she was sent into service. Later she left her country with the family where she was employed. All her life she had done domestic work. She was neat and quick and clean and her hands were rough like nutmeg graters and she knew all there was to know about people and their ways of living.

Weekly lived in a rented room, it was covered with brown linoleum which she polished. The house was built a long time ago for a large family but now the house was all divided up. Every room had a different life in it and every life was isolated from all the other lives.

Except for the old car she bought, Weekly, the Newspaper of Claremont Street, had no possessions. Nothing in the room belonged to her except some old books and papers, collected and hoarded, and her few washed-out and mended clothes. She lived quite alone and, when she came home tired after her long day of work, she took some bread and boiled vegetables from the fly-screen cupboard where she kept her food, and she sat reading and eating hungrily. She was so thin and her neck so scraggy that, when she swallowed, you could see the food going down. But as she had no one there to see and to tell her about it, it did not really matter. While it was still light, Weekly pulled her chair across to the narrow window of her room and sat bent over her mending. She darned everything. She put on patches with a herring-bone stitch. Sometimes she made the worn out materials of her skirts firmer with rows of herring-boning, one row neatly above the other, the brown thread glowing in those last rays of the sun which make all browns beautiful. Even the old linoleum could have a sudden richness at this time of the evening. It was like the quick lighting up of a plain girl's face when she smiles because of some unexpected happiness.

It was when she was driving out to the country on Sundays in her old car she began to wish for some land, nothing very

big, just a few acres. She drove about and stared into green
paddocks fenced with round poles for horses and scattered
in the corners with red flame-tree flowers and splashed all
over with white lilies. She stopped to admire almond
blossom and she wished for a little weatherboard house,
warm in the sun, fragrant with orange trees and surrounded
by vines. Sometimes she sat for hours alone in the scrub of
a partly cleared piece of bush and stared at the few remaining tall trees, wondering at their age, and at the yellow tufts
of Prickly Moses surviving.

The advertisements describing land for sale made her so
excited she could hardly read them. As soon as she read one
she became so restless she wanted to go off at once to have
a look.

'Yo' should 'ave seen the mess after the Venns' Party,' she
called to Mrs Lacy. 'Broken glass everywhere, blood on the
stairs and a whole pile of half-eaten pizzas in the laundry.
Some people think they're having a good time! And you'll
never believe this, I picked up a bed jacket, ever so pretty
it was, to wash it and, would you believe, there was a yuman
arm in it . . .' The Newspaper of Claremont Street talked all
the time in the places where she worked. It was not for
nothing she was called Newspaper or Weekly, but all the
time she was talking she never spoke about the land. Secretly
she read her advertisements and secretly she went off to
look.

She first went to the valley on a Tuesday after work.

'Tell about Sophie Whiteman,' Diana Lacey tried to
detain Weekly. Mrs Lacey had, as usual, gone to town and
Diana was in bed with a sore throat.

'Wash the curtains please,' Mrs Lacey felt this was a pre-
caution against more illness. 'We must get rid of the nasty
germs,' she said. 'And Weekly, I think the dining-room curtains need a bit of sewing, if you have time, thank you,' and
she had rushed off late for the hairdresser.

'Well,' said Weekly putting away the ironing board. 'She
got a pair of scissors and she went into the garding and she
looked all about her to see no one was watching and she cut
up a earthworm into a whole lot of little pieces.'

'What did her mother do?' asked Diana joyfully, knowing from a previous telling.

'Well,' said Weekly, 'she come in from town and took orf her hat and her lovely fur coat, very beautiful lady, Mrs Whiteman, she took orf her good clothes and she took Sophie Whiteman and laid her acrorss her lap and give her a good hidin'.'

'Oh!' Diana was pleased. 'Was that before she died of the chocolate lining in her stomach or after?'

'Diana Lacey, what have I told you before, remember? Sophie Whiteman had her good hidin' afore she died. How could she cut up a worm after she died. Use yor brains!'

Weekly was impatient to leave to find the way to the valley. She found a piece of paper and scrawled a note for Mrs Lacey.

'Will come early tomorrow to run up yor curtings W.'

She knew she had to cross the Medulla brook and turn left at the twenty-nine-mile peg. She found the valley all right.

After the turn off, the road bends and climbs and then there it is, pasture on either side of the road with cattle grazing, straying towards a three-cornered dam. And, on that first day, there was a newly born calf which seemed unable to get up.

She saw the weatherboard house and she went up there and knocked.

'Excuse me, but can yo' tell me what part of the land's for sale?' her voice trembled.

The young woman, the tenant's wife, came out.

'It's all for sale,' she said. They walked side by side.

'All up there,' the young woman pointed to the hillside where it was steep and covered with dead trees and rocks and pig sties made from old railway sleepers and corrugated iron. Beyond was the light and shade of the sun shining through the jarrah trees.

'And down there,' she flung her plump arm towards the meadow which lay smiling below.

'There's a few orange trees, neglected,' she explained. 'That in the middle is an apricot. That over there is a pear

tree. And where you see them white lilies, that's where
there's an old well. Seven acres this side.'

They walked back towards the house.

'The pasture's leased just now,' the young woman said.
'But it's all for sale too, thirty acres and there's another eight-
een in the scrub.'

Weekly wanted to stay looking at the valley but she was
afraid that the young woman would not believe she really
wanted to buy some of it. She drove home in a golden tranquillity dreaming of her land embroidered with pear
blossom and bulging with plump apricots. Her crooked feet
were wet from the long weeds and yellow daisies of the damp
meadow. The road turned and dropped. Below was the great
plain. The neat ribs of the vineyards chased each other
towards the vague outlines of the city. Beyond was a thin
line shining like the rim of a china saucer. It was the sea,
brimming, joining the earth to the sky.

While she scrubbed and cleaned she thought about the
land and what she would grow there. At night she studied
pamphlets on fruit growing. She had enough money saved
to buy a piece of land but she still felt she had no right.

Every Sunday she went out to look at the valley and every
time she found something fresh. Once she noticed that on
one side of the road was a whole long hedge of white wild
roses. Another time it seemed as if sheep were on the hillside
among the pig sties, but, when she climbed up, she saw it
was only the light on some greyish bushes making them look
like a quiet flock of sheep.

One evening she sat in the shop in Claremont Street, sucking in her cheeks and peering into other people's shopping
bags.

'Last week yo' bought flour,' she said to a woman.

'So what if I did?'

'Well you'll not be needing any terday,' Weekly advised.
'Now eggs yo' didn't get, yo'll be needing them! . . .'

'Pore Mr Kingston,' Weekly shook her head and addressed the shop 'I done 'is puzzle today. Mr Kingston I said
let me do your crossword – I doubt he'll leave his bed again.'

Silence fell among the groceries and the women who were

shopping. The silence remained unbroken for Weekly had forgotten to talk. She had slipped into thinking about the valley. All her savings were not enough, not even for a part of the meadow. She was trying to get over the terrible disappointment she had just had.

'If you're prepared to go out say forty miles,' Mr Rusk, the land agent, had said gently, 'there's a nice five acres with a tin shack for tools. Some of it's river flats, suitable for pears. That would be within your price range.' Mr Rusk spoke seriously to the old woman even though he was not sure whether she was all right in the head. 'Think it over,' he advised. He always regarded a customer as a buyer until the customer did not buy.

Weekly tried to forget the valley, she began to scatter the new land with pear blossom. She would go at the weekend.

'Good night all!' She left the shop abruptly without telling any news at all.

On Sunday Weekly went to look at the five acres. It was more lovely than she had expected, and fragrant. A great many tall trees had been left standing and the tin shack turned out to be a tiny weatherboard cottage. She was afraid she had come to the wrong place.

'It must be someone's home,' she thought to herself as she peered timidly through the cottage window and saw that it was full of furniture. Disappointment crept over her. Purple pig face was growing everywhere and, from the high verandah, she looked across the narrow valley to a hay field between big trees. There was such a stillness that Weekly felt more than ever that she was trespassing, not only on the land, but into the very depths of the stillness itself.

Mr Rusk said that it was the five acres he had meant.

'I've never been there myself,' he explained when she told him about the cottage. 'Everything's included in the price.'

Buying land takes time but Weekly contained herself in silence and patience, working hard all the days.

She began to buy things, a spade, rubber boots, some candles and groceries and polish and she packed them into the old car. Last of all she bought a pear tree, it looked so wizened she wondered how it could ever grow. Carefully she

wrapped it in wet newspapers and laid it like a thin baby
along the back seat.

On the day Mr Rusk gave her the key, Weekly went to
work with it pinned inside her dress. She felt it against her
ribs all morning and in the afternoon she drove out to her
piece of land.

The same trees and fragrance and the cottage were all
there as before. This time she noticed honeysuckle and roses,
a fig tree and a hedge of rosemary all neglected now and
waiting for her to continue what some other person had
started many years ago.

She thought she would die there that first day as she opened the cottage door to look inside. She looked shyly at the
tiny rooms and wandered about on the land looking at it
and breathing the warm fragrance. The noise of the magpies
poured into the stillness and she could hear the creek, in
flood, running. She sank down on to the earth as if she would
never get up from it again. She counted over the treasures
of the cottage. After having nothing she seemed now to have
everything, a bed, table, chairs and in the kitchen, a wood
stove and two toasting forks, a kettle and five flat irons.
There was a painted cupboard too and someone had made
curtains of pale-blue stuff patterned with roses.

Weekly wanted to clean out the cottage at once. She felt
suddenly too tired. She rested on the earth and looked about
her feeling the earth with her hands and listening as if she
expected some great wisdom to come to her from the quiet
trees and the undergrowth of the bush.

At about five o'clock the sun, before falling into the scrub,
flooded the slope from the west and reddened the white
bark of the trees. The sky deepened with the coming evening. Weekly forced her crooked old feet into the new
rubber boots. She took the spade and the thin pear tree and
went down to the mud flats at the bottom of her land.

Choosing a place for the pear tree she dug a hole. It was
harder to dig in the clay than she thought it would be and
she had to pause to rest several times.

She carried some dark earth from under a fallen tree over
to the hole. Carefully she held the little tree in position and

scattered the dark soft earth round the roots. She shook the
little tree and scattered in more earth and then she firmed
the soil, treading gently round and round the tree.

For the first time in her life the Newspaper of Claremont
Street, or Weekly as she was called, was dancing. Stepping
round and round the little tree she imagined herself to be
like a bride dancing with lacy white blossom cascading on
all sides. Round and round the tree, dancing, firming the
softly yielding earth with her new boots. And from the little
foil label blowing in the restlessness of the evening came a
fragile music for the pear tree dance.

Adam's Bride

Over its own sweet voice the stock dove broods . . .
(Wordsworth)

All small towns in the country have some sort of blessing.
In one place there is a stretch of river which manages to
retain enough water for swimming during the summer; in
another, the wife of the policeman is able to make dresses
for bridesmaids, and in yet another, the cook at the hotel
turns hairdresser on Saturday afternoons. The little town
below the escarpment had its blessing, it had its own court-
house. Built just after the turn of the century, it was sedately
ornamental outside and freezing cold inside for most of the
year. On very hot days the court-house heated up amazingly
and stayed hot and airless for longer than any other building
in the town. For the townspeople the court-house sup-
plemented the cinema. It had two advantages over the cinema: the characters were alive and often known by or related
to the audience, and the entertainment was not confined to
three evenings a week. It started early in the morning and,
on good days, went through continuously till three o'clock
in the afternoon. There was nothing the people liked better
than coming to the court-house. Some came daily in the
hope of witnessing the degradation and, even better, the
punishment of either strangers or their neighbours. And
there was always the hope that some person, in a high position respected by all, would be brought down by foolishness
or indiscretion for all the world to see and to talk about.

There were two small windowless rooms at the side of the
court-house. Both were uncomfortable and cold and both
had doors which opened directly onto the street. These

10

doors were kept locked. The noise of heavy traffic penetrated the thick walls of the small rooms as the law courts
were situated beside some overgrown acacias at the meeting
and crossing of three main roads. The moments of silence
were filled with the soft voices of the doves in the roof as
they talked to each other, without stopping, to and fro, like
middle-aged couples in bed.

At the end of the afternoon the young lawyer, Robinson,
went into the smaller of the two rooms carrying his brief-
case. He waited while the neatly dressed older man chewed
and sucked at an orange. He ate noisily spitting out the pips
and throwing the peel across the room. Ignoring the young
man, as soon as he had finished the orange, he danced round
the small table holding the corners of his neat jacket, kicking
out his legs and pointing his polished oxblood toes. He
twirled and pirouetted like a dancing teacher demonstrating
the steps of a new dance. While he danced he sang, forcing
his voice. Young Robinson said, 'I've brought the papers you
wanted.'

To which Armstrong, The Bench, replied, 'Robinson! Did
you know that all magistrates suffer horribly from
haemorrhoids? Strange hotels, unhealthy foods, impossible
lavatories. What is a man, in any case? A man is simply a
tube with a sphincter at each end. And what happens to that
tube and its sphincters when it's kept quite still in the cold,
hour upon hour, up there behind the bench?' He did not
wait for a reply. 'I ache with constipation and I ache with
the cold!' he exclaimed. Then, very gently, 'I can't reconcile
myself to my work, and I can't reconcile myself to my
upbringing.' He looked at Young Robinson with tenderness.
'I can't reconcile myself to my feelings either. Perhaps, you
don't quite understand what I am saying.'

'I think –', Young Robinson began but The Bench interrupted him. 'I never have an extra place laid at my table,'
he said, 'I always hope that no one will drop in. That's how
I live! There's not room at my table! And if my neighbour's
children come I can't stand them. I shout at them to get
their bloody tennis balls quickly and get out. You see, Young
Robinson, I can't seem to live any other way. I don't try to

live any other way . . .' He took another orange and sucked
at it noisily. 'But you know,' he said, spitting a pip across
the floor, 'not a day passes without my questioning my way
of living. What's the use?' he shouted, 'what's the use of
questioning if you don't provide answers?'

'Yes, I do think –', Young Robinson began, but again The
Bench interrupted him.

'You don't have to answer my questions on my life', he
said softly. 'It's enough that you furnish those legal details
here.' He paused, and then intoned, 'Somebody soweth,
somebody else watereth, but God alone giveth the increase.'
He stood looking at Young Robinson, who waited as if to
be given some kind of permission.

'It would be pleasant to sit back and murmur things to
this God,' The Bench said, 'but what if He isn't there? What
if He doesn't exist!' He lowered his voice almost as if talking
to himself. 'I seem to have lost or ceased to notice the tranquillity of my house,' he said, 'the pleasant harmony of
chairs and tables standing on polished wood and window
after window filled with green leaves in repose. I don't know
whether my house is in order or not. Once it was something
I thought I looked forward to, a kind of secret pleasure. But
I think my wife talks too much,' he said. 'She starts to talk
as soon as she wakes up, she talks as soon I come home and
she talks on into everything we do.' He sighed. 'When a
woman talks through kisses there's something wrong, that's
why I'm so busy, I never go home –'

'I'm sure it's – , Young Robinson felt he should speak, but
The Bench said, 'The apparently slight details of human
life, the pulse, the respirations and the temperature, the
matching size of the pupils of the eye for example, these
small details are watched over constantly in the care of the
human being. It's as if in recording these things, one human
being actually feels he is saving the life of another.'

'I suppose that's –', Young Robinson was interrupted by
The Bench who said, 'The one thing that really matters is
so very simple,' he said, 'it's having enough to eat and then
being able to get rid of what's eaten in a dignified and controlled way.'

'Symbolically –', Young Robinson put the brief-case on the table.

'Put the control another way,' The Bench went on talking, his face white with fatigue, 'I put a man inside for thirty days, for three months or for seven years or for twenty but, with your help, he gets off and is fined four hundred dollars instead.'

'Well?' said Young Robinson, putting the brief-case back under his arm.

'Well, it's then I begin to question,' The Bench said, 'and there are no answers to my questions. Not only does he have to find the four hundred dollars, he has to go back, as he is, to his terrible life, unemployed, no driver's licence, a houseful of dirty crying children and a sick wife.' He looked hard at Young Robinson, 'Without your help, Young Robinson, the man would be rebuilding his health in a prison farm, earning money. His wife would be much better off without him. People like that shouldn't see each other too much.' The Bench cleared his throat noisily. 'God! listen to my silly answers!'

The two men, neat in the chosen clothes which fitted their profession, stood facing each other. For a moment both seemed perplexed, the young one by the bitterness of the older man, the older man by life itself. When The Bench smiled, his face, instead of being happy, showed deeper lines of sorrow; and more bitterness was in his voice.

'Mr and Mrs Dove in the roof!' he said looking upwards. 'Safe suburban regularity!' He looked at the younger man in a kindly fashion, but said, 'Did you know, Young Robinson, that if doves are put together in a cage they'll peck each other to death? It's the same with men and women. They don't peck, but they expect from each other. Marriage is like a cage. Sometimes people expect from each other the un-expectable, the ungivable, and then they are not any better than the doves ... This enviable harmony of pulling up weeds together changes into a terrible bitterness which –' He stopped talking suddenly, and cleared his throat as if embarrassed. 'Get to bed early, Young Robinson,' he said, with a dismissive gesture. 'Call in the morning, will you, and fetch

me please, I have a need to be fetched, please, from Green's
Hotel.' He turned away abruptly and left the small room by
the narrow door which opened straight onto the street. A
few steps behind Young Robinson followed, carefully lock-
ing the door behind him. He had to wait to cross the busy
street. The Bench had made his way already through the
traffic and had disappeared from sight.

Music out of doors is frail, it hovers uncertainly, joy is more
elusive and sadness is deeper. Tremulous notes climb the
thick green veins of pale sap and fall softly as the petals fall
from blossom. Every note is muted by the foliage and by the
earth through which other sounds make their way to mingle
with the sound of the morning.

Because of the music, everything in the green dilapidated
yard had an air of unreality as a stage looks unreal when the
curtain is raised on the stillness of some scene before the
actors move and speak.

Carrying a black jacket carefully over his arm, Young
Robinson went quietly up to the man who was sitting at the
table with his head resting on his folded arms. He coughed
politely, and put out one hand as if to shake or touch the
older man, but he did neither; his hand remained outstretched as if he had often contemplated the action of
touching but had never gone beyond the contemplation.

'It's time to go,' Young Robinson said softly. 'I've been
all through the hotel looking for you. I don't know how you
find your way about,' he said, 'the verandahs look and feel
as if they are about to collapse, and your room seems to be
leaning right away from the rest of the house.' He waited
a moment. 'Here's your coat,' he said. 'I've brought your
coat, I hope you don't mind, I've been in your room. It's
time to go!'

'This morning I betrayed the rooster!' The Bench spoke
into his folded arms and then he raised his head. 'Look at
him!' He glanced across from Young Robinson to the bantam rooster who stood close by, drooping, as if trying to sink
nearer to the earth. The bantam was so covered in dust it
was impossible to see what had once been a proud metallic

arching of green and black feathers. On his comb were dark
spots of congealed blood. He stood drooping lower in his
shame, bedraggled and dirty beside the glowing apricot colour of the freshly cut wood.

'A cockfight?' Young Robinson glanced at the rooster.

'Yes,' The Bench said. 'My neighbours back home
complained of his noise, so I brought him with me. He has
never had a fight in his life. He hadn't had any food and
water, he'd been in a box for a day and a night and, in this
unfamiliar place he displays great courage. He had no
choice!' The Bench spoke harshly, 'This was the betrayal. He
depended on me, don't you see? I tried to separate them
with the shovel.' The Bench added, getting up, 'And then
an old woman came out from the house with a pail of water.'
He laughed, and stood with his back to Young Robinson
with his arms out waiting to be helped on with his jacket.

The Bench took a last look at the rooster. 'He's bewildered and wounded,' he said, 'he's too ashamed and strange
to take grain and water. I've tried to offer him both, but he
turns away.'

The two men left the rooster alone under the cape lilacs
and the honeysuckle. The peaceful surroundings, instead of
comforting, seemed only to enhance the hurt. Work was in
progress on the road and they had to go by a track, a kind
of detour. The pushing over of great trees, the forming of
the road, reminded The Bench of a dream. The trees were
being torn out by huge machinery.

'I had a horrible dream last night,' he told Young Robinson. 'Someone was trapped, I seemed to hear dreadful
screaming, I didn't know if . . . but it's bad manners to tell
dreams.'

They had reached the crossroads, and, carefully looking
all ways, they stepped into the shadows of the acacias and,
from there, they walked across to the court-house.

'Here,' said The Bench, fumbling in the pocket of his neat
black jacket. 'Here have a bit of this rosemary, there's mint
here too, go on, take some. I suppose you've noticed this
habit of mine, this peculiarity.' Young Robinson shyly took
the dried up bits of leaves and stalks being offered.

'May I say,' The Bench said in pompous tones, as Young
Robinson unlocked the side door, 'May I say that this fragment of green, this herb, this tiny fragrance helps me in its
inarticulate way to make raids on the human difficulties
which are presented daily without any hope of reaching
some kind of blessedness!' He laughed and stepped in front
of Young Robinson, who was standing aside to let him enter
the cold dark place first.

When The Bench took his place directly under the pale
shaft of early morning sunshine several people, who rose to
their feet out of respect at his entrance, were unable to sit
down again as too many bodies had packed themselves into
the available space along the narrow forms and benches pro-
vided for spectators. By the time the commotion of re-
seating had subsided, the pale shaft of light from the tiny
window had crossed the polished jarrah and lay briefly
on the bald head of the clerk who sat in readiness at a
table below. The court-room was crowded and it was very
cold.

There were policemen everywhere, some busily writing
and others in charge of the small side door through which
a patient stream of offences shuffled. They came through
one after the other, well-washed and in clean clothes appearing in these moments with flashes of the pale cold sunshine.
One predicament after another stood before The Bench,
who bowed his head and flapped his fingers against the palm
of his left hand as he dismissed them one by one with appropriate fines or punishments. This parade, which was like a
monotonous dance, was accompanied by the coughings and
creakings of the spectators and the mutterings of those
people whose voices are never still. Even in a court-house
there are operations to describe, recipes to exchange, and
there are always those people who recall with enjoyment the
disasters heard in this very room in previous weeks, months
or even years.

Sometimes there were little silences, perhaps following
the furious roaring of machinery as a semi-trailer outside
failed to take the three-road crossing seriously enough. In

these little silences the contented bedroom conversations of
the doves drifted down from the roof.

Sometimes voices were raised in reverberations through
the back places as on this particular morning. There were
faint stirrings throughout the court as an official voice called
'Evelyn May Adams! Evelyn May Adams!'Another voice
called for silence as undisciplined human curiosity started
up in different corners.

'Evelyn May Adams!' The startling accusations which followed penetrated even the dimmest understanding, and
spread with the stirrings which were like crowded insects in
long grass, all over the room. The woman was accused of
driving without a licence, driving an unregistered unlicensed
vehicle, the said vehicle being stolen by the accused.
Accused was accused of murder. Here the stirrings became
consternation; those present raised themselves so as to be
able to glimpse the woman – perhaps she was recognizable,
someone they knew or had heard of, or related to someone
once known. Accused was accused of murder on two counts.
Through the official mutterings came the name of the wife
of the vermin officer. She kept a store in a small country
town. It became clear to those who could hear well enough
that she had been killed, together with the accused's own
little daughter, at twenty minutes after two. A piercing
shriek from a corner of the court-room and the restless agi-
tation spreading through the crowd prevented any mention
of the date being heard.

There were calls for silence. Suddenly the double doors
at the back of the court-room were thrown open, and the
spectators became contortionists in order to see who had
come in. Voices subdued, but excited, were whispering,
'Who is it?' and, 'Who can it be?'

A man came in, a stranger; in spite of his ragged and bleeding
state it was clear he was not an uneducated man. Worn out,
exhausted, he was yet a man who in some way commanded,
perhaps from desperation, attention. For a moment he
leaned into the court-room, still holding one of the brass
handles of the door; he took in the packed room with his

head lowered, like a starving dog who expects someone is about to take away his food.

'I want to stand here beside her,' cried the stranger. 'I want to be her spokesman. She's too stupid to speak for herself. I want to tell you it's all because of me she's done those things.' He went to where the woman was standing, dishevelled and drooping towards the ground, and he stood beside her as if it were their wedding day, but not proud and smiling as people are for weddings. The staring crowd were not wedding guests.

'I want to tell you, Your Honour,' he began. The Bench bowed his head slightly. Since the woman appeared he had never taken his eyes from her, except to glance quickly in the direction of Young Robinson, who stood in his accustomed place by the door which led into the ante-room.

'Your Honour!' the stranger said. The Bench bowed a second time. 'I'm not an old man. I want to tell you, it's poverty and continual hardship which makes me look old. What you see is the result of poor feeding, years of poor feeding and lack of the ordinary refinements men can expect. He paused and looked at The Bench, whose face was grey and deeply lined. The gaze was returned, steadily. The stranger's face was grey.

'I want to tell you this first, Your Honour,' The Bench bowed again, 'I want to get things straight. Take a look at her! Your Honour, look at the way she's dressed, washed-out, cast-off clothes. The way she is I doubt she's got much longer to live . . .' He paused, and then shouted: 'I've been walking all day yesterday and all night to get here in time. I knew I had to get down from the hills and across that wedge of forest. I knew no one would stop to give me a ride. If I'm walking, they'll say to themselves 'he's wanting to walk', and in any case who'd want to stop and give someone who looks like me a lift? There wasn't much time, so I went off the road into the forest. The tracks as I thought were tracks weren't, they were old fire-breaks put through years ago, turning back on themselves all the time, so I was lost before I'd hardly started.

'Your Honour! I took to the scrub and tried to go through

where no man ever goes through.' He paused, looking earn-
estly at The Bench, who inclined his head as though telling
him to continue. 'I kept thinking,' the stranger said, 'it's like
my life, this is, in the forest. And I pushed and struggled
through. The hakea was up to my shoulders. It's terrible in
there! I prayed out loud that it would give way to something
less tormenting. The forest is thick in places and it's frighten-
ing at night, and I was wet through . . . I haven't slept, Your
Honour. I only decided yesterday morning to try to get
here.' He paused, then suddenly exclaimed, 'I love her! You
won't believe this, but I know about love. This miserable
creature, I love her! I love my wife so much I'd like to be
able to marry her all over again. Only you see . . .' He hesitated. 'Only you see, I'd do it all again what I've already
done.' He rubbed his hands over his grey unshaven face.

'It's all my fault!' he shouted. 'It's all my fault what she's
done to the rat-catcher's wife. They, him, the rat-catcher and
his wife keep the store. They're gossips, the worst kind of
gossips. It's the rat-catcher's wife's fault too. Wait till I tell
you – and then there's our child, it's my fault what she's done
to our child!'

His voice crumbled into a sob and he covered his face with
both hands. There was a silence in the court-house; only the
happily married doves in the roof murmured their com-
placent and monotonous endearments.

Adams straightened himself. The Bench was sitting very
still, with both elbows on the polished jarrah, his hands
cupped to his face like hands held clasped for praying.

The Bench bowed slightly when Adams said, 'Your
Honour, I gave her an idiot baby. See? Our little girl
couldn't do for herself, not one thing could she do for herself, now do you understand? She hadn't any sense, not even
the sense poultry have. She couldn't put a bit of food in her
own mouth. Now do you see? My wife's not got much in
her head herself. I knew she was stupid when I married her,
though her mother never said so and it didn't show all that
much.' He glanced at Evelyn who had not moved, though
she was trembling.

'On our wedding day,' Adams said, 'Evie May here looked

like a pear tree in blossom, her eyes were spilling over with
tears of happiness. You know, the white blossom of the pears
can fill the whole sky if you can get to lie on the grass and
look up. Her frock was full and white and her hair was in
a thick dark plait, down her back. It was tied with a big white
ribbon. She was a great big dressed-up doll holding on to my
arm, and she was smiling with her tongue just poking out
at the edge of her mouth and her eyes so bright, as I said,
overflowing with tears and she kept looking at me, she
couldn't take her eyes off me. All the township came to the
wedding. Her mother and her aunty were well known there.
I'd been around for some time getting work here and there,
and sometimes not getting it.' Adams was quiet for a
moment, and then again came the invocation, 'Your
Honour!' The Bench, his face as white as paper, bowed his
head; the lines of his face seemed darker. He glanced at
Young Robinson as if to ask, 'What's to be done?' But
Adams was already telling.

'Your Honour,' Adams continued, 'five acres of land and
a house went with this bride.' He spoke slowly. 'I wanted
some land! There's people who are born with land and
others who buy it or sell it, and there's yet others who never
have the chance. Well, I wanted some land more than anything I've ever wanted.' He looked all round the court, holding up his head proudly. 'Five acres and a house came with
her!' he said. 'The wedding was something! As I said, her
mother's well known there, and her aunty. There were tables
full of food outside the hotel, and beer, plenty of it, the
whole town was at the wedding. Oh, it was a feast, only I
couldn't get Evie here to leave off playing with the children.
There were children everywhere, they seemed to be her
mates, and she seemed to be aunty to them all. I kept trying
to remind her it was her wedding day.'

By some strange accident which no one could ever remember, Evelyn Adams had an apple stick in the loose skin of
her elbow. The stick, about half an inch long, could be easily
felt and held and moved about too with the skin all round
it of course, between the finger and thumb of anyone who

wanted to feel and marvel at the strange things people could have in their elbows. As a child it had been to her advantage. A teacher, annoyed at her lack of reading ability and an even worse inability with numbers, could be diverted from instant wrath by being told of the presence of Evie May's apple stick and being allowed to feel it. Other children in similar difficulties frequently made use of this interesting elbow and its contents.

Evie May's mother was thankful to get Evie May married. She had lied about Evie May's age partly because of her daughter always seeming so young and because, as the years rushed by, there were not any men interested at all either in the hand of Evie May, or in the five acres of what she called the good rich salt flats she was offering, together with a substantial home, which needed only a little repair work to make it habitable. She had herself renewed a piece of tin on the roof, and patched the cracked west wall with some good second-hand asbestos. A lick of paint, she told Adams, was all that the house needed, a lick of paint. Of the fact that Evie May would be thirty-five on her next birthday, she said not a word, letting Adams think she was rising twenty-five. As she told her sister, Evie May's Aunty Deanne, 'He's not just a cockerel himself, looks forty-five if he's a day,' and her sister agreed. Both women felt that when he discovered what a good worker Evie May was he would look after her, and she did need looking after very badly. She couldn't set foot out of doors without the company of either her mother or her aunty, but she became pregnant straight away and the two women couldn't go on standing the responsibility of this for ever. Five children were boarded out in various farms around the township, and two more were in a farm school. Perhaps later, the two women discussed this with the temporary foster mothers, when Evie May was really on her feet in her own home, the children could come back either for holidays or for good; a lot would depend on Mr Adams, it was agreed. Everything would depend on Mr Adams.

Aunty Deanne and the proprietor of the hotel had an understanding, a close friendship, and it seemed an ideal place to celebrate the wedding. So there was the wedding

feast, in the street in front of the hotel and round the corner
in the gardens, and absolutely everyone in the township and
in the surrounding farms felt themselves to be invited. Evie
May had worked like a man for most of the farmers. She had
been in on the sheep-shearing for years, the fruit-picking and
the poultry dressing, and she had been nursemaid in count-
less homes to children during the absences of mothers for
their frequent confinements.

The wedding day was coming to an end. The children in
their white dresses were dancing and singing in the street,

> Poor Jenny sits a-weeping a-weeping a-weeping
> Poor Jenny sits a-weeping all on a summer's day

they sang, and then they shouted, 'Evie May, Aunty Evie
May you're in the middle now. Join hands all dance round
now, Poor Evie sits a-weeping a-weeping, poor Evie sits a-
weeping all on a summer's day.

The children laughed and clapped and one of them called
out, 'Aunty Evie, let's make posies!' and another voice
called, 'Aunty Evie, let's go down the paddock and throw
cow pats again!'

'I'll race you!' another child called, 'I'll race you to Aunty
Evie, first one to get to Aunty Evie can have a feel of the
apple stick in her elbow! Last one to Aunty Evie is a dilly!'

Evie May was nearly delirious with happiness and laughing on her wedding day. She became conscious of a dark
shadow on the edge of the day; the sun was leaving the
street, and Adams stood on the pavement by the doors of
the hotel.

'Come here, Evelyn May,' he said in a gruff voice; shyness
made his voice sound rough.

A woman's voice called out. 'Evie! Don't spoil your dress.'
It was her mother. 'Oh!' she exclaimed crossly, 'there's
manure stains all over your lovely white! Just you look, miss!
at all those smeary green patches and you're to have your
photo taken. Tidy yourself up, do! He's waiting for you.
Hurry now! Evie May, do you hear me? He's standing there
waiting! He's waiting there, standing, waiting –'

'Yes Mother,' Evie May said obediently.

'Now smile, everybody!' Evie May's mother helped the photographer, and there were a great many extra relations in the family photograph. Adams did not like being photographed. He was relieved to see the guests depart.

'Well, that's over,' he said roughly, 'I said, that's over! Come into the house. Come along home,' he said.

'Where's my mam?' Evie May was suddenly on the edge of tears; the broad familiar shapes of her mother and aunty were nowhere to be seen. 'Mam?' she called. 'Aunty? Where are you, Mam?'

'Come on now into the house.' Adams felt anger towards his bride. 'Come on,' he said impatiently. 'We're married, you and me. This is where we're going to live, you and me. Your mother's given us the land and the house. Remember? She's explained it to you. We'll have some pigs and poultry. Remember? We're married now. She's explained, she's gone to live with her sister, your Aunty, she's left here, she's not here in this house any more. Come on now, into the house.'

Evie May sobbed, 'Mam, I want my Mam. My frock's all spoiled. I've dirtied my good dress.'

'Shut up!' Adams raised his voice, 'Shut up and come inside!' How could he be pleased with his land or his house with her making all this noise? 'Never mind your dress,' he shouted, 'take it off!'

Evie May began to howl, 'Oh No, No, No!' She seemed terrified of Adams and she cried as if her heart was breaking.

In the silence the doves in the roof of the court-house continued their contented conversation. The people sat listening, and The Bench sat with his elbows on the polished jarrah, his hands holding the crushed herbs cupped to his face. From time to time he glanced at Young Robinson.

Adams spoke quietly. 'Your Honour!' he said, and The Bench bowed his head. 'Suddenly she stopped overflowing with happiness. In the night she started crying again. She was frightened, she didn't understand! She didn't understand anything, not even her time of the month. I seemed to make her cry, Your Honour, and she's never stopped crying, Your

Honour! She's showed her real stupidity by stopping with me, caring for the little girl and working herself to death in the all-night roadhouse at the sixty-two-mile peg. That's what her life is. She got food there which she brought home, and she got a lift to and from work in a delivery truck. Take a look at her,' Adams shouted and pointed at the woman. 'She's not slept properly for years. She's had to care for the girl, too. She did her best to help me on that good-for-nothing piece of land. We had our hopes with the pigs and the poultry, but in the summer there's no feed,' he paused and shouted, 'In summer the whole place goes bald!' He looked round the court-house with his head lowered.

'I tried,' he said, his voice breaking, 'I tried with sweet corn, a summer crop. Sweet corn,' his voice became pleasant, 'sweet corn's like a miracle when it comes. Sweet corn talks and whispers while it's growing, but I had trouble with the water. The tanks rusted through. No need for me to describe the hard ground and the withered dead stalks . . .' His voice became harsh. The corn whispered all right. While I tried to find just one cob, I could hear it whispering, only I didn't know what it was saying. The goats ate all the bark off the almond trees. We had nothing left. I tried to dig a few potatoes, but they had shrivelled in the hot hard ground.' His intensity rose as he added, 'Can you imagine what that's like? The disappointment of not finding any potatoes when you're really hungry, and you've been hoping for the smell and taste of boiled potatoes?' Adams paused. The Bench made no move except to incline his head a little, that faint bow which gave permission to speak. Adams continued.

'When the winter came I tried with broad beans,' his voice was pleasant with the memory, 'the bean patches were green and I let myself think about the pods. I remembered the scent of bean flowers from my childhood.' He spoke very softly. 'We never had the bean flowers, it was the frost, Your Honour, we had nothing but black stalks. So cold in winter and so wet. Our house? People have better sheds. It's hardly a house, so damp and mouldy in the winter, it stinks! And in the summer you feel you've got to get out, there's no air in there.

'As I said, she never stopped crying. I said to myself I'd never touch her again. Of course I did. The idiot child was our first and I said to myself, No More! But she got pregnant again. My fault! A woman can't get pregnant on her own. I couldn't stand it! And I can't stand it now, what I did to her. Wait till you've heard it all. I got home late one afternoon, it was very hot. She wasn't in the house.'

In the stillness of the long hot afternoon all life seems withdrawn, except of course the life a person carries inside herself. Evie May was big with child, and this child restlessly kicked in spite of the fact that Evie May was keeping very still herself. She sat outside the unhappy little house which was so ugly in its poverty. The house rested on the squalid earth so heavily that it was impossible to move the door; it stayed permanently partly open. The windows had no sills, and two of the windows out of the three had boards across them, the glass having been broken. At the back of this ashamed place was a vine. Every place on earth has one thing which saves it: a brightly painted chair, perhaps, or a square of light falling every afternoon on the floorboards from a small window facing the west, a path made by someone's love or a cushion with an unmistakeable air of elegance in its vanishing lace, the remains of venetian needlepoint, a single redeeming thing, nothing very great but there all the same in surroundings often too dreary to bear. Evie May's house had this vine. It was healthy, the roots grown during a great number of years probably touched down to that clear cold water which flows so mysteriously under the earth, a long way down beyond the reach of an ordinary man.

On this hot day Evie May sat under the green leaves of the vine. She had a pail of dirty water beside her and she tried to cool herself with a vine leaf, dipping the leaf into the water and splashing herself. All the time the cicadas kept up their endless noise, and a soft wind coming across the desolate brown paddocks carried the unconcerned calling of the crows. From somewhere quite close her little girl was crying and crying.

'Oh hush yer noise, do!' Evie May complained, 'I'm

coming in a minute. I'm coming in a minute. I just want
to rest a minute.' She splashed the water indolently; it ran
in warm itchy rivulets on her big arms and legs. 'Oh! It's that
hot in there! Oh! hush yer noise,' she called again to the crying child.

Adams suddenly appeared round the side of the house. It
was as if a shadow hung there, for a minute, as if there were
no sun. The shade was not welcome. Adams began to shout;
he had been looking for her and he was tired and dirty.

'Oh, so that's where you are! Can't you hear her bawling?'
he shouted. 'She's messed everywhere. Everywhere! Why
haven't you cleaned up? Where's my tea? Fire's not made,
no kettle on. What's you been doing?'

'It's too hot to light the stove.' Evie May sat back panting.
Clumsily she put one foot in the pail. 'I'm not well,' she
began.

It was all too much for Adams, the sight of her in dirty
clothing leaning her uncombed head against the asbestos,
the enormous belly, a reminder of what was so inevitable,
and the memory of the filthy house which soon they would
be forced to enter.

'Too sick to light the stove and get my tea,' he shouted.
'What am I supposed to do?'

He snatched the vine leaf and kicked away the bucket of
water. He grabbed her hair and she screamed as he pulled
her to her feet. Her scream and the crying of the child
seemed to blend into one great cry which spoke of all the
misery and disappointment a man can provide for himself
without meaning to. In a moment of violence he kicked her
in the fullness of her pregnant belly: she gave one more terrible scream as, in silence, she moved slowly, doubled with
the shock and the pain, round the side of the house to the
partly open door.

Just as quickly as the anger had come, so it left him. Bent
with shame and fear of what he might have done, he followed her.

'I kicked her in the stomach, Your Honour,' Adams said in

a broken voice. 'She stopped screaming. I'll never forget how she looked at me as she went round into the house. I cried while I drove her to the hospital.' In the silence, when Adams stopped talking, the doves could be heard, making love to one another up in their house in the roof.

'Your Honour!' The Bench, without any outward sign of weariness or disgust, bowed his head slightly and Adams continued.

'Your Honour! Weeds are terrible things. There's an unnamable despair about weeds. I couldn't keep up with them. The wild radish has long deep roots and the capeweed spreads itself over the ground. It's flat and wide and fleshy. Nothing can grow where these two are growing. And then there's the paspalum, you can hack at it till your eyeballs are straining out of your head, and when you've dug out a patch of it, spending all your energy, even enjoying the sharp smell of the earth, you're tired out, you can hardly breathe, let alone speak, and when you look at what you've done,' his voice became a hoarse whisper, 'there's a cleared space just big enough to dig a man's grave.' He rubbed his hands over his dirty scabby face. 'It was one expense and disappointment after another,' he said. 'For all that I wanted some land so much, I soon learned that a man can't live off a few acres. You can't keep starving goats fenced in. They got out, they ate poison weed or they were shot. Who wants starving goats trespassing? I'd had such hopes. Now, I want to tell you something, Your Honour.' The Bench barely bowed, but it was sufficient an inclination of the head to give permission.

'One day,' Adams said, 'I went down to the store to get a few things and,' his voice became suddenly relaxed and pleasant, 'and there was a box of pencils on the counter. New pencils, red ones and blue, shiny ones like we had years ago at school. A new pencil has a smoothness, a smell of refinement.' His voice was tender. 'Suddenly, I wanted to lick the new dark point and write my name somewhere. In my hands, the pencil felt like a mysterious tool, something special, something to hold delicately, to caress. And, I wanted a

sheet of paper to write on. I waited there for the store
woman, the rat-catcher's wife, they keep the store, she's,
well, you'll see what she is –'

In an atmosphere of kerosene-washed boards and the smell
of cheap sweets the country storekeeper knows everything
about the people who come for bread and suppositories and
yards of hosepipe, for axe heads and mattocks and babies'
feeding bottles, for remnants of dress material and paper-
back novels of space fiction, romance and crime.

In the country store, where Adams waited for the rat-
catcher's wife who had gone up to the shed at the back for
potatoes and kerosene, every kind of merchandise was for
sale. On the back of the door were cards of safety pins and
hair nets; a tray of shop-soiled birthday cards sat in the window; loaves of bread were in a glass-sided cupboard, and on
the counter next to the bell jars of yellow tarts and dough-
nuts was the box of pencils. He stared at the faded advertisements for cigarettes and old-fashioned toilet requisites, and
at the paint peeling from the ceiling, but always his glance
came back to the pencils. Shyly he took one, and held it
between his thumb and fingers, poised as if ready to write.
He longed to write something, perhaps just his name on a
smooth clean sheet of paper.

The outside door banged, and the rat-catcher's wife stood
on the other side of the counter.

'It's a long way from that shed,' she said, out of breath.
'Everythin' you arssed for was up in that shed!' She moved
heavily and stacked things on the counter. When she spoke
she often did not stop. 'There's your kero and there's your
potatoes and there's your pumpkin and your tin of jam.
That's the lot and that's all I can let you have Mister Adams.
I'll tot them up in the book in just a minute. There's bread
owing and tea and soap and milk and onions I'll have to tell
you it's weeks now since any money was paid me and let me
tell you straight away that so-called farm of yours is no good
the soil what there is of it is all salt and it's sour you won't
get anything to grow it's been like that for years it's either
a flood or a drought and anything that's born there has some-

thing wrong with it. There was a cow there in labour only larst year with one hoof poking out for days and do you think anyone would touch her? Not a soul would have a bar of it because of the price on a calf three hundred dollars worth of calf see and no one wanted to be blamed so there that poor creature was her sides all scraped raw in the dirt. Nearly lorst her as well as the calf. Had to be butchered out in the end. Not like yoomans is it I mean there's never a price put on a yooman baby is there but a calf's different it's a question of money isn't it. There are some places where nothin' thrives like a kind of curse, see, some places have a blessing and others if you see what I mean well there's a curse like I always say . . .'

'I'll have this pencil too, please.' Shyly Adams interrupted the rat-catcher's wife.

'What?' She hadn't heard, 'You'll what?' Surely she hadn't heard properly.

Adams even more shyly repeated, 'This pencil, I'll have this pencil too, please.'

'Oh, all right,' the rat-catcher's wife said grudgingly. 'I suppose I'll put it down in the book.' Curiosity got the better of her. 'A pencil?'

'Yes,' Adams said, and he pulled a cheap writing pad from a rack near the door, 'and I'll have one of these, please.'

'You want a pencil and a writin' pad?' Her voice was filled with suspicion and curiosity. 'Whatever for? You writin' a book, then?'

Adams did not offer any definite answer, he merely bent his head over the cardboard box into which his dull but necessary shopping had been dumped. He gathered up the box and left the shop, leaving the door to swing to in a way which made the bell tinkle quite madly.

The rat-catcher's wife opened the door at the back and yelled up the yard to the shed, 'Fred, are you there, Fred? Fred, did you hear that? He's writin' a book!' Her feelings of curiosity almost got the better of her and she felt the palpitations in her heart, 'Him! writin' a book!' She wished so much for a customer just then, someone with more intelligence than Fred, with whom she could enlarge on this new

little bit of knowledge about that man Adams. She came
round the counter, out of breath, and opened the shop door
and looked up and down the street. Adams had gone round
the corner, and there wasn't a soul in either direction.

Sometimes there are those silences which are so remarkable,
in the middle of the noise of living. And when the silences
include a court-house crowded with people, it is incredible.

Adams tried to neaten himself. He tried to pull his
woollen vest straight and to button it, but there were no but-
tons. He tried to stand straight and still, but he could not.

The doves in the roof seemed to be brooding over the
voice of Adams.

He spoke up again, 'I let her do everything, Your Honour!'
The Bench bowed slightly, and Adams continued, 'A change
came over our family life. Evelyn here seemed suddenly different. She seemed happy! Unbelievable! She got up even
earlier than usual. She scrubbed and cleaned the house and
took the child with her every day, I suppose, to the roadhouse cafe. She seemed to work longer shifts than before.
She left meals for me. She made pumpkin scones, she even
got butter and put them ready with the butter in a clean
dish covered with a washed cloth. I noticed she'd moved the
furniture too. She'd put the table by the window. She put
a cloth on the table, one I'd never seen before, and she put
a chair with a cushion she'd made, you know, a chicken-feed
bag stuffed with dried grass.' His voice became pleasant as
he continued, 'The room smelled sweet because of this grass
cushion. She covered the whole table with a second cloth
. . .' He seemed to be lost in his thoughts for a moment. 'She
never moved the cloth,' he said. 'The days went by with the
pumpkin scones and the butter and the cleaned house and
no child. I was there alone with the heat and the quietness
and the clean tidy table . . .' His voice sounded almost as if
he were smiling. 'Down in the store the rat-catcher's wife
started to call me "Sir", and she looked at me with the kind
of respect which made me able to look straight back at her.'
His voice took on another quality, it was almost as if he were

happy. 'When I walked through the main street I felt the people were admiring me. I was somebody after all, and I held my head up. You see, Your Honour,' here The Bench bowed his head slightly, 'They all thought ... They all thought I was doing something. Evelyn never asked me about it. I know she never looked under the top cloth. She just worked harder than ever. She waited on me and admired me and did her best to see that I was in peace to write.' He paused, and then as if perplexed, added, 'I even got to thinking I would write a book, I even thought that I was actually writing a book, and when I was down there in the store with the rat-catcher and his wife I'd seem as if I was deep in thought and had forgotten the trivial things of shopping because of the big things in my mind, the things I was writing about. The rat-catcher's wife would try respectfully to remind me about tea and sugar. More than once she slipped a bottle of wine in with the groceries, nothing expensive of course, a red wine, she said, to help me with my inspiration. It was a good way to live, being built up like this.' He paused. 'This poor stupid creature here was working harder than ever,' he said, 'and I hadn't-even-tried-the-pencil-to-write-my-name, even though I wanted to, really wanted to feel the new pencil on the clean new sheets of paper.' His voice was hoarse, and he spoke as if he couldn't really believe he was talking about himself. 'Sometimes when I was alone on the farm I used to think I could hear a car coming, you know, the noise of the wheels turning slowly on the loose gravel. I imagined a visitor coming, someone who'd heard I was a writer, and wanted to know about my work. I dreamed of some visitor coming because of the book I'd written. I pictured to myself what fame and success would be like. But of course, no one ever came to our farm, never! All the summer I longed for the rain,' he continued in a flat voice. 'I thought once the rain came I'd really write something. All the summer this went on and then this poor fool picked up an infection and was too ill to go to work. Something in the bowel. She was really ill. Her stomach pains were terrible. She groaned all night and the child was ill too. She lost her job in the cafe, because these days if you're ill someone else can take your place and then you can't get back to it. You can't get your job back!

'The house got dirty, and I kept charging things on the book at the store. We had to eat and Evelyn here needed things. The rat-catcher's wife was respectful enough at first, but people give up their respect for the thing they've trapped, and it doesn't take long to owe five or six hundred dollars. I'd got used to the wine and the butter and the real coffee. We never touched the table and we never touched the table cloth, but I saw Evelyn look at it sometimes, sideways she'd look towards it, and she'd look at me when she thought I wasn't looking at her. Then the rain came.'

Wishing away the existing season is more than a symptom, it is the complaint, the illness itself. As in the world of fashion where fur coats have to be tried on in midsummer, the man working his acres has to deal with an existing problem keeping in mind the one which hangs over the months to come. In the middle of the longed-for heat of the summer there is a wish for the rain, and this wish becomes an obsession. A man cares more about the state of his dam than he cares whether his son is in bad company or not. Brackish water oozing up with a mysterious persistence through the rough white clay of a newly excavated dam is more serious than any family calamity a man can bring to his mind during a sleepless night. It is something he dares not speak about. If the dam would only yield fresh water during the early rains then he would have been better pumping water from the stream. As he walks round the glaring white embankment, he looks into the dry creek bed and wonders painfully if the full flood of the creek, when it comes, will take with it this far mound of the dam wall. He does not speak about this either, but takes short moody walks to the particular place and speculates on his shortage of money, his shortage of water and perhaps even his shortage of sense. Perhaps someone will drown in the dam, or alternatively perhaps it will never fill with water, he can only wait now for nature and her 'holy plan'.

And then all at once there is the smell of the rain on the

wind and everyone is quite unprepared. Barn doors dropped
and wedged on the summer hard earth are still open and the
rain, in splendid form, drives in to places which are better
kept dry. Old water courses re-open, and overnight the contours of a man's piece of land change. Earth and stones, valuable topsoil, are washed relentlessly from their assumed per-
manence. Twigs, leaves and branches are drifted to places
where they will be a nuisance. Tender tributaries swell and
rejoice the earth, but a poor quality house suffers from a
kind of rheumatism in which every weakness, known and
unknown, gets worse from one rain-washed day to the next.
Every ill-fitting joint becomes more immovable, forgotten
leaks force themselves upon the memory unpleasantly,
damp rises, mould appears on walls and ceilings are curiously
decorated; even the bread is graced. And with the mould
comes the dreadful smell of it.

Evie May's poor quality house was no exception and this
place, which was intolerable in the heat, was, perhaps, even
worse in the winter. Evie May, hardly recovered from the
infection in the summer, found herself plunged into the cold
wet filth of the sudden winter. It was too much. Gaunt and
weak she struggled with sodden shabby washing. She made
a tremendous effort, and tied a white ribbon round her head.
For some reason this piece of ribbon, which should have
been an improvement, darkened the circles round her eyes,
sharpened her bluish nose and, furthermore, would not stay
in position but slipped crookedly on her hair, which was lifeless with poor health.

Greedily and noisily she sucked and chewed at an orange,
spitting the pips out or rather letting them fall from her slack
mouth; the peel lay all over the greasy floor. The little girl
kept crying.

'Hold yer noise,' Evie May said to her child. 'Hold yer
noise! Here, have a bit of orange. There's a good girl, have
a bit of mommy's orange,' she pleaded with the dirty crying
child, 'Go on then! Have a bit of mommy's nice orange.'

As she held out a torn-off piece of orange to the child, she
was aware that a shadow filled the half-open door. She
turned quickly to see Adams coming in. He was returning

from an inspection of the place in the bottom corner of his
five acres where he would have liked to have a small dam
made. The rain, just as he thought, was washing down to
that place, rivulets of precious water down the slope, and
water actually swirled as if laughing in places as it poured
and ran on beyond the boundary of his land to the grateful
creek bed. As he stood, wet through in the rain, he imagined
what it might have been like to be on the steep slope of a
newly excavated dam, the rough white clay slippery with the
water as it flowed down to fill the deep rough basin. As he
stood sinking in the salt mud flats of his land he tried to picture the change in the landscape such an excavation could
make, the great white turned-back mounds which would
form the walls of the dam, and the water itself stored to be
used to make his land useful instead of the ache of disappointment it had become. His imagination turned again
to the steep slippery slopes of white and rusty clay; perhaps
a person might get drowned in his dam. He'd have to put
a row of star pickets and a stout nylon rope, something which
would not rust or rot, between them.

He pulled his feet out of the mud, and knowing he could
not work with the earth in such a sodden state, he made his
way back to the house.

'I'm soakin' wet,' he bellowed from the doorpost. 'D'you
hear me? I'm soakin' wet, get me a towel will ya?'

'Nothin's dry,' Evie May whimpered, handing him a dingy
cloth.

'How can I dry myself on this?', Adams roared, 'it's wetter
than I am!'

'Nothing's dry,' Evie May said, 'I can't get the clothes dry.
She's under the table,' she added, indicating the child who
was hidden by the fringes and tassels of the undisturbed
table cloth.

'As if I care where she is!' Adams paced about the small
untidy room. 'It's like a cage in here,' he said, 'It's filthy, too.
I don't care where she is!' he shouted. 'Clear up this mess.
Chuck that mess out of here! I can't stand the smell of
oranges in here.' He shivered like a sick man. 'It's cold,' he
complained. 'There's no fire, why isn't there any fire?'

'The wood's all wet,' Evie May said in a whining tone. Adams, with a look of despair, said, 'God, it's cold! I'll get the wood. Get cleaned up a bit,' he said, softening. The white ribbon slipping on her head made him angry, but he realised why she had put it on. She stood for a moment, pondering a response to his gentler tone.

'I, I suppose you can't work when we're in here,' she said timidly, 'I mean, at the table there. I suppose we're in your way all the time. I'll try and get something. I'll try and get back to the roadhouse.' She looked at him pleadingly.

The child, remaining hidden, suddenly let out a noisy wail of crying, as if the softened voices frightened her. As she yelled she crawled out from under the table, and with both hands pulled off the top table cloth.

Adams and Evie May stood staring at the table. There was a moment of horror between them. It silenced the child.

Evie May cried out in an unnamable despair.

'Oh! she's pulled the table cloth off! Oh! there's the pad and the pencil just as they was on the bottom cloth. You've never touched them! She said, Missis Westcott, the rat-man's wife, she said as you was writin' a book.' She drew in a long tremulous breath in a snivel, the way a child gathers breath to cry after a hurt, and added, 'You haven't been writin' a book at all, then!' She began to cry, a sort of hopeless crying with all the sadness and bitterness of disappointment.

'Don't stare at me like that, then,' she sobbed. 'And don't just stare at the table like that. All this time I thought, I was thinkin', I was believin' . . .' She sobbed in a heartbroken way as the child started to whimper and pull at her mother's uneven hem.

Adams saw again the refinement of the pencil. The cheap writing pad was small and pathetic. The rain was coming more heavily. The water would, as usual, flood the bottom of his land, more than two acres would be under water and of no use and all that water going to waste. The rain rattled on the tin roof. Somewhere in the bedroom it was plopping into an overflowing bucket. The pencil was new and shiny, it lay on the cloth, innocent.

'Shut up! Shut up!' He trembled with uncontrollable rage.
'I'll kill you if you don't shut up!' An inheritance of shame
welled within him, but how can a man know or even think
about what he is or what he inherits? 'I'll smash you through
that wall! I'll smash you through that wall, and that idiot
kid too!' Evie May raised her tear-swollen face.

'I thought you was writin' a book!' she said, and let out
a howl of despair. 'All this time I thought you was writin'
a book.'

Adams took her by the hair.

'Let go my hair!' she shrieked.

Holding her by the hair Adams lost himself in his rage.
Somewhere, as if in another room, he seemed to hear a
woman crying 'No, No, No,' and begging, 'Leave me alone.'

He heard the noise of the weeping and the sound of the
child crying gradually getting fainter and fainter.

Over their own sweet voices the doves moved to and fro in
the roof of the court-house. Brooding back and forth, to and
fro.

'Yes, Your Honour,' Adams said in a voice breaking as if
he would cry. The Bench bowed slightly.

'Yes, Your Honour,' Adams said, 'I did all those things,
I took her by the hair and I threw her against the wall, and
the child, I threw her too.' He paused and then continued,
'I couldn't stand the way she looked at me in her disappointment, and I couldn't stand my own shame. I knew all the
time she thought I was doing something special. The rat-
catcher's woman will have told her, will have put the idea
in her head and kept it there. I even half-believed it myself.
But of course there was nothing there on the table, not one
word, not even my own name.' He waited a moment and
looked around the court. 'I'll never forget her look of fear,'
he said in a low voice, 'I'll never forget the fear in her face.
It will be always there, this look. I could never be punished
enough for this and, in itself, it is my punishment. She was
terrified of me as if I was a wild animal. Well that's what
I was,' he shouted, 'a wild animal, not as good as an animal
because they act as animals do, but a man can think and

decide how to behave. Well, Your Honour,' The Bench bowed his head, 'Your Honour,' Adams said in a low voice, 'she took the child and she ran from me. She ran from the place crying out loud like someone gone mad, down the slope through all the mud on the salt flats, through the flooding creek, it's dangerous there, rough, and there's deep holes, a man could drown there. She got across to another property and it was from there she took that good-for-nothing old truck, a condemned thing with no brakes. Somehow she got it going, and she must have driven it straight down the hill to the crossroads to try to get to the main road, I suppose, to get over to her mother and her aunty.' He paused, and then very slowly and deliberately he said, 'If she ran down the store woman, the rat-catcher's wife, it was that woman's fault for telling Evelyn here things that raised her hopes beyond all possible hope. The rat-catcher's woman is a gossip and a liar, and it's like her to be out in the middle of the road just out of spiteful curiosity when there's a truck with no brakes coming down the hill. And if Evelyn killed our child it would have been because she didn't see the child. The child must have got down off the truck and been behind it when Evelyn backed it off the bloody mess she'd made of that vermin, the rat-catcher's woman. She wouldn't have seen the child when all she could see was the bloody mess she'd made of that woman.'

Adams stopped speaking. It was as if he expected some kind of reaction from The Bench and from the people who were packed along the court-house benches, but only a little restless movement like the soft sighing of the wind went through the room.

It's not her fault, Your Honour,' Adams said in a hoarse whisper. The Bench gave a slight bow from the neck. 'If she made all that bloody mess down there at the crossroads,' Adams said, 'it was because she . . . It was because,' he continued, 'she had to get away from me. She was frightened to death of me and the terrible temper I was in, in my own shame. Because, Your Honour, I want you to know, and all these people in here to know, I am ashamed. If she's done all those things it's because of me and, because I'm the only one she's got in the whole world to look after her, that's why it's so much worse. That's why I've come to speak for her. She's all alone! And take a look will you at the creature who is the only person she's got!' Adams turned to one side and putting one arm across his face, like a frightened boy in a school playground, sobbed aloud in the court-house.

No one moved. The tired sobbing quietened, and the doves caressed each other with their sweet monotonous voices as if there were nothing in the world except tender conversation.

The Bench sat looking with dismay at the inextricable mess of human misery standing before him. He made no attempt to clear the court, though he could have done, simply by rising to his feet. He looked across at Young Robinson, who was standing in his usual place near the door of the ante-room. It was as if a moment of understanding passed between them, as if both men, the older one and the younger one, understood something for the first time. After such an understanding there can be nothing more.

With a slight movement of his hand, The Bench dismissed Adams and his wife.

'She needs water,' Young Robinson said to The Bench in the ante-room. 'Yes, of course,' The Bench said, and he offered Young Robinson the cup of water he was holding in his hand. 'Yes, of course,' The Bench said again. He told Young Robinson to find out what needed to be done. 'I'm leaving it all in your hands,' he said, and then he asked, 'You'll come when you've finished? You'll come to me? I need . . .' Instead of asking Young Robinson, as he usually did, to call for him the next day, he simply broke off, looked at him, and left by the side door.

Young Robinson heard the roar of the engine. He heard the noise of the brakes and the shouting in the street. He heard a girl screaming and screaming. He heard the noise of the accident, but he did not realize. He did not go out to The Bench. He stayed in the small windowless room offering the fainting woman water which she could not drink.

Hilda's Wedding

Everyone said Night Sister Bean was a witch.

'Never let her look at a transfusion,' Casualty Porter said to me my first night on duty.

'Why ever not?' I asked him.

'Never let her look directly at a blood transfusion,' he said and he refused to say more and I waited for him in the doorway of the night porters' pantry.

'What harm can a kipper do?' Smallhouse was asking Gordonpole. The men were having their meal and took no notice of me. Gordonpole got up from the table and bashed about in the cupboard looking for the chutney.

'It's a shabby world,' Smallhouse continued. 'You want to look at the prison farms,' he said ignoring the noise. 'Just you watch what stock they put in their paddicks and do the same yourself,' he said. 'Whatever it is the Government's doing, just you do the same as them because, I'll tell you this, prices will alter to suit what they have to sell. And, if you sell when they sell you'll be a rich man. Take a case in point, take beef now, there's no price at all just now for it, but you go out there and take a look at the beef cattle running and fattening on the pasture of the Crown.'

Smallhouse and Gordonpole polished the whole hospital every night. It took them all night. They emptied the bins too and they were allowed to smoke which was fair enough when you saw what was sometimes thrown away from the operating theatres.

'Do they own land?' I asked Casualty Porter later and he laughed at my reverence. He shook his head.

'Not even a window box,' he said. 'It's all in the mind,' he said and then he introduced me to Feegan, an old man dressed in black. He was engaged for ever in an endless dance up and down and across, back and forth all through and over the whole building all night long. With a special clock strapped to him he checked the fire-fighting equipment. He looked like a little black machine.

Everyone said this thing about Sister Bean.

'Always stand between Sister Bean and the drip,' they said. They said if she looked directly at it something would be sure to go wrong with it. An air bubble would develop or it would go through too quickly or too slowly or stop altogether causing the patient to deteriorate rapidly perhaps even to death.

It seemed I was always to be on special nursing in some dark screened-off corner of the ward working stealthily beside a doctor busy with an unknown person, someone I'd never seen before and probably would never see again. That's what it was like being a relieving night nurse.

This thing they said about Sister Bean was hard to believe because she'd been so intimately concerned with life and death for over forty years. She had black coffee every night at ten past twelve and I was supposed to take it to her; so on top of all my other worries I had to think of this too.

I thought I would discover the truth about Night Sister and I stood aside on purpose when I heard her coming. She always came accompanied by the little breezes of her own rapid movement. She muttered too, a kind of hoarse whispering of names and diagnoses. It was like a dispensing of spells and curses as she came scurrying through the half-dark ward. All at once she was beside the bed and stood with her head bent while I told her about the patient. She nodded twice, her starched cap seemed top heavy on the small withered bean stick of her body.

I looked sideways in the frail light to the transfusion and waited for her to follow my sidelong look. The life-giving drops, quivering red berries were trembling and falling with promise, drop dropping steadily one after the other.

It was a faultless transfusion and the patient was warm and asleep. No one knew I was throwing away the ultimate chances of the transfusion and gambling with a man's life. No one at all knew what I was doing. I handed her the special charts.

Night Sister flicked her torch over them and handed them back.

Instead of standing between Sister Bean and the drip I looked sideways at it again silently inviting her to follow my look. It was as if, fully acquainted with her witch-like powers, she either refrained from using them, or at this time, did not choose to do so.

The hospital building glowing with subdued light in the night was like a great ship forever in harbour. Human life in this ship was divided into blocks. One block for hearts and one for chests, a block for bladders and one for bowels, a block for bones, one for women's troubles, one for mental disorders, one for births and all for deaths. I spent the nights in all the different parts of the hospital busy with the post-operative care of patients and worrying about Sister Bean's little white starched tray-cloth.

When I went through the half-lighted basements of the kitchens I met Maggie the hairless cook. Her head was always tied up in a greasy cloth. With her was Hilda, the fat maid who was always pregnant and a Boy. He had no name and no one knew how old he was. He worked all night quietly going about setting steam gauges, cleaning out ovens and bread crocks. He scoured the milk churns and prepared enormous cauldrons of peeled potatoes. He raked and stoked the boilers and he never spoke to anyone. No one had ever heard his voice.

'All nurses must show their little pink forms before entering,' Smallhouse said when I went down to the pantry to fetch Casualty Porter.

'What did the gynaecologist say to the actress?' Gordon-pole said. He was coiling lengths of cable flex.

'Oh I haven't time for your silly riddles!' I said to him. 'Listen!' I said. 'I think Hilda should be married. It's time Hilda was married.'

'Good idea!' said Smallhouse. 'I'd be only too glad to give her away,' and he roared his head off. They had to hold each other up they laughed so much.

'Oh! my! Mind my polisher!' Gordonpole clutched his sides.

'No listen!' I said. 'I'm serious. I think she needs a nice kind husband, a father for her children.' They all looked at me and they all looked at each other.

'Sister Bean's had an operation, she's safely away in the women's surgical ward,' I said. 'So now's the right time for the ceremony and, in any case, as you can see for ourselves we haven't much longer.'

'But the trouble is, we're all married already,' Smallhouse said. And then we all looked at Casualty Porter who seemed to have lost something under the table.

'It's very informal everywhere tonight,' I told them. 'There's a chocolate cake in Matron's office and someone's fixed a wireless in the broom cupboard, there's to be dancing later.'

Smallhouse and Gordonpole were enthusiastic and in a short time we managed to get Casualty Porter to be agreeable. He even went and fetched flowers from the passage outside the private wards. He put a poinsettia in his buttonhole and then we dressed Hilda in one of the gowns they use in X-ray.

'It's a lovely green,' I told her. 'You should always wear this colour.' I made her a veil with three packets of sterile surgical gauze.

'You look a treat!' I told her.

We had to wait until Feegan, bound by the checking clock, could make a brief appearance in the kitchens to perform the ceremony before being forced to set off again on his light prancing up the well of the first staircase.

Smallhouse would give the bride away and Maggie was to stand in as mother of the bride.

'Oh,' I said, 'you haven't got a hat for the wedding.' We

all looked in dismay at Maggie's lack of suitable clothes.

'Wait,' I said and I rushed up to the linen room by the out-patients' hall and quickly searched the shelves. 'There that suits you very well,' I said, pinning one of Sister Bean's caps on to the greasy head-cloth.

'It's really you!' I said when she began to protest she wouldn't be seen dead in one of them.

'Well,' I told her, 'You're not dead yet.' I pinned a draw sheet on to Hilda's plump shoulders.

'Gordonpole can be a page,' I said and I made him hold the end of the sheet like a train. Hilda was delighted. She stood swaying and her melon-coloured face shone with a big smile.

'I've lost my way in the seasons,' Smallhouse muttered while we waited impatiently for Feegan. He consulted his diary. 'Hm I see shearing time is nearly with us,' he snapped the little book shut.

'That's just like you farmers,' Casualty Porter said with his customary good humour. 'You look at a date and you shear your sheep no matter what the weather is and you let them starve with cold! I've seen it with my own eyes. It's the same with burning off, that's why the whole country gets burned to a crisp just because a date is set for being able to burn no matter how dry the season.'

Smallhouse looked coldly at the bridegroom and turning away he addressed Gordonpole. 'How are things up at your place?' he asked.

'Terrible,' Gordonpole sighed. 'It's the poultry,' he said. 'They lay one egg between them, it's union rules, you know, the "State Amalgamated Fur and Feather", one egg only in twenty-four hours, it's a sort of lay to rule they've started. There's nothing I can do.'

'Too right!' Smallhouse nodded. 'As if there isn't enough farmyard stress already. Mine have gone off their heads too, lost their minds completely. They're eating their own eggs!'

'That's because you're not feeding them right,' the bridegroom interrupted again. The father of the bride and the page turned angrily towards the bridegroom.

'Now!' I said quickly, fearing a threat to the domestic

harmony. 'I think we should move that trolley with the bins.'
Smallhouse and Gordonpole lit their cigarette ends and
tidied the stinking bins into a corner. They had just finished
when Feegan came in stepping lightly between the buckets
of carnations and roses.

'Did you remember a prayer book?' I asked Casualty
Porter. Of course he had forgotten.

'I've got this,' Feegan said pulling a small book from his
tight black pocket. 'It's a Cricketer's Manual,' he explained.
'It's very old, it's dated 1851, an heirloom, in a sense it's a
sort of treasure,' he seemed to apologize. We had never
heard him say so much before, his voice was very pleasant,
it was an agreeable surprise.

'Well then,' I said. 'Read a bit of it please.' We all sang
'Here comes the Bride', and Feegan read from his little
book, 'The moral character of any pursuit is best estimated
by its consequences to individuals and its effects upon
society. If the absence of evil be not a permissible proof of
innocence it ought to imply assent, when no positive evi-
dence stands in opposition –'

'That was very nice thank you,' I said quickly. I was afraid
time would run out.

'Anyone here object to this, er, marriage?' Feegan gave a
hurried glance round the assembled company. Somewhere
the other side of the kitchens the Boy dropped something
heavy, it sounded like a hod of coke.

Feegan hurried on. 'Dust to dust and ashes to ashes,' he
gabbled. 'I declare you man and wife.'

Hilda gave Casualty Porter such a hug he gasped for
breath.

The telephone was ringing and ringing in the outpatients'
hall and he had to rush off to answer it. Feegan danced off
into the darkness and we threw rice and bits of torn-up
coloured paper over the radiant Hilda.

While we were hurriedly eating some sausage rolls,
Smallhouse made a speech.

'Unaccustomed as I am,' he said, 'I would like to make
a few comments on the cauliflower which is perhaps the
oldest sex symbol known to man. We should', he said, 'in
this shabby world look to the prison farms. The prison farm,'

he drew breath, 'and the coins of the realm,' he seemed lost in thought and chewed his sausage roll gloomily. 'Coins of the Realm,' he said.

'That was very nice thank you,' I said anxiously looking at the clock.

'Coins of the Realm,' Smallhouse said again and shook his pockets. He was still searching in his pockets when Hilda clutched herself and gave several great moans. We all looked at her in dismay.

'Her waters have been and gone and broke,' Maggie said knowingly. I told Gordonpole to get the trolley and I rushed to the phone.

'Archbishop here,' Casualty Porter answered it in an over-developed Oxford accent. 'On behalf of Royalty and ourselves we wish the bride all happiness, a message from the Queen herself reads, "We are amused", telegrams are arriving from –'

'Get me maternity quick!' I interrupted him.

'Ward 4 speaking.'

'Hilda's in labour,' I said.

'How frequent are the pains?' came the competent reply.

'It's all one big pain,' I said.

'Where's the head?' said the cool voice.

'What?' I said. 'Oh I think, somewhere between the stove and the sink.'

'The head,' the Charge Nurse on Ward 4 said patiently. 'Is it on the perineum?'

'Oh that head! Oh yes I should think so,' I said, dreadfully afraid Hilda would be delivered on the kitchen floor.

'Nurses never think. They know,' the Charge Nurse said coldly. 'Bring the patient straight up.' And she rang off.

Hilda's baby was born while we were in the lift.

'Turn the blanket back', she said, 'so as I can get a look.' Somewhere in between Hilda's big thighs and her coarse underwear a small damp wrinkled creature gave out a great cry and Hilda smiled. 'Isn't he lovely,' she sighed and her big face was surprisingly sweet and fresh.

We hurried the trolley along as quickly as possible.

'Keep still,' I said sharply to Hilda. I was afraid she would crush her own baby.

Hilda and the baby and all the muddle of wedding clothes and flowers were swept off into the antiseptic fragrance of the maternity ward.

On the way down I called in at the women's surgical ward and I peered round the first screen inside the door. Sister Bean looked smaller than ever lying on her pillow without her big white starched cap. She turned her bright little eyes to me. And, as if she knew why I had come to visit her, she gave a withered little smile.

'Since when did varicose veins get a transfusion nurse?' she said. 'All the same, thanks for coming to see me.'

I went on down into the underworld of the kitchens. I saw the Boy standing alone in the mess of makeshift confetti and scattered rice. Bruised and dying flowers were all over the place and the Boy was just standing in it all, his broom and dustpan on one side as if he'd forgotten them. His face was all puffed up and, from where I was, it looked as if slow heavy tears were crawling down his smeared cheeks.

The fresh milk had come so I stopped and drank a basinful.

The empty milk churns were being taken away from the ramp outside the kitchens and the city beyond was beginning to wake up. A thin trickle of tired sad people left the hospital. They were relatives unknown and unthought about, they had spent an anonymous night in various corners of the hospital waiting to be called to a bedside. They were leaving in search of that life in the shabby world which has to go on in spite of the knowledge that someone who had been there for them was not there any more.

The air was surprisingly sweet and fresh at the edge of the kitchens where the inside of the hospital flowed out to meet the outside world. I stood there, full of fresh milk and I took deep breaths of this cool air which seemed just now to contain nothing of the weariness and the contamination and the madness of suffering.

It seemed too that it was more of a certainty than merely a possibility that at some time Night Sister Bean would be admitted for major surgery and then we would know once and for all the truth about this thing everyone said about her.

Two Men Runni

In a minute they'll be here. I can hear them coming, one each side of the gallery, unlocking the doors one after the other. In a minute it'll be my door.

They're coming nearer, faster, it's like a race between them to get all the doors unlocked. Metal against metal echoing along the gallery; and then the noise of all the feet running back and down the iron stairs; no voices, just the solid drumming of all those feet let loose pounding and reverberating.

I'm running down now to a kind of freedom just like all of them. Even my clothes and my canvas shoes are the same as theirs. Dark green. I don't know how much I am like them, except that like them, I need food and water, and I go to the toilet like they do and I have a shower, like they do, when it's my turn. I spend a lot of time wondering whether I am really like them, and if I am, how much and why.

Yesterday I had another session with the psychiatrist. He's got a bird in a cage. He says that, though the bird's in a cage, it sings and sings to him and it tells him everything.

I would have liked to ask him what it was the bird was saying about itself. But I didn't. I thought he would feel stupid sitting there making up things the bird was singing about. So I never said anything just as the week before I didn't speak nor the week before that.

'Cigarette?' he made sure politely that I was at ease. 'I

want you to be comfortable in here,' he said smiling, showing flashes of gold in his back teeth. He smoothed his hair and smiled at the bird in the cage and it sang and sang as if its little chest would swell and burst.

'Now what would you like to tell me this week?' he asked me.

I couldn't think of anything intelligent enough to say so I smoked the cigarette and looked out of the window. Behind him, through the window, there were streets and houses and I could see a road going on and on into the distance, out to the hills. Not being used to smoking I had to concentrate on the cigarette, and then I began thinking if I could just be out on that road, perhaps I could go back and simply straighten everything out. A half-remembered song went round and round in my head. I seemed to be singing it, not aloud of course.

> country road take me home
> to the place where I belong
> take me home country road

And then suddenly I felt terribly tired. 'Really,' I thought, 'it's easier in here. There are things I should be doing out there; like everyone else I have my responsibilities but while I'm in here I can't attend to any one of them. Even if I could go back, out there,' I told myself, 'there's nothing at all I could do.' Thinking like this I realized that everything had been lifted off me. So I finished smoking the cigarette.

As I looked towards the hills the song in my head turned into a little gate opening on well-oiled hinges, quietly opening, so close it seemed to be that I stretched out my hand to it and then quickly withdrew my hand and the gate turned in my head with the song and the voice of a very clean woman I had known once somewhere out there far away . . .

'I can't stand having people around the house before breakfast,' her voice came down her nose, thin and hard. 'Dot dot dotty dot,' she said, 'what kind of language is that!' Song and gate and voice turned and turned in my head. 'If I could go back,' I thought, 'I'd do it all again, but I'd do

it somehow differently.' And, as I sat there, I tried to think
out the changes I might have made.

The psychiatrist interrupted my thoughts.

'Nothing you want to tell me about?' He smiled and, with
both clean palms, he smoothed back his already smoothed
grey hair.

I considered his question and, because I didn't have anything to tell him, I didn't answer.

'Don't worry about it,' he said kindly. 'Your memory will
come back. Your memory will come back.' He held the door
open for me and we shook hands and all the time that crazy
little bird was singing.

Now we're running on concrete. There's the whistle and the
voice.

'Running on the spot. One-Two-One-Two-Run-Run-
One-Two-Left-Right-Left-Right-One-Foot-Two Foot-Foot-
Foot-Foot-Foot-And Run and Run and Run . . .'

'Move over!' There's a man running at my side.

'Move over,' he says, he says it every time. 'Move over,
nearer the edge,' his voice is very low. 'Edge off a bit. Keep
on running,' he says, 'I'm coming.'

'I'm running too,' I tell him, and we are both running.
Two men running. Two men, in dark green, running.

Every day when I'm running all kinds of things go through
my head, words and places and people's faces. Today it's
poetry.

'*To know the change/ and feel it/ was never said* oh No!
That's not right! *To know the change/ and feel it/ when
there is none to heal it* . . . dot dot dotty dot . . . *was never
said in rhyme.*'

'What ever's that. What's that you're on about?' his
voice, out of breath, is indignant.

'It's a poem Hamish. A poe-em poe-ettry. *The poetry of
the earth is ceasing never*, er, Keats.'

'Cut it out willya. My name's not Hamish!' Out of breath
he finds it hard to talk. 'I never knew you was a pote, I
thought you done operations.'

'Backyard only dear Hamish,' I answer in my fruitiest

voice. 'And, as you will perceive, unsuccessfully. Ultimately, unfortunately, ultimately, I failed, Hamish.'

'You cut out that Hamish! I'm not Hamish! How d'you mean backyard? I mean it would be dirty to operate on someone out in the yard, out in all that dirt.' He's gasping for breath.

'Well kitchen table would be more accurate,' I change from the fruity to the pompous. 'Among other things, so to speak, as well as being a poet, I am an abortionist.'

'But however did you?'

'It's a matter of technique,' I say with no little pride. 'Once you've done one, you've done them all. They're all the same. There's nothing to it. My life, my dear fellow, has been full and varied. Used car salesman in the mornings, afternoons abortions, er, by appointment only, and, in the evenings, Poet.'

'Garn with you! There's all kinds of wimmin, there's fat and thin; pretty and ugly and old and young . . .'

'There may be differences superficially,' I interrupt him. 'But basically the design is similar. They're all the same. Such a bore really!'

'Well if it's so easy why did you give it up?'

'I haven't.'

'Well yo'm not doin' it now. Yo'm not a abolishinist now.'

'Mother didn't like it.'

'Aw Gerroff! Yer mom's dead. You said so before.' He pants and groans. 'Aw Gawd!'

'You always get out of breath at this part,' I tell him. 'Now easy, take it easy, easy there. Breathe right out before you breathe in. Hold and Breathe!'

We are running together. One foot two foot breathe in breathe out, running and running.

'I only failed because I wanted to,' I explain to him.

'Then why did you say it's unfortunate?'

'Everything has its unfortunate side.'

'Too right it does!'

'All the same I have my regrets you know; breathe in, breathe out, right out, breathe in, there's something pleasant about being a lady's pet poet. Breathe! There was

never an evening when I was not invited to some grand
house or other, either as Poet in Residence or Personal Abortionist. Breathe in, breathe out. In and out. For my poetry
I used Keats freely.'

'What's that? Some kind of flea powder or something?'

'Oh never mind!'

Breathe in. Breathe out. I'm singing now,

> One day the man I used to be
> Will come along and talk to me.

He's shouting now. Somewhere behind me he's shouting,

'Will you? Will you know the way in the dark?' I slow
down for him.

'Of course I'll know the way,' I tell him in my ordinary
voice. 'Of course I'll know the way. It's the way I've come.
I know the way from when I was a boy.'

'Tell me about when you was a boy,' as always he asks me
to tell him, and as always, he can hardly speak. We're still
running, but slowly.

'Well, everything was different then,' I say. 'I was different in those days. I used to play at horses and carts on the
kitchen table.'

'Aw, gettaway with you yo' never!'

'Yes, I had a jar, a preserving jar with a lid, it was full of
nuts and bolts and nails and screws.'

'Screws!'

'Yes, the other sort. I had them all sizes, brass ones big
and little.'

'But what did you do?'

'Just that.'

'What?'

'I played at horses and carts on the kitchen table. I had
the screws and nails and bolts arranged, you know, dotted
up and down as if the table was the road. I used to walk them
– dot – dot – dotty – dot along the table.' He's laughing and
I'm laughing with him. Laughing and running and running
and running.

'The operations? They was much later?' he manages to

ask. I don't want to talk about them, the operations, not now, so I don't answer. I'm running faster.

'Wait!' he calls. 'Wait for me! Tell me about the place.'

I'm running faster now and faster.

'Wait!' he calls again. 'Wait, oh wait for me!'

'You'll have to keep up,' I shout. 'It's a long way. We'll have to run for a long time.' I look back at him. 'Well, perhaps not all that long, listen!' I say just loud enough for him to hear. 'Listen, there's a creek, you'll be able to wash your feet. There's a barn. It's full of hay. We can rest up; we can sleep. Just wait till you smell the hay. It's safe in the hay.'

'What if someone comes?' he's panting and anxious.

'No one will come. I've told you before. There's no one there now. Just keep on running. Keep up! Easy. Breathe right out. Out! Before you breathe in.'

And so we're running. I feel quite fond of this unknown man. Because of the running we do not really see each other, but I feel fond all the same.

'You'll like the place when we get there,' I tell him. 'It's very quiet in the wheat in the mornings. In the wheat in the mornings it's always the same. There's a rushing of wind. I used to wonder where the wind came from. It's a cold wind and the sunrise is pink. Have you ever seen the sun rise in the wheat?' I shout at him, 'Have you ever seen the sunrise pink?'

'No. Never,' he's gasping for breath.

'Slow down a bit,' I say, 'and I'll tell you something. There's a group of white gums by the gate. They're lovely trees, they make a special place to think about and to get back to. The sun lights up the white and grey bark. It's like a patchwork of pink and white and grey, a sort of picture embroidered all up the trees. The wind rushes. It always rushes there and the pink and grey galahs scream from one group of trees to the next. Those birds! You'll see their rosy breasts and greedy necks. My father often stood at the edge of the road, I saw him standing with his head turned upwards as he enjoyed the fresh air.

' "Just look at all those birds," he would say. "Those birds must be getting their food from somewhere to have all that

energy." Nearby the windmill clicked and the birds seemed
everywhere, in the trees, in the sky and on the windmill.
Swiftly they flew towards the rising sun and, just as swiftly,
they circled round, their colours changing so that one minute they were like a pink cloud and the next minute they
could not be seen at all. It seemed to me then as I watched
the flocks of birds with my old man that the birds suddenly
came out of the clear morning air and, just as suddenly, went
back into it.'

The feet are pounding. Running feet. Our feet seem separate from the rest. Running and running. He asks me, 'What
did yer ole man do?'

'My dad? What did he do? Oh yeah. He sold medicines
and spices. I went with him.'

'Where?'

'Everywhere. He travelled everywhere, selling. I went with
him. I helped him, unpacking and selling and packing up
again. We camped out or stayed at farms. He did fixing jobs
around the farms sometimes.'

'Did he do operations too?'

'Course not! The women bought things off him.'

'What things?'

'Oh you know, cough syrup, ointment, powder and lipstick and he used to get stockings for them, all kinds of
things, he had in his cases. They used to bake things . . .'

'What?' He's dropped behind and can't hear me.

'They used to bake things.' I'm shouting at him.

'Like what?' He's shouting back.

'Like apple pies,' I'm shouting. 'Treacle tarts, ginger cakes,
banana cakes, fruit loaf . . .'

'Stop! Stop!' he's shouting. 'Stop, I'm hungry oh stop!'

'Keep on running,' I call to him gently. 'Come on don't
get left behind. Just keep on running. Breathe right out
before you breathe in. Just keep on till you smell that hay!'

'Yeah, you make it like I can smell it orlready,' he's gasping for breath. 'But go on telling me abour yor ole man.'

'We'd go on and on,' I explain, 'till there was a township

or a farm. We'd have dinner or tea depending on the time of day.

' "Just look at the cherries in this tart," my Dad would say, "what a picture it would make painted and stuck all round the walls!"

' "Have you brought my embroidery silk and my knitting wool Mister Enderby?" And, "Mr Enderby you have remembered the stockings, are there any stockings?" the women asked.

'Dad had everything they asked for, and we ate cake with raisins and cherries as big as birds' eggs.'

'Tell me some more about the farm,' his voice is strangled into a whisper. 'Tell me some more about the farm. Gawd!' he cried, 'I – can't – run – any more. Wait for me!'

I have left him too far behind.

'Wait! I'm getting lost! I'm lost!' he's calling. I slow down, running still, running in one place, running on the spot.

'Of course you're not lost,' I feel strong and my voice is deep, sustained by some unknown strength. 'Of course you're not lost. You can run. Run like this, lightly, one foot, two foot, one foot-two foot-breathe-in-foot-breathe-out-foot. In and out. You can run. This running's like flying. How can you be lost on the way home?'

'Wait oh wait! Oh wait for me. I can't keep it up.'

'This next part's easier,' I tell him. 'The road goes flat between paddocks. You'll hear the creek, the water rushes over the rocks, it's like music. And, if you listen, you'll hear the frogs and perhaps a fox cough-barking along the bank to call another fox.'

'I'm lost! I've lost the way!' he's wailing.

'Keep on running. I'm telling you about the farm.' I'd like to reach my arm out round his shoulders but I don't. 'Come on, run here close beside me. You can see the farm from a long way off, from the road. It looks like a toy farm. Up on the hillside there's a harmony of farm buildings, house and barn and sheds. The sheep and poultry are like toys spread out on a kitchen table. There's farm machinery too, that's something for a man to play with. The whole place is a place of pleasure if you're just visiting.

'It's a different matter if you're there all the time.' I hold out my arm as if to draw him on, to keep him running close. 'I'll tell you about the cock fight,' I say to him. 'One evening we reached Parks' farm just about tea time. We were tired out. No one was about.

' "Hullo!" Dad said. "It's very quiet." And so it was. There was a sort of hush over the place. There were no little silver eyes darting in and out of the vines round the house. Marge Parks didn't come out to meet us and there was no sound from the dogs or the poultry. And then just in front of the shed I saw two bantam cocks, the young cock had his head across the bent back of the old one and every time the old one moved, the young one attacked. Oh it was fierce! Blood trickled from their dusty combs; most of the blood was from the old rooster who seemed to be sinking towards the earth, really tired and resigned. My old Dad tried to separate them with the handle of a fork but they were locked together. He sent me for a bucket of water which he threw over them. The shock parted them and Dad chased the young cock into the pen where the little brown and white hens were waiting and watching. The young cock stood in a corner, his feathers ruffled, and he seemed to me to look uncomfortable and guilty. We tried to offer the old rooster some grain, Dad held it out to him in the palm of his hand, but it was just as if the old bantam had given up. It was as if he knew the end of his life had come and he sank down nearer to the ground. He refused food and water and stood there sad and ashamed and we didn't know what to do for him.'

We are running lightly, now, one foot-two foot.

'It's a different matter,' I say again, 'if you're there all the time. There's all kinds of problems, broken fences, cattle diseases, weeds and thieves, and then there's floods and droughts.' I pause, he's calmer, he always is calmer when I tell about the cock fight, he's calmer when he's listening to me. I go on talking.

'When you're running to the farm then it's different; it's pure enjoyment like it was when we used to turn up there

with all the boxes and display cases; lipsticks, powder, sham-
poo, dress materials, lace trimmings and cases of dresses and
hats and stockings . . .'

'Go on!' he says, 'I want to hear about when you was a
boy.'

'Yes. I'll tell you, there was something special in the qual-
ity of the air and in the arriving and in the going away too.
We were on the move the whole time. We lived like this.
It was his living.'

'Why did he give it up then? Why?'

'He couldn't go on for ever, no one can, he had a little
dream of settling down on a farm of his own. He loved the
Parks farm. Marge Parks always used to say to him, "When
you going to settle down George? When are you coming
George? You know the place needs a man George." She had
been a widow for years. We always stopped a while at Marge
Parks' place and he always said he'd finish up at that farm.
It was home to him.'

'And did he?'

'Yes.'

'So?'

'Well it turns out sometimes that a man dreams just a bit
too much. His dream outsteps what he is really able to
expect and do. I'll explain. He always said if ever he got confused in his sense of direction, then it would be time to pack
in the whole thing.

' "Boy," he said to me more than once, "if ever I arrive
in a township, no matter where it is, if I can't remember,
in that town, which side of the highway the hotel is and
which side the railway is, if it comes to this, if at any time
I turn up somewhere and don't know where I am, then that's
it!" And that's exactly how it happened. One evening we
drove along the wide empty street of a wheat town. The
place was windswept and clean in that pearly light before
dark. The hotel, the railway and the petrol pump, the shire
hall, the store, the hospital and the grain silo he had them
all mixed up.

' "By rights –" Dad turned the car round, "the hotel
should be here and the railway across there, but I've lost my

way!" His face was white as he looked at me. "Boy!" he said, "I'm packing in." '

'He knew Marge Parks was waiting for him. He said a widow with her own acres and a tidy farm was home. He was looking forward to it. He said my life would be better too. He'd been worried for a long time he said about me not being at school. Sales weren't too good either, he often said that there was too much competition. The women he said were going down to the city themselves and doing their own shopping and having things sent from the big stores.'

We're running, our feet pounding. We're breathing hard and running, I run faster.

'Say!' he calls me, 'I've had a thought. Forget yor ole man for a minnit.'

'You always have a thought about something just about now. I've told you before, it's all right,' I'm shouting at him. 'It'll be all right.'

'Wait!' he's calling. 'I know you've said there'll be no one there. I know you've said that we can have the place to ourselves to hide – I mean, to rest up in,' he's running closer now, 'but what if there's someone there?'

'I've told you before,' I tell him. 'I've told you, there won't be anyone there.'

'Well,' he's shouting, 'how will we get in? We'll need to get in won't we. I've caught you now haven't I! You're caught!'

'I've told you before. I've told you, the key'll be there, it'll be hidden.'

'But you've said, more than once, you've said it'll be a different woman. It can't be the same one so how shall we know where she's hid the key?'

'Calm down!' I tell him. 'There's all sorts of women but their hiding places are the same. Now come on. Keep on running. There isn't much time left.'

'Aren't you going to tell me what happened?'

'Yes if you'll shut up, I'll tell you.'

We're running. My voice goes up and down, up and down as I tell him.

'By the time we reached the farm the car was steaming. Dad drove non stop, he was determined to get to Parks Farm before the car boiled out. He drove all night and it was just beginning to get light when we drove up to the white gums by the gate and on into the yard.

'Marge Parks came out in her dressing gown. Pink and grey quilted and crumpled she appeared through the slight mist. Her face was crumpled and lined with being asleep. I had never seen her early in the morning before. I was shocked at her and looked at the ground. She was always so clean and smart.

' "George! Whatever are you doing here at this time of the night?" Her voice shocked me too.

' "Hallo! Hallo! Hallo!" my Dad called out. "Hallo Margie Girl! It's our day, our day today!" my silly old man said. And then he told her he'd finished up on the roads and he'd come for good as he'd always said he would. He knew she was expecting him he said because she'd always said she was.

'I saw her face go like concrete, all the lines and creases set really hard. She fixed her look somewhere behind Dad.

' "Oh yes, of course George park your van and your trailer," her voice came down through her nose, thin and hard. "Yes of course George, you can park your stuff on my land. But George, I'm warning you, I'm not having all that scrap iron and rubbish here for long." She did not look at me at all.

'It's her stiff back I've always remembered most about her when I've thought about the farm.

'My old man began to tremble. I'd never seen him shake before. He seemed to shake all over. He tried to offer her things, all at once, pushing them at her with both hands.

' "Look," he said to her, "Margie look! Here's all the lipsticks, you can have them all, I told you, Marge, didn't I, that I'd bring everything to you one day."

' "Yes George, you did. But not in the night . . ."

' "Well," he took no notice of her, "well, the lipsticks are your colours, here's the Burnt Orange and the Miami. Oh, and here's Parasol, a bit pink but pink's your colour isn't it Marge, you're very fair. And Marge," he rushed on, "here's

stockings to last you the rest of your life. And here's a spice
rack, look there's ginger, cinnamon, cloves, pepper, garlic
salt, celery salt – the lot. And here's bath salts for you Marge,
in plastic urns, pink and blue, aren't they pretty?"
' "It's hard to say George at this hour of the day. You
know me, George, I don't like having people around before
breakfast." Her long cold stare fixed just beyond him made
me shiver. "There's no need to come up to the house," she
said then. "There's a tap down by the bottom shed," she
said, "you can use that."
'He couldn't believe it. He stared at her.
' "My energy's gone Marge."
' "I can see that George."
' "No need to come to the house, Marge, is that what
you're saying, Marge?"
' "It is George."
' "No need to come to the house, Marge, after I've been
coming all these years and we've always said . . ."
' "Dad," I said to him, "Dad, don't! Don't go on." '

We're running still, lightly now, one foot-two-foot-one-foot-
two-foot-foot-foot-breathe in breathe out breathe in. Side by
side we're running, easily.
'What about the kitchen table?' he asks me. 'Where did
you put your nuts and bolts?' his breathing's easier.
'Where'd you put yer horses and carts of a night time?'
'I knew you'd ask that,' I say. 'I'll tell you. My Dad made
me a bit of a table out of an old box in the trailer and every
night I set out my horses and carts, dot-dot-dotty-dot up and
down, to and fro along the road, fast and slow, my horses
and carts passed each other, stopped to let each other go by,
they turned in the roadway and sometimes they collided.'
'An' what did yer Dad do? Go on tell what yer Dad did.
'He just sat there.'
'While you played?'
'Yes. While I played with my horses and carts, in the evenings, he just sat there. There seemed to be no life in him
at all. You see, he'd looked forward so much to being there
and it was quite clear Marge Parks didn't want him around

the place. He'd sit and stare at my horses and carts as if they
weren't there. You see, he didn't know like I knew just why
she didn't want him there. He didn't seem to understand.'

We're running. Running.

'I told him things about the horses,' I say. 'I'd pretend one
was lame to get him to join in. "The milk horse Dad, she's
lame!" I'd shout to him.

' "A lame milk horse," he'd say at last, "put her on clay
Boy, clay's the thing Boy, that'll fix her." But mostly he just
sat there shaking his head.'

We're running still. I'm running faster.

'Hey wait, you're leaving me behind,' he's shouting, 'Hey
wait! My feet hurt and I can't run any more,' he's wailing
now, 'oh my feet!'

'Come on,' I'm marking time, running on the spot. 'Come
on.' I tell him. 'Keep it up, forget your feet. Breathe! That's
better. Try to remember what the grass feels like, the soft
grass. And try to remember the wind blowing in your face.
The grass,' I remind him.

Lightly on the grass, one foot-two foot-one foot-two foot-
run-run-running in the wind.

'Tell me what happened next.'

'You know what happened next.'

'Well, tell me again, you know, what you saw through the
winder. Tell what you saw through the winder.'

'Ah yes, the window. But first,' I say, 'I must tell you about
Franz Heiss.'

'What about him then?'

'Well, he'd never been there before. And this time we
didn't see him straight away though once or twice I thought
I saw someone, but when I said so to Dad he just laughed
and said no one was there, Marge ran the place herself, he
said, and only hired men when it was time to do certain
things.'

'What was he like then this Heiss?'

'All right in his way,' I tell him, 'he couldn't speak much

English. He seemed to work the place. He was a big man, young and very sunburned. When he saw me he would smile and offer me an orange or a handful of nuts. When he met with Dad he would smile and give a little bow and say "Fine day Mister Enter," he never managed our name properly. Dad always said 'Gooday' to him, I never saw my Dad be rude to anyone.

'It was clear Heiss was doing everything that needed doing and Dad got busy with his car. I think he had it in mind to get it on the road again. He stripped it all down; bits of the car were everywhere and, in a confused sort of way, he sat in the middle of it all.

'One night he told me to go up to the house to borrow an adjustable spanner. "I can't set eyes on mine Boy," he said.

' "But it's dark Dad," I said.

' "Yes, but I'll have it to use first thing in the morning," he said. "Off you go."

'I think I was afraid of Marge Parks coming down the backyard. She was such a tidy woman, everything was scraped clean on her place and everything put away. Heiss worked clean like that. I was afraid of Marge Parks seeing the old car spread over the top end of the grass. So I went for the spanner.

'I went up through the paddock and into the yard. I remember the smell of the grass, sweet and fresh. I went through her tidy garden, the little side gate was so well oiled it never made a sound. I thought I must get the spanner. I knew we must get away from there. I somehow felt the adjustable spanner was all that was needed to get the car back together and we'd be off on the road again, laughing and talking and stopping along the roadside whenever we wanted to, watching the clouds and the birds, listening to the lonely singing of the wind in the telegraph wires and knowing again that wonderful feeling of having the whole countryside to ourselves. And then the pleasure of turning up at a farm just as the woman there was opening her oven.

'I longed to be safely in a farm kitchen again helping to

unpack the cases. Sometimes we spread out the dresses and
blouses over chair backs and the girls of the house tried to
make up their minds which to order.

‘ "I can't decide Mr Enderby, the tartan is so smart and
the lace on the white one is so pretty!"

‘ "Have them both then my dear," my old Dad would say,
"pay me something now and I'll make out a docket and you
pay a little more next time."

‘There was a smell of fresh new cotton . . . but to get back
to the adjustable spanner; I knocked on the door but I
knocked too softly and no one came. I knocked again and
waited. I stepped into the flower bed trampling all over
whatever was there and I looked through the window. It was
the bedroom.

‘ "No one came to the door," I told him when I got back
down to the paddock. "Come in off the damp grass," I said
to him. I could see his face white there in the middle of the
wreckage. "Come in off the damp grass," I said again.

‘The bedroom window sill was low into the flowers, I kept
thinking about it as I set out my horses and carts in the
trailer.

‘Dot dot dotty dot the horses moved, dot dot, up and
down their little road, dot dotty dot.

‘ "Dad," I called him. "I think the stallion's standing." I
waited but there was no reply, he was just sitting there,
shaking his head sometimes.

‘ "Dad!" I tried again, "I'll have to write out a stud notice,
the stallion's standing."

‘ "Oh?" he raised his head, making an effort for my game,
"and is the mare reluctant?"

‘ "I don't think so," I told him.

‘In the morning he sent me up to the house to borrow the
giant wrench.

‘He sat all day in the parts of the car and he didn't eat
anything. I made him some bread and butter and picked my
way over to him, but he shook his head.

‘ "You have it," he said to me.

‘ "I've got a sick horse," I told him that night in the trailer.
He was lying in his bunk.

' "Sick or just old?" he asked me at last.

' "A bit of both," I said and it was then that I burst out crying. He seemed surprised. He got up quickly.

' "Put her on grass," he said to me, taking the horse out of my hand. "Where's your grass?" he asked me. "Here," I said, showing him a corner of the box. Carefully he put the nail on the right place.

' "There's no need to cry," he said. "Just give her a spell on grass."

'The next night he asked me, "How's that little old horse of yours?"

' "She's on the grass like you said," I told him. He picked up the horse and examined her carefully.

' "I'm afraid it's the knacker's yard for her," he said, "but they'll give you something for her," he added. I took my horse from him and in my hand I held a rusty nail.'

Running. Running. Running.

'What happened next?' he asks me.

'That's all,' I tell him quietly. 'My old man was not strong enough for the giant wrench, to use it, I mean and Heiss, Franz Heiss used it instead. He had the muscles.

'Self defence I suppose they called it.'

'Yeah, self defence that's it.'

Run. Run. Running, breathing in and breathing out, breathe in breathe out, run-one foot-two foot-foot-foot-foot-foot-

'So that's why I went back there,' I tell him very quietly, the words coming out as a breath. 'That's why I went back there,' I say. 'I went back there not so long ago. That's why I've done what I've done.'

We're running easily, breathing easily, breathe in, breathe out right out. This running's life.

'Like this,' I tell him softly. 'Like we're running now I went back to the farm alone one night. I wanted to thank Marge Parks for all she'd done.'

'You wanted to thank her!'

'Yes. In a way I owed a lot to her. When I was running back there that night I didn't know just how much I owed.'

'Life? you mean?'

'I'm paying that back now aren't I?'

'Yeah.'

'I wanted to thank Marge Parks for putting me through school and through university because she did all that with all the right clothes and money in my pocket and poetry books, the lot! And I wanted to sort out just what she had done to my old man. I could never, all through the years, get out of my mind her face and the look in her eyes when she came out of her house early that morning when, after driving all night, we had just arrived. It was a confrontation I have never been able to forget, a confrontation of hope on the one side and no hope on the other. I have never, in all the women I have met since, seen the same terrible, hard, careless stare. Because of who she was, it's even worse.

' "What's wrong with the boy?" she asked later that day, it was in the evening of that first day. She had come wandering through the yards down to the top end of the paddock where she'd told us we could camp.

' "What's wrong with the boy?" she asked my father the same question, tipping her yellow metal curls in my direction.

' "Dot dot dotty dot," my horses and carts were thick on the new road we had made for them.

' "Dot dot dotty dot," Marge repeated. "Whatever is that? What language is that?" and she fixed my father with her stare. "Dot dot dotty dot!"

' "He's only playin' Marge," Dad said to her. "It's only a little game he has that's all."

' "Dot dot dotty dot," Marge just stared her long cold hard stare.

' "Dad!" I called as I watched her stiff back disappearing towards the house. "Dad, there's a new gelding, he just came down the paddock. Dot dot dotty dot – there he is, he's gold coloured."

' "Where's your paddock Boy?" Dad leaned over the box.

' "Here," I said, "alongside the road."

' "Which one is he?" he asked.

' "This one," I said. He picked up the horse.

' "He's no gelding Boy. I'd say he was a stallion, a fine stallion, he's no gelding!" He gave me back my horse and in my hand I held the brass screw, like gold it was.'

We're running and running and breathing steadily.

'Like this,' I tell him again, softly, 'like we're running now I went back to the farm alone one night. It was pitch dark. I hoped she'd be alone. She'd be older, I thought she'd be older and weaker but I was older too and much bigger and a lot stronger. Even if Heiss was standing there, bronzed, tossing back his bright gold hair, moving with all the easy strength and urgency I'd seen through the window, I knew I'd get him too. I knew I could deal with him, especially if he was, by chance, serving her in the same way again. That way he'd be easy to catch, she had him caught, see, she had him caught tight; her fat white legs were crossed behind his neck. It was very possible that she might have him trapped like that ready for what I had to do.'

We're running side by side. He's gasping for breath.

'Go on, go on tell me!' he manages to speak, 'Go on! Go on!'

'I got to the place,' I tell him. 'I came up through the paddock and into the yard. Nothing was changed except that it seemed to be a much smaller place, compact even. I remembered the smell of the grass, sweet and fresh. I think of the grass very often now. Grass, and the smell of it is something you miss very quickly, something you can really long for.

'I went through her tidy garden and over her mown lawn, over her herbs and flowers and roses. I trampled on them all.

' "Make a lot of noise," I thought, "to scare the old Bitch." And then I knocked on her door. And I went on knocking on her door till, terrified, she came and opened it. I hid in the roses and she called out, "Who's there? Who is it? Who are you? What d'you want?" I could tell by her voice she was alone there.

'I breathed in and I breathed out, louder and louder,

panting and very heavy, breathing in and breathing out. I rustled in the bushes to scare her. She was terrified all right.

' "Get off my porch!" she yelled. "Get off my land! Whoever you are, get off! Off! Get off I say and I mean it."

'I came out then laughing straight in her face.

' "Madam" I said bowing low like Heiss, "Madam!" I went down on one knee, and in my fruity voice I said,

> But to the girdle do the gods inherit,
> Beneath is all the fiends;"

that's Shakespeare but you wouldn't know. I've come to thank you for Shakespeare. Marge, listen!

> There's hell, there's darkness, there's the sulphurous pit,
> Burning, scalding, stench, consumption; fie, fie, fie, pah, pah!

Shakespeare on women! He knew what he was talking about. And thanks to you, Marge Parks, I too know."

' "Why Alfie," she said, "is it you? What are you doing here?" She gave a little laugh. "You had me properly scared." Her face was very white. Still laughing I walked right in.

' "I've come to see you," I said to her – hair curlers, cold cream, face pack and all. "I've come to thank you for all you've done for me and to settle with you once and for all about my father. I've come to see you about him."

'I only meant to tell her straight out what I thought and to frighten her a bit, you know, to sort of shake her up. I've discovered all sorts of things about people now and quite a lot of people need a good shaking. But when I saw her straddled across her hall with her selfish bedroom so comfortable behind her, I knew it was for some other reason I had come there.

'She screamed the whole time. I've never heard, not even in what I've done with women, any woman scream like that. Her screams drew me on. I couldn't get my clothes off quick enough, hers too, I didn't take too much trouble.

'She stopped screaming and suddenly all I could see or think of was the tiny gate, so well oiled and quiet when it opened into her neat garden all those years ago, the night I'd been sent for a spanner. Because of remembering the gate and because of the way it turned, slowly opening, round and round in my head, her moans and crying afterwards gave me a shock.

' "What you crying for?" I asked her, trying to close the gate in my head to close off the confusion. I sat down on the bed.

' "Oh!" she cried and cried and caught hold of my arm. "Oh Alfie," she said, "there's something I've got to tell you." She tried to draw the pink quilt up over her, "there's something . . ."

'God! I knew then I had to tidy things up. I had to be even tidier than she was. You know finish up the whole thing.

' "No! No!" she screamed. "Not a knife!" And I stood there and said, "Yes! Yes! A knife." '

We are running close side by side.

'You had to do her in then?' he asks me.

'Yes. Yes I had to.'

We're running and running, trying to get breath. It sounds as if he's crying but it's me making all the noise.

'I can't get it out of my mind,' I tell him, 'she told me, she cried out, she told me something I never knew before. I never knew before that she was my mother.'

We're running and the tears are flying off my face. Running and running.

'That why you give up the pote-ry and the abolishins?' he's gasping.

'That's why I gave up the poetry and the abortions and, of course, the second-hand car business. That's why I gave them up, yes and no.'

'You got two answers.'

'Not really. There aren't any answers. I have given up. If I could go back and re-do everything I would do it all differently, I'd say different things. I might even think different things. But who knows what I would do . . .'

We're running together easily. Tenderly.

'How far's the farm now?' he asks.

'The gravel pits, the hills, the catchment and the foxgloves in the catchment. Did you know,' I ask him. 'Did you know that where the water collects and runs off the rocks there are different flowers growing there? Did you know that, because of this water, a paddock can be deep purple like a plum? And then, if you think about plums, the different colours range from deep purple through to the pale pearly green of the translucent satsuma before it ripens. Because of water that's how a paddock can look from one end to the other. It's the same with people . . .'

'Hey!' he shouts, 'how far's the farm now? From here, how far's the farm?'

'The farm? From here?' I pause. 'The same as last time I suppose.'

We're running steadily. Every day when I'm running all kinds of things go through my head, words and places and people's faces.

Today it's poetry. I have a special voice for poems.

'*To know the change/and feel it/was never said* oh No! That's not right. *To know the change/and feel it/when there is none to heal it* . . . dot dot dotty dot . . . *was never said in rhyme.*'

'What's that you're on about?' he's indignant. 'I asked you how far's the farm. The farm, how far away is it now?'

'It's a poem, Hamish. Keats, I use him freely.'

'Aw! Cut out that Hamish! I'm not . . .' There's the whistle and the voice. The feet pound on the concrete. There's the whistle and the voice.

'Off right – off left – off right – off left –off right – off – off – off – off.' Now we're running off the concrete and up the iron stairs.

'Move up!' There's a man running at my side.

'Move up – up – up – up – up,' he's always out of breath.

'If a man is deprived of freedom,' I say to him, 'that's punishment. Right?'

'Right!'

'Right agreed!' I say. 'But is it right on top of that to sub-ject a man to extra punishment?'

'Extra punishment? What d'you mean? We got TV, fans, smokes them's not punishment.'

'Yes, I know,' I say, 'but they're just sops to hide and cover . . .'

'What d'you mean?' He's out of breath on the stairs. 'Hide and cover what?' He's dropping back, he's several steps below me.

'All the uncertainties,' I'm talking to myself. 'All the fears. Never knowing what's to happen next. Never having any privacy or any memories; everything is washed away – hosed out, everything, walls floor ceiling shelf bench everything is hosed. There are no memories.'

I'm running up and up the iron stairs and up back along the gallery; no voices just the solid drumming of all these feet on their way back pounding and reverberating.

The doors are being locked, one after the other, faster and faster. In a minute it'll be my door. They're coming nearer. In a minute I'll be locked in.

I'm having another session with the psychiatrist today.

He's just the same, clean and smooth and kind. He shakes hands with me and offers me a cigarette and tells me to sit down comfortably.

It occurs to me as I sit there that a man can learn a great deal during these interviews. A stupid brute could become, in time, a clever brute. This is something for a man in my position to consider carefully. 'If I listen to him,' I think to myself, 'if I take in everything he talks about and explains, his mind and my mind fitted quietly together could make something which will ultimately be very useful to me.' This thought is remarkably satisfying especially as it is accom-panied by another thought; and this is that he is getting nothing from my mind to fit into his.

'Your memory will come back,' he tells me in his interes-ting explanations about human behaviour. I look beyond him through the window to that long road I can see going back into the hills. A bit of a song goes round and round in my head, it's only a fragment, I seem to be singing, not out loud of course.

>   country road take me home
>   to the place where I belong
>   take me home country road
>   take me home country road

The words are turning round in my head with the easy opening of the well-cared-for gate. The words and the little gate turn together in the clicking of the windmill. There's a rushing of wind and a singing in the telegraph wires. The wires stretch for miles across the wide paddocks and alongside the endless roads. The wind rushes and sends the loneliness humming along the melancholy wires.

'*I can't stand having people around the house before breakfast,*' the thin hard voice coming down her nose breaks up the smooth soft things turning in my head. '*There's no need to come up to the house, there's a tap down ...*'

'Your memory will come back,' the psychiatrist interrupts my thoughts. 'Your memory will come back. This reluctance to talk is quite normal.'

Because I am not used to smoking I have to concentrate on my cigarette and, all the time, the little bird in the cage is singing and singing.

Tomorrow when all those feet pound down to a kind of freedom, it will be simply as if two men are running.

Uncle Bernard's Proposal

'How can a man feel sorry for his food,' Uncle Bernard said when his nephew, Walter, asked him, 'Uncle do you feel sorry for the fish?'

'No I don't feel sorry for the fish,' Uncle Bernard continued. 'How could I live if I feel sorry for my food.' He snapped his fingers. 'Spik Enklisch now, remember you have to learn to spik. Otherwise how you manage?' He picked his teeth with a sharpened match. His white hair showed like a bandage beneath the brim of his hat. He wore it all the time indoors because of the draught.

Uncle Bernard travelled in macaroni. Every day he set off with his heavy cases stopping first on one doorstep and then, patiently walking up the path to another door, offering his wares to the housewives. Fondly he described the merits of his macaroni, noodles and ravioli. He had thick strips and thin, long spaghetti tubes and short fat ones; some were shaped like shells and others were flavoured with caraway seeds and yet others were reinforced with egg. Mostly he ate plain macaroni himself, always using a spoiled or broken packet from the case, he prepared it simply by boiling it in salty water. For years he lived like a poor man, saving and saving because he wanted to buy a vineyard, and now his second nephew had come out to help him in the new life. They sat together in the ugly rented room.

'But hurry!' he said. 'You must go to your chob. Late is no gut. Time is money! But first for you the dentist.'

'Back home in Holland –'

'Spik Enklisch! Forget old tooth, forget old life!'

'Mr Oons! Mr Oons!' the shrill voice of the landlady rose above the noise of the cisterns across the shabby hall. 'When you pay me? Today you pay me?'

'All right. All right. No troubles,' Uncle Bernard raised his voice to hers. 'Today I pay. You will see!' To Walter he said, in his voice the promise of a treat, 'Tonight Claus comes home. He has been away a whole year! We have nice room here, I make nice meal tonight. Forget Holland. Gut bye and gut lock. All day I denk on you. Tonight you will see Claus after all this time.'

Walter stood at the edge of the good-humoured crowds as they made their way in their best clothes down the jostled alleys of the Show Grounds. All night he had not slept because of the pain of a toothache, at times it seemed as if his jaw must split in half so great was the pain. Mingled with the toothache and the sleeplessness was a longing for the smells and sounds of his home, he wished he could hear his mother's voice, she would have known what to do for the pain. Uncle Bernard also knew what to do.

'Dentist!' he said after peering into Walter's mouth. 'Out!' he snapped his fingers.

Walter stood now quietly watching the people, the pain over at last. He had spent the morning behind frosted windows in a suburban dentist's waiting room watching small fishes floating in a glass tank of greenish water. The gentle movements of the fish and the steady flow of bubbles streaming in a chain, one after the other from a device in the corner of the tank calmed his nerves a little. He was a stranger, he couldn't understand what people said and, in any case, he feared examinations and injections and medicines. He moved uneasily on the bench so that the other people waiting should not see him trembling.

'It's rotten,' the dentist said. 'It'll have to come out,' and Walter clasped his arms across his chest and found afterwards that he had broken his fountain pen, the farewell present from the neighbours back home, with the fierce bracing against the pain.

People were now on all sides of him, walking to and fro

eating candy floss and hamburgers as they stared at the enormous wheels of the farm machinery and pushed their hands and forearms into the deep fleece of the Grand Champion Ewe of Western Australia as she lay panting inside the promise of the biggest wool clip ever to come from one sheep. The people were all enjoying themselves.

His work, his first work in the New Country was cleaning up at the Show Grounds. It was well paid and it had the advantage that it did not require any conversation. He worked late this first night, the dull ache in his jaw reminding him, with relief, that the bad tooth was out.

Forgetting where Uncle Bernard's lodgings were and not even knowing the name of the street, he wandered after work in the dark not knowing how to set about finding the house with its crazy toppling verandahs among all the other houses. He had not expected it to be so cold at night. Back home everyone said it was a wonderful climate, blue sky and sunshine, summer all the year round.

The policeman who found him gave him hot tea and bread and two grey blankets. And the next morning Uncle Bernard came to claim him.

'Claus is come!' Uncle Bernard's face was creased in smiles. It seemed his cheeks would burst bulging with smiles when the two brothers met after such a long time. All three men wept a little together in the privacy of the ugly room.

'Mr Oons!' Mrs Schultz, the landlady, called through the door. 'I bake little cake for celebrate tonight.' She came in, 'Oh my Gutness!' she said. 'How he grow in the Wheat!' It was true Claus seemed to fill the room with his height.

'His shoulders look beeg enough to carry the whole Vorld!' she said. 'You mosst take your brozzer there and make him grow too.'

'She denks of all the money you get there.' Uncle Bernard laughed a little after she had gone. Then he made Walter read aloud from the bit of newspaper the vegetables were wrapped in to teach him English.

A week later the two brothers left for the wheat belt where they were to work. They slept on the ground beside their machinery, they ate boiled wheat and red jam and saved all their money. Quite soon Claus was able to buy a truck.

By the time enough money was saved for Uncle Bernard's vineyard all the land which had been ribbed and patterned all over with rows of vines and edged with the living lace of almond and plum blossom had been made into an aluminium refinery with streets leading off into new housing estates. There were no fig trees left, the olive groves were gone and where there had once been wooden trestle tables piled with sweet muscat grapes and watermelons, an icecream parlour stood beside a fish and chip shop. The little land which remained was far too expensive for them, so the three men began to look at places further out from the city.

At last it seemed as if Uncle Bernard's life-long dream was about to come true. They found ten acres, a fine slope facing the west with a creek curving on to the bottom end in two places. About half way up the slope was a clearing where there was a little weatherboard cottage and a shed.

'All the furniture is included in the sale,' Uncle Bernard was so excited he could hardly speak. 'And look at the great trees!' he said.

'Needs some repairs!' Claus reached up easily with one great arm, it looked as if with one movement he could lift off the rusty iron roof in readiness to put on a new one.

'No troubles!' Uncle Bernard stood still as if enchanted in the fragrance which came from the warm earth. It was as if he expected some great wisdom to come to him from the Bush. Wild oats, waist high, and the yellow-daisied cape weed had taken over the parts which had once been cultivated. Years of neglect waited for their strength.

'Only denk!' Uncle Bernard said. 'When these trees were saplinks no white man had ever set foot here!'

Walter and Claus had never seen their Uncle so happy. He inspected the fence posts and planned where he would plant his orchard.

'All land is somebody's land,' he said. 'And this land is ours.'

In the evening they packed up their few things in the ugly rented room and Uncle Bernard wrote letters to firms about fruit trees and vines and tools and machinery.

'I wonder if the stink wort of Western Australia', he mused aloud, 'is any relation to the sour sob of South Australia.' He sounded like one of his text books, he had a great many old text books which he had collected. Every night, for years he had been studying and making notes from them, in particular he was interested in vines and the making of wine.

'What if the grapes don't grow?' Walter was a little anxious. 'Would something else be easier to grow?'

'All crops, if they come, are certain crops,' Uncle Bernard said and, as there was no reply to this, they went to bed early to bring the morning more quickly.

'Mr Oons, Mr Oons!' the shrill voice of Mrs Schultz penetrated their happy preparations the next day. 'I have small present for your farm,' she spoke the word farm with a kind of reverence and dragged a cardboard box into the room. In it were two fowls huddled under a small piece of wire netting.

Uncle Bernard was touched. 'But thank you!' he said. 'Frau Schultz with all my heart, I must thank you.'

'They look sick,' Walter said as they all peered into the box.

'Yes Yes,' Mrs Schultz agreed. 'One, Cecilia her name is, is a bit sick, but the other is well. I have suggestion,' she continued. 'You kill the good hen and make soup for the sick one and then you will see, she too will be well!' Mrs Schultz nodded happily and her thick-lensed spectacles, catching the morning sun, sparkled. 'Chick'n soup can't hurt a hen! Is gut for hens as is gut for peoples!'

'She denks I leave without paying her,' Uncle Bernard laughed a little after Mrs Schultz had gone to the back part of the house. 'I go now to pay and then,' he snapped his fingers, 'is the vineyard!'

'You'll not do much up there,' the woman in the post office said to them bluntly one day soon after they had moved in. She kept the General Store, the post office part was a piece of the counter at one end with iron bars all round it. She leaned forward in her little cage, her bosom resting comfort-

ably on the dark red jarrah polished smooth with years of
many such comfortable restings.

'The creek floods in winter and dries up in summer and
the water's salt, even if you sink a well ever so far down the
water's salt.' She watched Claus and Walter as they watched
Uncle Bernard understand this awful truth.

'Your soil's all salt and clay,' she continued, 'and up the
hill with all those outcrops of granite the earth's washed
away so nothing'll grow there. And,' she went on, 'There's
poison weed all over the pasture so it's no use your putting
stock there, your sheep'll be dead in a week.' She handed
Uncle Bernard his stamps.

'What the rabbits don't get the bandicoots and crows will
have. There was a snake up there last summer and I daresay
it's still there and where there's one snake there's usually
another,' while she drew breath, Uncle Bernard looked
down at his money and carefully counted out the coins on
the palm of his hand.

'Pity you've no family,' the post mistress said suddenly, it
was as if she softened a little towards the newcomers. 'Pity
you've no family, it's a waste of a good man.'

They walked back together along the old railway line, all
the rails had been removed but the heavy jarrah sleepers
were still embedded in the earth, half hidden in the withered grass twisted and trodden down now and sharply
fragrant after the dampness of the night.

'Here is good wood Oncle,' Walter tried to attract and
comfort, but Uncle Bernard strode on ahead of them, he
seemed to be swallowed up in the brightness of the spider-
webbed morning. On all sides of them the stillness was filled
with crows and cockatoos, and from time to time the deep
lonely lowing of far away cows came along the quiet valley.
And all the time the voices of the magpies fell in the clear
air rippling like the water of the creek below them pouring
over washed stones. As they walked they failed to see the
morning sun wrapping the colour round the bark of the
trees, and for them, no birds were singing.

Uncle Bernard was very quiet and thoughtful all day. In
the fragrance of eucalyptus leaves burning slowly, he stood

resting on his rake rather than using it. Walter, clearing the ground, threw bark and bits of blackboy on to the fire and the frail blue smoke rose like incense all around them. As a rule Uncle Bernard loved this smell and always said so but now he seemed not to notice it.

'I go indoors to study,' he said after a time to his nephews. They thought he might have an idea for a new wine label. He had an exercise book full of his own designs, plump ladies mostly, rather naked and wreathed in vine leaves drawn and smudged in red and blue ink; the names of his wines were familiar, 'Claret Bernard' and 'Bernard Burgundy' and 'Bernard Rosé Sec', and all had impossible dates and descriptions of soil conditions copied from his various books.

Walter and Claus put off going indoors for a time in case Uncle Bernard wanted to think about his wife and family, it was a long time since he had seen them and, as Aunt Mitzi put in her last letter, soon she would be too old to travel.

'Potatoes!' Uncle Bernard said happily when at last the two brothers entered the tiny kitchen of the cottage. 'We break up clay with potatoes.' He tapped an old book which lay open to his thin knees. 'We plant now in time for first rains.'

So the three men planted potatoes, rows and rows of them till their backs were breaking. Later they stood in the tranquillity of the long golden afternoons earthing up the precious green haulms. They looked with satisfaction upon their work, it was so neat and so successful.

'What is a man?' Uncle Bernard said, 'Josst a little bit of meat and some bones put together and no one can know how long he can walk on the world and no one can know what he can do in the world!' he smiled at the potatoes with real pleasure.

'You plantin' potatoes?' It was surprising to them that the post mistress always seemed to know what they were doing. She stacked their groceries on the counter. 'You can be sure the frost'll get them. Terrible cold nights and frosts we get up here. It's not like down in the city up here you know. Oh the frost!' she acted a shiver and turned her eyes up to the ceiling so that only the whites showed. 'Just you wait!'

And it was as if to show them she had spread her own frost-laden hands, the fingers crackling with blue ice, over their land for, by the following week the bright green tops were all withered and blackened and seemed as if trying to shrink back into the warm earth underneath the cold rim of her promised frost.

They were forced to acknowledge their failure especially after the potatoes sprouted for a second time and then, in one night, were completely burned away by an even more severe frost. It was hard to believe any stalks had been there at all.

'Lorst 'em again?' the post mistress said. 'Ah well that's life!' She handed Uncle Bernard his stamps, and again as if she was a bit sorry she said, 'It's a great pity you've no family.' She shook her head. 'It's sad to think as some woman could be well looked after for the rest of her life. It's a waste of a good man.'

They walked home along the old railway line carrying their packages.

'Perhaps you tell her you have wife and family to bring out,' Claus said. 'Otherwise, Uncle, perhaps she hopes you will marry her!'

'She has good idea!' Uncle Bernard nodded his head. 'Her good idea gives me good idea. Two heads often better than one!' he laughed out loud. As they climbed the slope to their cottage, the evening sun reddened the white bark of the wandoo trees.

'Get dressed, nicely dressed,' Uncle Bernard said, 'Both of you, very nice. Tonight we make visit.'

He washed himself carefully, they could hear him noisily blowing in the water and he took longer than usual, he put on his good jacket and his yellow tie.

'We visit widow on next property,' he said. 'She is rich farm widow from New South Wales, we visit her,' his voice deepened. 'I make proposal to her.'

'But Uncle how can you make marriage in this place and bring out your wife and family as well. How can Aunt Mitzi and the girls come if you have second wife?' Walter was agitated.

Uncle Bernard laid one finger alongside his nose. 'We make proposal all the same,' he said. 'Claus, you make yourself very nice. Very nice! I lend you my other tie. But hurry! Only hurry please! Darkness is so quickly coming here.' He hustled his nephews through their washing and dressing.

'Sometimes a man by himself is a waste,' they heard him mutter. 'Sometimes a woman can give a man an idea.' He pushed his nephews out of the cottage.

'We make proposal, now Claus how do you look?'

'Me Uncle?'

'Two properties is better than one.' Uncle Bernard led the way, his boots crushing fragrance from fallen eucalyptus leaves.

'But Uncle we don't know what she is like,' Claus protested, he knew his Uncle was very disappointed about his soil and he wanted more than anything to help but this was too much.

'I can't do this thing Uncle,' he said.

'Come on,' said Uncle Bernard. 'Leave everything to me.' They picked their way through the scrub on their own land and stepped over the bedraggled wire fence.

'Oh my Gutness!' Uncle Bernard surveyed the widow's property. 'She has indeed conquered her land!' And indeed the whole area was chopped down and burned off, the ground was still black and ashy neatly to the boundary line on all sides, scraped and burned and cleared of every living thing.

'Not a leaf!' Uncle Bernard scratched his chin. 'Well Claus she is a tidy widow.'

Claus refused to smile or even look at his Uncle.

The widow opened the door herself, for in a three-roomed cottage there is no need to keep a maid. She was elderly and grey and weather-beaten like her old house and sheds. The tiny room had hardly enough space for so many people.

'Sit down, make yerselves comfortable,' the widow said.

'She's too old and ugly,' Claus wanted to whisper to his Uncle but there was no chance. Uncle Bernard introduced himself and his two nephews.

'Madam how is your health?' he enquired politely.

'I'm a ball o' dash,' she replied. 'How's yerself?'

'Madam I have come to make proposal,' Uncle Bernard continued.

'Fair enough,' the widow settled back in her chair. Claus mopped the sweat from his forehead and Walter wondered whether his Uncle had gone out of his mind expecting Claus to marry this old grandmother. Her land did not look any better than theirs. It seemed hard to believe that Uncle Bernard wanted to grow grapes so much he would go to any lengths to do so.

'Do not refuse me Madam, this proposal is very close to my heart,' Uncle Bernard said, 'I spik on behalf of my nephew –'

'Oh Uncle No!' Uncle Bernard silenced Claus with a look.

'What I want to say means a great deal to me,' Uncle Bernard ignored the protest from Claus. The widow listened attentively sucking in her cheeks and mumbling a little with her toothless gums.

'My proposal', Uncle Bernard said, 'will bring great personal gain on both sides,' he leaned forward eagerly. Walter thought Claus would faint, he was too big for his chair and he kept moving uneasily and every time he moved it seemed as if the chair would fall to pieces beneath him. Uncle Bernard was smiling, his cheeks looked as if they would burst with his smile.

'Our properties adjoin one another, our fences are in very poor shape. What say you Madam,' Uncle Bernard leaned forward, 'What say you Madam if we tear out our old fences and join our two properties and together we start an amalgamated company and sell our terrible soil to be made into clay fire bricks. In very short time we shall all be rich!' he snapped his fingers as if to show how quickly the wealth from the soil would be theirs.

Claus slowly relaxed, his body gave a long slow movement which was continued in the long slow creaking of his chair, his relief spread in a smile to Walter.

The widow sat quietly, munching her gums and thinking.

'Fair enough,' she said at last. 'It's not a bad idea, let's get ahead with the whole thing as soon as possible.'

'No troubles Madam,' Uncle Bernard said, 'Leave every-ding to me.'

The moon was climbing quickly, they could see the clean brightness of it through the little window.

'Tonight we sleep,' Uncle Bernard said. 'Tomorrow is clay bricks!'

On the way home Uncle Bernard walked a little way in front of his nephews. And, in the darkness and the stillness of the night, they were unable to know really whether he was laughing softly to himself or sighing deeply.

Paper Children

Clara Schultz lying alone in a strange hotel bedroom was suddenly confronted by the most horrible thoughts. For a woman accustomed to the idea that she would live for ever, having lived, it seemed for ever, these thoughts were far from welcome. For instead of being concerned with her immortality they were, without doubt, gravely about her own death.

Perhaps it was the long journey by air. She had travelled from Vienna, several hours in an aeroplane with the clock being altered relentlessly while her own body did not change so easily. She was on her way to her daughter. She had not seen her since she was a baby and now she was a grown woman, a stranger, married to a farmer. A man much younger than herself and from a background quite unknown to Clara and so somewhat despised by her. She confided nothing of this thought, rather she boasted of her daughter's marriage.

'I am going to visit Lisa, my daughter, you know,' she told her neighbour Irma Rosen. Sometimes they stopped to talk on the stairs in the apartment house in the Lehar Strasse and Clara would impress on Irma forcefully, 'My daughter is married to an Australian farmer and expecting her first child. All these years I have only a paper daughter and now my paper children, my daughter and son-in-law, they want me to come, they have invited me!' And Irma whose smooth face was like a pink sugar cake on the handworked lace collar of her dress nodded and smiled with admiration.

It was only when she was alone Clara despised the farmer husband, she was able to overlook completely that her despising was in reality a kind of fear of him and his piece of land.

'We are in a valley,' Lisa wrote to her mother. Clara tried to imagine the valley. She had in her mind a picture of a narrow green flower-splashed place with pine trees on the steep slopes above the clusters of painted wooden houses, like in the Alps, very gay and always in holiday mood. She tried to alter the picture because Lisa described tall trees with white bark and dry leaves which glittered in the bright sunshine, she wrote also of dust and corrugated iron and wire netting and something called weatherboard. Clara found it hard to imagine these things she had never seen.

No one can know when death will come or how. Alone in the hotel, Clara thought what if she should go blind before dying. She thought of her room at home, what if she had to grope in that familiar place unable to find her clothes, unable to see where her books and papers were. She lay with her eyes closed and tried to see her desk and her lamp and her silver inkwell, trying to place things in order in her mind so that she would find her way from one possession to the next.

What if she should go blind now here in this strange room, not knowing any other person here? In a sudden fear she pushed back the bedclothes and put her small white fat feet out of the bed and stood on the strange floor and groped like a blind person for the light switch.

'Lisa,' she said to her daughter gently so as not to startle the girl. Lisa turned, she had a very white face, she moved awkwardly and her face was small as if she was in pain. She was much younger than her mother expected her to be. Beside her was a little girl of about two years, she had fair hair cut square across a wan little forehead. The child had been crying.

'What a dear little girl,' Clara said as pleasantly as she knew how. 'What do you call her?'

'Sharon.'

'Cheri?'

'No Sharon.'

'Ach! What a pretty name. Come here to Grossmutti my darlink,' but the little girl hid behind the half open door.

'What a pretty place you have Lisa,' Clara tried. 'Pretty! Pretty!' She waved her short plump arm towards the desolate scene of the neglected hillside, cleared years ago, scraped and never planted; patches of prickly secondary growth littered the spaces between collapsing sheds and the tangles of wire netting where some fowls had lived their lives laying eggs.

The house, in decay, cried out for mercy, it was a place quite uncherished. The rust on the iron roof was like a disease, scabs of it scaled off and marked the verandah as if with an infection. Clara wondered why. Poverty perhaps or was Lisa feckless? Clara had no patience with a feckless woman. If they were poor, well she had money, and she would find out the best way to spend it. She wanted to help Lisa. All the tenderness stored up over the empty years was there to be poured forth, now on her child and her child's property.

'Have you hurt yourself Lisa?' Clara tried again, softly gently as if speaking in a dream. She had not expected a little girl. She knew only that her daughter was pregnant.

'Lisa wants me to be near when she has her baby, my paper children want me,' Clara told Irma on the stairs and Irma nodded her approval. 'So I burn up my ships as they say in English and go.' Clara had taken many big steps in her life but never such a final one as this one might be. Australia was such a long way off from Vienna, it almost could not exist it was so remote.

'They have fifty cows and sheeps and chickens.' Such space was not to be imagined on the dark stairs of the apartment. 'Such a long way!' Clara said 'But air travel, you know, makes the world so much smaller.'

'Have you hurt yourself Lisa?' Gently she approached the pale young woman who was her unknown daughter.

'Aw it's nuthin',' the girl replied. 'He threw me down the other night, I kept tellin' him "You're hurtin' my back!" but he took no notice. "You're hurtin' my back," I shouted at him!' She rubbed the end of her spine.

Clara flinched with a real hurt.

'Pete, this is my mother,' Lisa said as a short thick-set young man, very sunburned and bullet shaped came round the side of the house. He threw a bucket to his wife. 'Mother this is Pete.'

As they stood together the sun slid quickly into the scrub on the far hillside and long shadows raced one after the other across and along the sad valley. Clara had never seen such a pair of people and in such dreary hopeless surroundings. She felt so strange and so alone in the gathering darkness of the evening.

The little muscular husband shouted something at Lisa and marched off with hardly a look at his new mother-in-law. Clara couldn't help remembering the Gestapo and their friend, they thought he was their friend, the one who became a Gauleiter. That was it! Gauleiter Peter Gregory married to her daughter Lisa.

'This man is my father's friend,' proudly Clara had introduced the friend to her husband only to experience in a very short time a depth of betrayal and cruelty quite beyond her comprehension. Friends became enemies overnight. Lisa's husband somehow reminded Clara unexpectedly of those times.

'Have you something to put on your back?' Clara asked.

'Like what?' the girl looked partly amused and partly defiant.

'Menthol Camphor or something like that,' Clara felt the remoteness between them, a kind of wandering between experience and dreams. She moved her hand in a circular movement. 'Something to massage, you know.'

At first Lisa didn't understand, perhaps it was the unusual English her mother spoke, Clara repeated the suggestion slowly.

'Aw No! Had a ray lamp but he dropped it larst night! Threw it down most likely but he said he dropped it. "The lamp's died," he said. I thought I'd die laughin' but I was that mad at him reely I was!'

'Should we, perhaps, go indoors?' Clara was beginning to feel cold. The Gauleiter was coming back. 'I just have these few packages,' Clara indicated her luggage which was an untidy circle about her. But the young couple had gone into the cottage leaving her to deal with her baggage as well as she could.

Trying to hear some sort of sound she heard the voice of Gauleiter Peter Gregory shouting at his wife, her daughter Lisa, and she heard Lisa scream back at her husband. Voices and words she couldn't hear and understand properly from the doorway of the asbestos porch. She heard the husband push the wife so that she must have stumbled, she heard Lisa fall against a piece of furniture which also fell, a howl of pain from Lisa and the little child, Sharon, began to cry.

Clara entered the airless dishevelled room. Because of all she was carrying it was difficult, so many bundles. 'One cannot make such a journey without luggage,' Clara explained to Irma as, buried in packages, she said goodbye to her neighbour, 'Goodbye Irma. Goodbye for ever dear friend.'

Besides she had presents for Lisa and even something for that husband.

Lisa looked up almost with triumph at her mother.

'I'm seven months gone', she said 'and he wouldn't care if he killed me!' The husband's sunburned face disappeared in the gloom of the dirty room.

'Oh,' Clara said pleasantly, 'she is too young to die and far too pretty.'

'Huh! me pretty!' Lisa scoffed and, awkwardly, because of the pain in her back, she eased herself into a chair.

'Who's young!' the husband muttered in the dark. Clara didn't know if he was sitting or standing. 'Well, we women must back each other up,' she said, wasting a smile. Whatever could she do about Lisa'a pain.

Clara fumbled with the straps of her bag.

'Come Sharon, my pretty little one. See what your Grossmutti has brought for you all across the World.' The child stood whimpering as far from Clara as possible while the parents watched in silence.

And Clara was quite unable to fasten the bag.

She had never been frightened of anything in her whole life. Dr Clara Schultz (she always used an abbreviation of her maiden name), Director of the Clinic for Women (Out Patients' Department), University Lecturer, wife of the Professor of Islamic Studies, he was also an outstanding scholar of Hebrew. Clara Margarethe Carolina, daughter of a Baroness, nothing frightened her, not even the things that frightened women, thunder and mice and cancer.

Even during the occupation she had been without fear. They were living on the outskirts of the city at that time. One afternoon she returned early from the clinic intending to prepare a lecture and she noticed there was a strange stillness in the garden. The proud bantam cock they had then was not crowing. He was nowhere in sight. Usually he strutted about, an intelligent brightly coloured little bird, and the afternoons were shattered by his voice as he crowed till dusk as if to keep the darkness of the night from coming too soon. The two hens, Cecilia and Gretchen, stood alone and disconsolate like two little pieces of white linen left by the laundress on the green grass.

Clara looked for the little rooster but was unable to find him. His disappearance was an omen.

Calmly Clara transferred money to Switzerland and at once, in spite of difficulties and personal grief, she arranged for her two-year-old baby daughter to be taken to safety while she remained to do her work.

A few days later she found the bantam cock, he was caught by one little leg in a twisted branch among the junipers and straggling rosemary at the end of the garden. He was hanging upside down dead. Something must have startled him Clara thought to make him fly up suddenly into such a tangled place. When she went indoors, missing her baby's voice so much, she found her husband hanging, dead, in his study. She remained unafraid. She knew her husband was unable to face the horror of persecution and the threat of complete loss of personal freedom. She understood his reasons. And she knew she was yearning over her baby but she went on, unafraid, with her work at the clinic. Every day, day after day, year after year, in her thick-lensed spectacles and her white coat she advised, corrected, comforted and cured, and, all the time, she was teaching too, passing on knowledge from experience.

But now, this fearless woman trembled as she tried to unfasten two leather straps because now years later, when all the horror was over for her, she was afraid of her daughter's marriage.

As Clara woke in the strange bedroom, it was only partly a relief.

There was still this possibility of blindness before death, because of course she would die. Ultimately everyone did. For how long would she be blind, if she became blind? Both her grandmothers had lost their sight.

'But that was a cataract,' Clara told herself. 'Nowadays one can have operation.'

Again in imagination, she blundered about her room at home trying to find things, the treasures of her life. But alone and old she was unable to manage.

And another thing. What if she should go deaf and not be able to listen to Bach or Beethoven any more? She tried to remember a phrase from the Beethoven A Minor String Quartet. The first phrase, the first notes of caution and melancholy and the cascade of cello. She tried to sing to herself but her voice cracked and she could not remember the phrase. Suppose she should become deaf now at this moment in this ugly hotel with no music near and no voices. If she became deaf now she would never again be able to hear the phrase and all the remaining time of her life be unable to recall it.

Again she put her small fat white feet out of the bed and stood on the strange floor and began like a blind and deaf person to grope for the light switch.

'Travelling does not suit everyone,' she told herself and she put eau de Cologne on her forehead and leaving the light on, she took her book, one she had written herself, *Some Elementary Contributions to Obstetrics and Gynaecology*, and began to read.

This time it really was Lisa, with joy in her heart Clara went towards her. The real Lisa was much older and Clara saw at once that the pregnancy was full term. Lisa walked proudly because of the stoutness of carrying the baby. Though Clara knew it was Lisa, she searched her daughter's face for some family likeness. The white plump face was strange however, framed in dark hair, cut short all round the head. Mother and daughter could not have recognized each other.

'Oh Lisa you have a bad bruise on your forehead,' Clara gently put out a hand to soothe the bruise. Supposing this husband is the same as the other one, the thought spoiled the pleasure of the meeting.

'It's quite clear you are a doctor, Mother,' Lisa laughed. 'Really it's nothing! I banged my head on the shed door trying to get our cow to go inside.'

'One cow and I thought they had many,' Clara was a little disappointed but she did not show it. Instead she bravely looked at the valley. It was not deep like the wooded ravine in the Alps, not at all, the hills here were hardly hills at all. But the evening sun through the still trees made a changing light and shade of tranquillity, there was a deep rose blue in the evening sky which coloured the white bark and edged the tremulous glittering leaves with quiet mystery. Clara could smell the sharp fragrance of the earth, it was something she had not thought of though now she remembered it from Lisa's letters. All round them was loneliness.

'Where is your little girl?' Clara asked softly. Lisa's plain face was quite pleasant when she smiled, she had grey eyes which were full of light in the smile.

'Little girl? Little boy you mean! He's here,' she patted her apron comfortably. 'Not born yet. I wrote you the date. Remember?'

'Oh yes of course,' Clara adjusted her memory. 'Everyone at home is so pleased,' she began.

'Here's Peter,' Lisa said. 'Peter this is my mother,' Lisa said. 'Mother this is Peter.'

The husband came to his mother-in-law, he was younger than Lisa so much so that Clara was startled. He seemed like a boy, his face quite smooth and it was as if Lisa was old enough to be his mother.

Peter was trying to speak, patiently they waited, but the

words when they came were unintelligible. His smile had the
innocence of a little child.

'He wants to make you welcome,' Lisa explained. She
took her husband's arm and pointed across the cleared and
scraped yard to a small fowl pen made of wire netting.
Beside the pen was a deep pit, the earth, freshly dug, heaped
up all round it.

'GO AND GET THE EGGS!' she shouted at him. She
took a few quick steps still holding his arm and marched him
towards the hen house. 'QUICK! MARCH!' she shouted.
Gauleiter Lisa Gregory. Clara shivered, the evening was cold
already. Her own daughter had become a Gauleiter.

'QUICK! MARCH! ONE TWO! ONE TWO!' Lisa was
a Führerin. The valley rang with her command. 'DIG THE
PIT!'

The sun fell into the scrub and the tree tops in the middle
distance between earth and sky became clusters of trembling
blackness, silent offerings held up on thin brittle arms like
starved people praying into the rose deep, blue swept sky.

Mother and daughter moved in the shadows to the door
of the weatherboard and iron cottage.

'I am very strong mother,' Lisa said in a whisper and in
the dusk Clara could see her strength, she saw too that her
mouth was shining and cruel.

In the tiny house there was no light. Clara was tired and
she wondered where they could sleep. In a corner a cot stood
in readiness for the baby, there seemed no other beds or furniture at all.

'When my sons are born,' Lisa said in a low voice to her
Mother, 'it is to be the survival of the fittest!' She snapped
her thick fingers. Clara had no reply. 'Only the strong and
intelligent shall live,' Lisa said. 'I tell my husband to dig the
pit. I have to. Perhaps it will be for him, we shall see. Every
day he must dig the pit to have it ready. There will be no
mercy.'

Clara reflected, in the past she had overlooked all this, she
had taken no part in the crimes as they were committed but,
ignoring them, she had continued with her work and because
her work was essential no one had interfered. Clara reflected

too that Lisa had never known real love, taken away to safety she had lost the most precious love of all. Clara took upon herself the burden of Lisa's cruelty now. She wanted to give Lisa this love, more than anything she wanted to overlook everything and help Lisa and love her. She wanted to open her purse to show Lisa before it was too dark that she had brought plenty of money and could spend whatever was necessary to build up a nice little farm. She wanted to tell Lisa she could buy more cows, electricity, sheds, pay for hired men to work, buy pigs, two hundred pigs if Lisa would like and drains to keep them hygienic. Whatever Lisa wanted she could have. She tried to tell her how much she wanted to help her. She tried to open her purse and Lisa stood very close and watched Clara in severe silence. The cottage was cold and quite bare, Clara longed to be warm and comfortable and she wanted to ask Lisa to unfasten her purse for her but was quite unable to speak, no words came though she moved her mouth as if trying to say something.

She had never been so stupid. Of course she would feel better in the morning. Women like Dr Clara Schultz simply did not fall ill on a journey. It was just the strange bed in the rather old-fashioned hotel. Tomorrow she would take her cold bath as usual and ask for yoghurt at breakfast and all she had to do then was to wait for Lisa and Peter.

The arrangement was that they were driving the two hundred miles to fetch her to their place. Of course it was natural to be a little curious. Lisa was only two years old when she was smuggled out of Vienna. The woman Lisa had become was a complete stranger, and so was the husband. Even their letters were strange, they wrote in English because Lisa had never learned to speak anything else.

Clara knew she would feel better when she had seen them. All these years she had longed to see Lisa, speak with her, hear her voice, touch her and lavish love and gifts on her. She still felt the sad tenderness of the moment when she had had to part with her baby all those years ago.

'Lisa, my bed is damp,' Clara said 'The walls are so thin. I never expected it to be so cold.'

Lisa had been quite unable to imagine what her mother's visit would be like. In spite of the heat and her advanced pregnancy she cleaned the little room at the side of the house. She washed the louvres and made white muslin curtains. There was scarcely any furniture for the narrow room but Lisa made it as pretty as she could with their best things, her own dressing table and a little white-painted chair and Peter fetched a bed from his mother's place.

Lisa tried to look forward to the visit, she knew so little about her mother, an old lady now after a life of hard work as a doctor. Every year they threw away the battered Christmas parcel which always came late, sewn up in waterproofed calico. There seemed no place in the little farmhouse with its patterned linoleum and plastic lamp shades for an Adventskranz and beeswax candles. And the soggy little biscuits, heart shaped or cut out like stars, had no flavour. Besides they ate meat mostly and, though Peter liked sweet things, his choice of pudding was always tinned fruit with ice cream. The meaningless little green wreath with its tiny red and white plaster mushrooms and gilded pine cones only served to enhance the strangeness between them and this mother who was on her way to them.

Of course her mother was ill as soon as she arrived. She had not expected the nights to be so cold she explained and it was damp in the sleepout.

'My bed is damp,' she said to Lisa. So they moved her into the living room.

'No sooner does your mother arrive and the place is like a 'C'-Class Hospital,' Peter said. He had to sit for his tea in the kitchen because Clara's bed took up most of the living room. She had all the pillows in the house and the little table beside her bed was covered with cups and glasses and spoons and bottles and packets of tablets.

'It is only a slight inflammation in my chest,' she assured Lisa. 'A few days of rest and warm and I will be quite well, you will see!'

Lisa worried that her mother was ill and unable to sleep. She tried to keep Peter friendly, but always a silent man, he became more so. She stood in the long damp grass outside the cowshed he had built with homemade concrete bricks, waiting for him at dusk, she wanted to speak to him alone, but he, knowing she was standing there, slowly went about his work and did not emerge.

From inside the asbestos house came Clara's voice. 'Lisa! Another hot water bottle please, my feet are so cold.'

Lisa could not face the days ahead with her mother there. She seemed suddenly to see all her husband's faults and the faults in his family. She had never before realized what a stupid woman Peter's mother, her mother-in-law, was. She felt she would not be able to endure the life she had. Years of this life lay before her. Fifteen miles to the nearest neighbour, her mother-in-law, and the small house, too hot in summer and so cold and damp once the rains came, and the drains Peter had made were so slow to soak away she never seemed able to get the sink empty. This baby would be the first of too many. Yet she had been glad, at her age, to find a husband at last and thought she would be proud and happy to bear a farmer a family of sons.

'A spoonful of honey in a glass of hot water is so much better for you!' Clara told them when they were drinking their tea. She disapproved of their meat too. She was a vegetarian herself and prepared salads with her own hands grating carrots and shredding cabbage for them.

Peter picked the dried prunes out of his dinner spoiling the design Clara had made on his plate.

'I'm not eating that!' he scraped his chair back on the linoleum and left the table.

'Oh Peter please!' Lisa implored, but he went out of the kitchen and Lisa heard him start up the utility with a tremendous roar.

'He will come back!' Clara said knowingly nodding her head.

'Come eat! Your little one needs for you to eat. After dinner I show you how to make elastic loop on your skirt,' she promised Lisa. 'Always I tell my patients, "an elastic loop, not this ugly pin!" ' she tapped the big safety pin which fastened Lisa's gaping skirt. 'After dinner I show you how to make!' Lisa knew her mother was trying to comfort her but she could only listen to Peter driving down the track. He would drive the fifteen miles to his mother and she would, as usual, be standing between the stove and the kitchen table and would fry steak for him and make chips and tea and shake her head over Lisa and that foreign mother of hers.

She listened to the car and could hardly stop herself from crying.

Living, all three together became impossible and, after the birth of the baby, Lisa left Peter and went with her mother to live in town. Clara took a small flat in a suburb and they went for walks with the baby. Two women together in a strange place trying to admire meaningless flowers in other people's gardens.

Lisa tried to love her mother, she tried to understand something of her mother's life. She realized too that her mother had given up everything to come to her, but she missed Peter so dreadfully. The cascading voices of the magpies in the early mornings made her think as she woke that she was back on the farm, but instead of Peter's voice and the lowing of the cows there were cars on the road outside the flat. She missed the cows at milking time and the noise of the fowls. And in the afternoon she longed to be standing at the edge of the paddock where the long slanting rays of the sun lit up the tufted grass and the shadows of the coming evening crept from the edges of the Bush in the distance.

'Oh Liserl! Just look at this rose,' her mother bent over some other person's fence. 'Such a fragrance and a beautiful deep colour. Only smell this rose Lisa!' And then slowly, carrying the baby, on to the next garden to pause and admire where admiration fell lost on unknown paving stones and into unfamiliar leaves and flowers unpossessed by themselves. The loneliness of unpossession waited for them in the tiny flat where a kind of refugee life slowly unpacked itself, just a few things, the rest would remain for ever packed. Only now and then glimpses of forgotten times came to the surface, an unwanted garment or a photograph or an old letter reminding of the reasons why she had grown up in a strange land cared for by people who were not hers.

In the evenings they shaded the lamp with an old woollen cardigan so that the light should not disturb the baby and they sat together. Lisa listened to the cars passing, in her homelessness she wished that one of the cars would stop, because it was Peter's. More than anything she wished Peter would come. Tears filled her eyes and she turned her head so that her mother should not see.

'Oh Peter!' Lisa woke in the car, 'I was having such an awful dream!' She sat up close to the warmth of her husband feeling the comfort of his presence and responsibility.

'Oh! It was so awful!'

She loved Peter, she loved him when he was driving, especially at night. She looked at his clear brow and at the strong shape of his chin. He softly dropped a kiss on her hair and the car devoured the dark road.

'You'll feel better when you actually meet her,' he said. 'It's because you don't know her. Neither of us do!'

Lisa agreed and sat in safety beside her husband as they continued the long journey.

Clara was able to identify Lisa at once. She had to ask to have the white sheet pulled right down in order to make the identification. Lisa had two tiny deep scars like dimples one on the inside of each thigh.

'She was born with a pyloric stenosis,' Clara explained softly. 'Projectile vomiting you know.' The scars, she explained, were from the insertion of tiny tubes.

'Subcutaneous feeding, it was done often in those days,' she made a little gesture of helplessness, an apology for an old-fashioned method.

In the mortuary they were very kind and helpful to the old lady who had travelled so far alone and then had to have this terrible shock.

Apparently the car failed to take a bend and they were plunged two hundred feet off the road into the Bush. Death would have been instantaneous, the bodies were flung far apart, the car rolled. They tried to tell her.

Clara brushed aside the cliches of explanation. She asked her question with a professional directness.

'What time did it happen?' she wanted to know. She had been sitting for some time crouched in a large armchair, for some hours after her yoghurt, wondering if she could leave the appointed meeting place. Outside it was raining.

'Should I make a short rain walk?' she asked herself. And several times she nearly left the chair and then thought, 'But no, any moment they come and I am not here!'

A few people came into the vestibule of the hotel and she looked at them through palm fronds and ferns, surreptitiously refreshing herself with eau de Cologne, wondering, hopeful. Every now and then she leaned forward to peer, to see if this was Lisa at last, and every time she sat back as the person went out again. Perhaps she was a little relieved every time she was left alone. She adjusted her wiglet.

Back home in Vienna she was never at a loss as to what to do. Retirement gave her leisure but her time was always filled. She never sat for long hours in an armchair. Back home she could have telephoned her broker or arranged with her dentist to have something expensive done to a tooth.

'Time? It's hard to say exactly,' they said. 'A passing motorist saw the car upside down against a tree at about five o'clock and reported the accident immediately.'

There were only the two bodies in the mortuary. Beneath the white sheets they looked small in death. Dr Clara Schultz was well acquainted with death, the final diagnosis was the greater part of her life's work. And wasn't it after all she herself who, with her own hands, cut the dressing-gown cord from her own husband's neck. She had to put a stool on his desk in order to reach as she was such a short person, and furthermore, his neck had swollen, blue, over the cord making the task more difficult.

They supported the old lady with kind hands and offered her a glass of water as she looked at the two pale strangers lying locked in the discolouration of injury and haemorrhage and the deep stillness of death.

Clara looked at her daughter and at her son-in-law and was unable to know them. She would never be able to know them now.

'I have a photograph, and I have letters,' she said. 'They

were my paper children you know.' She tried to draw from the pocket of her travelling jacket the little leather folder which she took with her everywhere.

In the folder was a photograph of them standing, blurred because of a light leak in the camera, on a track which curved by a tree. And on the tree was nailed a small board with their name on it in white paint. Behind the unknown people and the painted board was a mysterious background of pasture and trees and the light and shade of their land. She pulled at the folder but was unable to pull it from her pocket.

Not being able to speak with them and know them was like being unable ever again to hear the phrase of Beethoven, the cascade of cello. It was like being blind and deaf for the rest of her life and she would not be able to recall anything.

Dr Clara had never wept about anything but now tears slowly forced themselves from under her eyelids.

'My daughter, Lisa you know, was pregnant,' she managed to say at last. 'I see she is bandaged. Does this mean?'

'Yes yes,' they explained gently, 'That is right. Owing to the nature of the accident and the speed with which it was reported they were able to save the baby. A little girl, her condition is satisfactory. It was a miracle.'

Dr Clara nodded. In spite of the tears she was smiling. As well as knowing about death she understood miracles.

As soon as it was decently possible she would ring for the chambermaid and ask for a glass of hot water. Of course she wasn't blind or deaf and no one had come in with any news of an accident. She was only a little upset with travelling. Her fear of the failure of her body was only the uneasiness of stomach cramp and the result of bad sleep. She would have her cold bath early and then only a very short time to wait after that. Country people had to consider their stock that was why they were driving overnight to fetch her. It might be a good idea to start getting up now, it would never do to keep them waiting. She put her fat white feet out of the bed and walked across the strange floor to ring the bell.

It was a good idea to get up straight away because the telephone was ringing. Dr Clara, in the old days was used to the
telephone in the night. Often she dressed herself with one
hand and listened to the Clinic Sister describing the intervals between the labour pains and the position of the baby's
head. A little breathless, that was all, she sat on the chair
beside her telephone, breathless just with getting up too
quickly.

'Dr Clara Schultz,' she said and she thought she heard a
faint voice murmur.

'Wait one moment please. Long distance.' And then a
fainter sound like a tiny buzzing as if voices were coming
from one remote pole to another across continents and
under oceans as if a message was trying to come by invisible
wires and cables from the other side of the world. Clara
waited holding the silent telephone. 'Clara Schultz here,'
she said alone in the dark emptiness of her apartment for
of course she had sold all her furniture.

'I have burn up my ships,' she told Irma. 'Clara Schultz
here,' her voice sounded strange and she strained into the
silence of the telephone trying to hear the other voice, the
message, her heart beat more quickly, the beating of her
heart seemed to prevent her listening to the silence of the
telephone.

'Lisa!' she said, 'Is it you Lisa?'

But there was no sound in the telephone, for a long time
just the silence of nothing from the telephone. 'Lisa speak!'
But there was no voice.

Clara longed to hear her daughter's voice, of course the
voice could not be the same now as the laughter and incoher-
ent chatter of the little two year old. Now as an old woman
holding a dead telephone she remembered with a kind of
bitterness that she sent away her little girl and continued her
work at the clinic paying no attention to the evil cruelty of
war. She knew she was overlooking what was happening to
people but chose to concern herself only with the menstrual
cycle and the arched white thighs of women in labour.

'It's a means to an end,' she said softly to her frightened

patients when they cried out. 'Everything will be all right, it's a means to an end,' she comforted them.

Clara knew she had neglected to think of the end. Now she wanted, more than anything, to hear Lisa speak. But there was no sound on the telephone. She went slowly out on to the dark stairs of the apartment house. On the second landing she met her neighbour.

'Irma is that you?'

'Clara!'

'Irma you are quite unchanged.'

Irma's pink sugar cake face sat smiling on the lace collar which was like a doily. 'Why should I change?' Irma asked.

Clara took Irma's hand, grateful to find her friend. 'Only think, Irma,' she said, 'I am bringing home my daughter's baby!' she laughed softly to Irma. 'My paper children had a baby daughter,' she said, 'I shall call her Lisa.'

When Lisa and Peter arrived at the hotel they were unable to understand how it was that Clara must have been crying and laughing when she died.

Irma Rosen tried to explain to them as well as she could with her little English, and of course she was very tired with making the long journey by air at such short notice.

'When I find her you know, outside my door,' Irma said. 'I know, as her friend, I must come to you myself to tell. On her face this lovely smile and her face quite wet as if she cry in her heart! While she is smiling.'

They were as if encapsulated in the strange little meeting in the hotel vestibule. Lisa tried to think of words to say to this neat little old lady, her mother's friend. But Irma spoke again. 'Your mother is my friend,' she said, 'Always she speak of you. Her paper children and she so proud to be preparing to come to you. She would want me to tell you. Now I suppose I go back. Your mother say always 'But air travel, you know, makes the world so much smaller.' Is true of course, but a long way all the same!' She smiled and nodded, pink, on her lace collar. 'Sorry my Enklisch iss not good!' she apologized. 'Oh you speak beautifully,' Lisa was glad to be able to say something. 'Really your English is very good,' Lisa shouted a little as if to make it easier for Irma to understand her.

The young couple wanted to thank Irma and look after her but as Lisa's labour pains had started during the long journey, Peter had to drive her straight to the hospital.

The Play Reading

'Whatever shall I get for Mr Hodgetts and Aunty Shovell for their teas?' Mother sat down at the kitchen table. She was so tired coming straight from South Heights the luxury apartments where she cleans every day.

'How about a nice mutton and sardine yoghurt?' my brother said. 'It might make them change their minds about coming here for tea every night.' Mother looked at him as if she was seeing him very tall suddenly there by the door.

All this winter Mother's been going to night classes. She says she can feel her brain expanding out of her head.

'I know!' Mother brightened up, 'We'll have a play reading.' She took her night-school book out of her bag. 'It's a play by a man called Ibsen. He had this idea that it's only when the body dies that people really come to life.'

'What's it called?' I asked.

'*When We Dead Awake*.'

'Is there any sex interest in it?' I asked.

'Nice girls don't ask questions like that.'

'It seems they've had it,' my brother turned the pages quickly. 'Here you are,' he said, 'page 226, *He* says, "It reminds me of the night we spent in the train on our way up here." And *she* says back to him, "Why you sat in the compartment and slept the whole way." And *he* says –

'That'll do,' Mother said. 'It's all highly symbolic. The writer sees the human body all laid out over the Bush and the fences and the paddicks.'

'How?' I asked.

'The human contours and emotions are expressed in the landscape,' Mother said, her voice all posh.

'Here you are,' my brother said. 'Page 252. It's *her* talking again, here she goes. "Right down there in the foothills, where the forest's thickest. Places where ordinary people could never penetrate –" ' Mother took the book off him pretty sharply.

'You'll understand when you're older,' she said to me. 'The play's like a quartet,' she said getting posh again, her nose turning red the way it does when she's excited about something.

'What's a quartet?' I asked.

Mother cut an apple into four.

'I'll explain,' she said spreading out the bits of apple. 'These are the four characters,' she said. 'Here's Professor Rubek and his young wife, Maia, sitting beside the teapot –'

'Why ever would they sit by a teapot!' my Brother said.

'It represents the hotel,' Mother said patiently. 'Professor Rubek and his wife are sitting drinking champagne after their breakfasts and these other two', she arranged the other pieces of apple further away on the tablecloth, 'are Irene and the bear hunter. And this banana here can be the hotel manager, just a minor part in the play. Oh! You've eaten Professor Rubek!' Mother accused my brother.

'Irene and the bear hunter have gone too,' I said.

'Why you son of a Bitch!' Mother jumped up and my brother ran round and round the kitchen table with Mother after him. Suddenly my brother turned and Mother crashed into him. He sat backwards into the wood box.

'Halp! I'm choking!' My brother put on his idiot's face, 'Halp!'

I thought we should all die laughing. The Professor's wife looked lonely there on the table cloth so I ate her.

'Whatever shall I get for Shovell's tea!' Mother sat down to get her breath back.

The door opened and Aunty Shovell and Mr Hodgetts came in with all their shopping.

'Talk of Angels!' Mother said, very white.

'Nothing I wouldn't say about myself I hope,' Aunty Shovell made herself comfortable in the best chair. 'Tea ready?'

'You're just in time for the play reading,' my brother said. 'The Professor and his wife are just getting stuck into the booze after their cornflakes.'

'Oh?' said Aunt Shovell.

'Oh yes,' Mother said quickly. 'Mr Hodgetts you can be Professor Rubek.' Mr Hodgetts smiled at himself in the mirror over the sink, he smoothed his hair and examined his tongue. 'Delighted Dear Lady,' he said, 'delighted.'

'Put this lace curtain round you,' Mother said. 'Professor Rubek wears a shawl over his clothes to show the audience he's getting old – it's a writer's symbol,' she explained.

'Mr Hodgetts isn't getting old,' Aunt Shovell said. 'Mr Hodgetts is in the Prime of Life. You've only got to look at his neck to see he's in his Prime.'

'I'll be Ireene,' Mother said ignoring Aunt Shovell. 'Ireene's the Professor's nood model. They haven't seen each other for quite a while. He wants her to come with him up the mountain –'

'That's enough!' Aunt Shovell began gathering up her shopping bags.

'Oh Cheryl lovey it's only a play!' Mr Hodgetts smiled from inside his lace curtain.

'Let Aunty Shovell be Irene then.' My brother consulted the book, 'It says here she's supposed to be mad with knitting pins stuck in her hair and a knife hidden between her –'

'Just you watch your language!' Mother said. 'Shovell,' she said, 'you can be the Nun, that's a lovely part, when they all get swallowed up in an avalanche at the end of the play, the Nun's the only one left.'

'How can I be a Nun when Mr Hodgetts and me have an understanding!' Aunty Shovell's nose was as red as Mother's. They both asked my brother if their noses were red as if he cared.

'Come along Herbert, we'll get the half-past-five bus.'

Aunty Shovell went out and Mr Hodgetts followed her. The
door banged shut.

'He's got the lace curtains on,' I said.

'Never mind!' Mother said. I didn't know whether she was
laughing or crying but she said she'd be all right directly. To
keep himself going while Mother went down the road for
three steakburgers my brother ate the hotel manager.

The Libation

The woman who was in this room last week is dead. The
Fräulein told me yesterday, after her little speech of welcome. She hesitated before telling me, afraid of spoiling my
holiday, our holiday I should say, because stupidly, I am not
travelling alone.

The Pension Heiligtum is run by an old woman and her
elderly daughter. Neither of them speaks much English.
Both do their utmost to make us comfortable.

'Euer Zufluchtstätte!' the old woman said knowing from
before how much I need sanctuary, especially when I am
travelling. All the rooms look out into the green arbours and
the lilacs of a small enclosed garden. The quiet hall is lined
with porcelain and hand-painted cherubs.

We have a double room without a bath and, in spite of
being in the shadow of the Stephansdom, without magic.
There has been no magic on this holiday. I knew there would
be none before we left. All the time I have been asking
myself why I ever made the suggestion that she should
accompany me.

Neither of us is young. Between us there is the inevitable
intimacy of bowels and false teeth.

This morning Miss Ainsley ordered quantities of hot
water to be brought to her. As soon as it was cool enough,
she gulped it like medicine from the little enamelled jugs,
explaining that she was constipated. Later she said, 'Excuse
me', and has not yet returned.

I have known Ainsley for a long time. For many years she

105

was my father's secretary and, after his death, when she found she could not attach herself to me or to my work, she left. Later, she came back, needing a home which I have grudgingly given her. I am not always kind to Ainsley. I am not even nice to her. She irritates me.

I have seen her tears, however, and that should be enough to alter my attitude. The point about her tears is that I was humbled by them. I don't love Ainsley and, what is worse, I don't like her. No one loves her, no one except perhaps an insignificant mother, a long time ago, has ever loved her. Her tears did not make me care about her but, for some strange reason, during one of my more prolonged and unpleasant remarks she, by crying, suddenly made me see myself as I really am.

Though I forget now what the incident was I remember all too clearly the huge tears trembling along her eye lashes. I couldn't help noticing too how the act of weeping distorted her slack cheeks and lips crumpling her face into a soft, red, puffed shapelessness.

'It's all right for you,' she sobbed to me then like an upset school girl, 'it's all right for you to say the things you say and to act the way you do. You're a sort of wealthy goddess. You've got everything going for you.' For some minutes she howled aloud uttering the most appalling clichés about me and about my selfish, cruel extravagant ways. Lately, I admit I have been guilty of the things she was saying. I stared at her with horror. I patted her quivering shoulder and, briefly, I felt real pity for her. Mixed with the pity was an unexpected curiosity as well as the distaste I knew I felt. That's why I did what I did to her and why I offered her the holiday.

'Don't cry Ainsley!' I said to her. 'Look here,' I said, 'of course you must come to Europe with me. Cheer up! I'll arrange everything.' I kissed her and stroked her and comforted her and she responded so quickly to my unwilling hands that even now, when I think about it, I feel ashamed. Ashamed of knowing her response to my unwillingness I mean.

So, while the hot water is dealing with Ainsley's inside I

am sitting here by the embroidered table cloth trying to imagine the last thoughts of the dead woman because I have discovered something about her which amazes me.

I do not want to be a tourist really. Travelling with Ainsley, being a tourist cannot be avoided. To anyone who can understand English, she explains that she finds a diet of campari and prunes very sustaining. Thus well nourished she stands, legs straddled, to be cultured, in the Beethoven Museum, in the Haydn Museum and in the Schubert Museum. Obediently she turns her head, chattering aimlessly, as we drive by, to gaze at the entrance to the ancient and famous hospital repeatedly entered by Schubert.

'*To wander is the miller's joy,*' she sings. 'We had this at school', she tells me and joins the crowd flocking to see the Schubert Sterbezimmer.

I made up my mind, years ago, never to travel again.

. . . 'there must be no letters, not even thinking,' I said once to a young woman with whom I was very much in love. 'I shall not come after you,' I told her then. And I meant it. I did not write and I did not travel across continents to follow her. We never saw each other again, though nothing could stop me from thinking about her. And now, all at once, in this apartment, dark with oiled wood and over-stuffed with heavy furniture, I am reminded of her because something which no one knows about, something belonging to the dead woman, was left in this room.

Since the discovery I made yesterday I have been unable to think of anything else.

All the time on the bus tour yesterday afternoon I was thinking of this woman while Ainsley chattered about the different ways of 'taking one's own life' as she calls suicide. We were making a tour through the Wiener Wald to Mayerling. Ainsley expressed her eagerness to see the hunting lodge where Crown Prince Rudolph and Maria Vetsera are said to have carried out a suicide pact. We were not able to see the Lodge as it has been converted into a chapel where an order of nuns are housed. All the way back Ainsley talked of what it must be like to 'take the veil' till her speech, thickened with campari, slurred off comfortably into sleep. Her round, blue-grey head bounced softly on my shoulder and unwillingly I smelled her soap.

The amazing thing is that we were so near. For some time, in fact the whole time while she was here in the Pension, we were journeying nearer and nearer. All the time while we were in the Hotel Traube in Salzburg eating ham with sauerkraut and dumplings or looking out vacantly over the wide view from the Hohensalzburg Castle, she was here in this room.

I am thinking back over those long evenings. While time was creeping slowly forward for her, we sat in suspended time gazing at the life-like figures in the marionette theatre listening to the radiance of love reflected in Mozart's music. Had I know she was here in Vienna at that time I do not think I would have remained a moment longer in Salzburg. And certainly I would have had thoughts other than those of longing to be back in the quiet paddocks at home. It is strange to think that in order to endure Ainsley during *Die Zauberflöte* and *Don Giovanni* I occupied my mind with complicated plans to end the holiday and get back to my farm as quickly as possible.

And the woman in this room must have been writing a letter to someone whose name I shall never know. She must have been contemplating, perhaps in this chair by this table, the action which led to her death and subsequent removal, with as little publicity as possible, from the Pension Heiligtum.

The letter has no beginning and no end.

The Fräulein, when she told me, was very grave and assured me, with dignity, that the room had been thoroughly cleaned and well aired since the unhappy event.

That I am the subject of a novel, possibly a rejected one, is incredible.

I asked the Fräulein what the name of the dead woman was. At first she felt she could not tell me. She uttered a name which had no meaning for me. It occurs to me now that the dead woman could have been travelling under an assumed name. Or she could, after leaving me, have married.

It is disconcerting being the subject of someone's fiction. To be the subject might be quite usual but it is not usually known or realized by the person who is the subject. My name is not Helena and the young woman with whom I was so deeply in love was not called Lois. That is of no consequence. The writer would naturally use made-up names.

All fiction springs from moments of human experience and truth. The writer of the story must have seen and observed and must have been completely aware of certain things about me and about my life. I have not seen the novel in question only some pages of an incomplete letter which is a reply to an obviously insensitive attack on the manuscript. I have seen in this half-written letter a desperate attempt at self defence.

In order to have written this book the writer must have perceived my most secret feelings, must have known everything about my farm, every detail of its geography, and everything about the derelict people with their avid intention in the wretched house adjoining mine. The writer must have known all the intimate details of my thoughts and feelings and my passion for this young woman which, for a time, altered my whole life. A life which was then so different from my boredom and disgust, yes disgust, which I feel now and which I envisaged then, at that time, years ago, and so brought our sensuous and idyllic happiness to an end before it could turn into a profane bondage.

Who can have written the novel? And who is the person who was writing the letter which I found?

The Viennese are very clean people. This room was thoroughly cleaned and aired, how then could I find the sheets of paper which have revealed to me so much of the dead woman – and so little. That she wrote a book and that the book was being rejected by someone unpleasant seems clear. Her name is not on any of the pages.

The Viennese are clean and they are thrifty too. I can follow the reasoning. The paper has been written on one side only and it is of good quality, new and white and clean. The drawers of the little chest and the writing desk have been carefully lined with the sheets laid flat and pressed into the corners. I discovered the handwriting on one of them by chance and then, one by one, drew out all the others.

I have them here, all the neatly written pages . . .

. . . Thank you for reading my book . . .

. . . Your notes and questions are anonymous so I do not know how to address you . . .

'What is the goddess?' This is your last question at the end of twenty-three pages of questions. 'What is the goddess? What is the goddess?' It's your last question typed out twice as if in exasperation.

You ask on the same page, 'Is "a deep spiritual and emotional experience" a euphemism for orgasm?' And still on the same page, 'What would Mr Byrnes and Helena be doing to the carcass if it had been trapped, struggling and in a panic on the fencing wire for several days and full of maggots? Surely not butchering it to eat? I can see that it provides an approach to drama but, please correct me if I am wrong, at the expense of realism? . . .'

I'll come to that part in a minute. I'll start at the end with your last question, the one about the goddess. She is an ornamental statue.

. . . In front of the Berghof is a wide gravel drive which encircles a white stone goddess seated in her water lily fountain. A car turning slowly here sounds like a car on the track at Helena's . . .

The sound of a car turning slowly and pausing and then turning again on the gravel path round the goddess reminds Lois of the same sound which she heard often at night when Helena was returning to the farm. Now of course she is not with Helena as they have parted for ever. Hearing the familiar sound in an unfamiliar place fills Lois with longing and sadness.

The goddess is both an image and a symbol. Earlier in the story Helena sings part of Schiller's *Ode to Joy*. She sings in the car when she is driving off with Lois taking her to the

farm. It is the middle of the night and she has rescued Lois
from an intolerable situation. She sings,

> 'Daughter of Elysium. We approach with hearts aflame
>   O Goddess your sanctuary.
>   'It's Schiller, *Ode to Joy*,' she explained.

As they approach Helena's farm it is as if they are approaching her sanctuary. Helena says,

'When I go through the gate and am actually on my land I feel
no harm can ever come to me . . .'

   She is a good deal older than Lois, perhaps she values
safety more after previous experience. She wants to share
this safety with Lois.
   The goddess in the poem and the safety of the farm represent the strength of Helena's love as the tender relationship develops between the two women. The goddess in the
lily pool suggests that love and safety are to be found, for
a time, in the seclusion of the vegetarian guest house. This
guest house in the mountains becomes, at the end of the
story, a sanctuary for Lois.
   The libation which you have failed to notice or mention,
belongs with the goddess and the sanctuary. Lois is describing her new and passionate friend,

Every morning Helena pours a little water carefully, a libation,
she calls it, into the tins and pots to sustain her little pomegranates and the myrtle and the rosemary . . . The water stays sparkling
to the brim of every pot for a few seconds and then disappears
into the grey sand . . .

From your notes I see that you want the goddess removed
from the book. I would like to keep her in as she is essential
to the story.
   Now, about the maggots and the carcass. There is a passage where Byrne and Helena deal with a sick ram. Lois is

watching from the house and the scene is described by her,

... I never saw Helena do anything violent before. I saw Helena
with the gun, she was behind Byrne's house, in a wired off yard
... I saw Byrne agitated ... and Helena at the edge of the barn
with her gun. I saw the strength and grace with which she took
aim ...

Helena shoots the ram, it is a mercy killing; and after the
shooting, Helena and Byrne clear away the carcass. For the
purposes of the novel it is not, as you suggest, just the pro-
vision of a dramatic moment, it is to show that certain cir-
cumstances require definite actions. Helena does not like
shooting. She does not want to kill anything, she says so. And
she does not want to end the idyllic happiness she and Lois
have together. The shooting of the ram shows that she will
do whatever is necessary at specific times. It shows too that
in spite of Helena being rich and· independent she knows
how much she needs a man like Byrne on her farm. The incident is there too to show that a change is coming and Lois,
fearing this and yet wanting it, is hysterical.

Your irrelevant question demonstrates your lack of understanding of quite simple and ordinary human needs and
human behaviour. To answer your question, no they
wouldn't eat the ram themselves, perhaps the dogs might,
but this has nothing whatever to do with the story.

The words 'a deep spiritual and emotional experience'
lifted out of context do not appear as they are meant to. The
words do not mean an orgasm. If I want to write orgasm I
will write it. The experience referred to means something
else as described in the text.

I do not understand your constant use of the word
euphemism. Three questions all together, you ask,
1 Love – is it a euphemism for sexual intercourse?
2 Sexual intercourse equals the highest form of love?
3 Do either of these concepts for the protagonists hold
water?
My answers are 'no' to question one.
'No' to question two.
I do not know what you mean in question three.

You are mistaken in your suggestion that Helena is black-
mailing Lois. Like other human beings Helena has her
needs. She is simply suggesting an arrangement which might
be of use to them both. Lois needs to be somewhere while
she has her baby. The views expressed on abortion and child-
birth are not necessarily my own. No, I do not wish to enter
into a correspondence with you about either.

Repeatedly you accuse me of being 'romantic' about pregnancy. The radiance I have written about is a fact of pregnancy. There are other observations about pregnancy in the
novel. Obviously you missed them because you did not
realize that Lois was pregnant.

Yes, Helena does have 'a past' as you call it but she would
never use it to push the publicity of a sensational book as
you suggest she might. Helena explains to Lois that now she
is no longer able to practise as a doctor and she lives in
seclusion because it is the only possible way she can live.

You must understand Lois! I can't put my name or my opinion
forward. I write but only for myself. I don't even have a trading
name here for anything I might produce. And I could never pub-
lish anything again.

No, I do not mention how the record player operates.
Does a novel have to contain every detail of a household?
Though I have described the big high comfortable bed and
the verandahs I have not stated how many cupboards the
house has, how many wash basins, lavatories, fireplaces,
doors and windows. Should a novel have an appendix with
these listed?

You say that the love scene between the two women is
'direct and purposeful' but the secrets of the two women
puzzle you. If everything was made clear in the first pages
there would be no novel.

Yes, the incestuous relationship with the brother is fact,
so is the murder of the elderly doctor, you are quite right,
neither of these are the secrets.

You say that the discovery of Beethoven is tiresome
because you discovered him on a wind-up gramophone in

1930. Your discovery does not mean that Beethoven has
been discovered for ever. Every day Beethoven is a fresh discovery for someone. For Helena a repeated discovery and
pleasure,

How wonderful to have her here with me. Her presence alters the
whole house. It is like the first cautious phrases of a Beethoven
Symphony, the Fourth perhaps, or the Ninth. I hope this cautious
movement lasts and goes forward as it must surely do, nothing
ever stays the same, with the same grace and harmony and
pleasure as the symphony does . . .

Your next note reads, 'Are the generalizations on the
mature woman and the pregnant woman, "the healthy
prima para", Helena's or your's? They are extremely romantic and idealized. The tender beauty of a pregnant woman
seems ludicrous. Is there never a depressed pregnant
woman? An ugly one? One with mottled thighs? One with
three chins? . . .'
Oh Get Stuffed! You clearly hate the idea of being pregnant! Of course the generalizations are not mine. I do not
use the novel to express my own views on any subject. I have
not tried to write a thesis or a dissertation on pregnancy or
on lesbianism. You seem to wish for or need a different kind
of book, one which I have not written. All sorts of pictures
of pregnancy are given quite early in the story. One is Mrs
Byrne's production of a wizened baby, almost out of spite,
and certainly for convenience. And, there is too the memory,
in prison, of the nauseating smell of pregnant women.
Later on as the loving relationship develops between the
two women, pregnancy is seen as a predicament –

But I didn't want her near me. 'It's too hot for that,' I said crossly.
'I'm too big! And I hate being pregnant, so big! It's awful Helena!
How can you think it's anything special! I hate it, I hate the baby.
I hate this hot wind! I hate everything!' I burst out crying . . .

How can you accuse me of 'perpetuating a myth about

lesbianism' it is just one person's views about love making.
Lois – and her thoughts about Helena,

Even in her love making she is controlled, she waits for me; very
occasionally, on purpose, I have made her lose control of herself
... and when this happens and it is over she is terribly sorry. Once
she wept and was afraid she had hurt me physically. I suppose it
seemed so violent to her. Love making with a woman is different.
What seems violent to her is not to me. She knows nothing of
the full violence of it, she doesn't know the hardness of a man's
body and the weight and fierceness of a man's passion ...

Lois is merely describing her own feeling and her own
experience and I do not consider her to be speaking on
behalf of all sexual partners.

You suggest in your notes that the book ends badly for
Helena and Lois. You ask why did I set up their lives with
such grim sordid (your words) backgrounds and circum-
stances.

In the writing I have tried to make it clear that the
relationship between the two women is a tender one with
healing qualities. Helena realizes that they must separate.
She knows that she cannot keep Lois with her for ever. The
life on the lonely farm, especially in the harsh summer, is
not right for Lois. Helena is afraid of the inevitable bitterness and unhappiness in the years ahead. She decides that
Lois should go away. Lois is remembering,

And she talked a bit about our lives. 'Once there was a German
poet, you'll have to brush up your German!' Helena said. 'He said
something like this: "if I can make a fruitful land between rock
and stream" or, "if I can find an orchard between rock and
stream", the idea appeals to me immensely. We can both be doing
that wherever we are ...'

Ainsley is looking forward so much to Grinzing. I am too
much occupied with thoughts to know exactly what I look
forward to.

Near my farm, where the road curves in a wide bend, there is an ugly dam. It looks as if the water in the dam is sloping towards the road. I have always been pleased to see this dam, even though it is not mine. It simply means I am near the boundaries of my place when I see it. Now I have no wish at all to go back to the farm. I am remembering all over again my return after I had taken her to the airport. I had never seen the farm before as I saw it then. The bald paddocks stretched into a dismal distance. The sheds and even the house itself seemed deserted, grey as if in perpetual twilight, empty beyond belief, without her.

The harsh voices of the crows cried loneliness into the still sad morning.

Ainsley has not stopped talking about the wine festival at Grinzing. The thought of the sentimental music and people wandering through the wine halls and the flower gardens, drinking and singing together, wearies me. Ainsley is excited because she has heard that wine is sold cheaply there in quarter-litre mugs.

Wine should be an offering, poured out in reverence.

I feel certain that the woman whose blood so recently darkened this oil-dark floor is the woman I loved years ago. The 'direct and purposeful love scene' was mine and hers. But there were many such scenes, not one.

I am the person who said those words quoted in the notes. I shot the ram too. There were other things as well, memories keep coming fast, one after another.

'You are so cool and smooth,' I told her once in a warm summer night. In our nakedness we did not need bed clothes. We seemed to only half sleep all night and the steady moonlight stripped the room of reality. She lay naked along my thigh with her little face pressed to my breast. Close outside the bedroom window the moon-ghosted loquats held their breath and our happiness in their stillness.

This Pension Heiligtum was a temporary stopping place in her long journey. I too am making this same pilgrimage though, when I set out, I did not know this.

'Ooo! Who's spilling her wine all over the place!' In reply, I tell Ainsley that she is drunk.

'Well Dear, perhaps a teensy trifle tipsy,' she agrees. 'But you are spilling your wine,' she insists. 'Here,' she says, 'have some more Dear. There's plenty more where that came from. I mean, that's what a wine festival's all about isn't it.'

'We never exactly made a suicide pact,' I tell her.

'No Dear! Of course not, why ever should we? Live and let live I always say.'

'I mean someone else, not you, someone else . . .'

'You need more wine Dear,' she says, 'you know it doesn't suit you not to have enough. Sit down here Dear, under these trees,' she says, 'while I toddle along and fetch some more.'

It's such a nuisance. I don't like having to depend on Ainsley. I don't like having to ask, in front of her, for hot water in a little row of enamelled jugs.

'Oops! You're spilling again Dear!'

'No, it's not spilling, it's only sloping.'

'There! What did I tell you. You have spilled it everywhere.'

'No, not spilled. It's poured, it's a libation.'

'What! It's a what? It's a whatter what?'

I want to be private from Ainsley. We have a double room without a bath. There is no privacy here. She will be the one to make the discovery. She will see the stain of the offering, renewing itself, darkening these oil-dark boards so recently and so carefully cleaned. I wonder if, when the time comes, I will be able to hear her frightened voice calling as she makes her way along to the rosy cherubs in the hall. She speaks hardly any German. She will have difficulty. There will be consolation if I am able to hear her having difficulty.

She might even cry. Knowing the effect her tears have on me I would prefer that she did not.

One Christmas Knitting

'Just you mind how you go on the horseway!'
(Missis Robbins)

Lately I've been thinking about my Anti Daisy and her peaceful death. She simply fell asleep in her chair by the fire and never woke up. My mother always said it was not right and that Anti Daisy should have drowned slowly with all her sins floating in front of her and herself weighted down with Grannie's silver spoons which were meant for me but which she, Anti Daisy, had refused to let me have as I was living through 'the shaded side of a well-known catastrophe' at the time and, because of this, she had as she said, cut me out of her will and would have nothing more to do with me, ever. My mother often said too that by rights the annuity which Anti Daisy bought herself with my father's share of some money should have contributed some pain to her death.

As far as we know Anti Daisy died a painless death.

But why wish pain on anyone.

The other day I received a letter from my mother in England. She had written,

I wish I could find words to tell you how much your father enjoyed your letters, how he looked forward to them and how he spent his time thinking about his replies, making little notes and asking me to remind him to tell you things.

At eighty-seven I wish he could have died in his sleep instead of that terrible road accident. They tell me he died at once but one of the policemen said he died in the ambulance. I hope he didn't see the tanker coming. He was coming home, there's half a letter he'd started to write to you, he'd chosen,

118

'*Die mit Tränen säen, werden mit Freuden ernten –*'
I'll send it later –

I can remember the place where he must have been crossing the road, it's the place where he always said to us, 'look
both ways'.

Now it's where heaven will have come down to earth to
gather him up. Because of his belief in something beyond
this life that's how he will have seen it. For myself, I am not
sure.

My mother is from Vienna. My father, after being in
prison for refusing to fight in the Great War of 1914-18 went
to Vienna with the Quaker Ambulance and Famine Relief.
He brought his Viennese bride into the household from
which his own father had earlier turned him out, in front
of all the neighbours, because of the disgrace of being in
prison.

'Your mother has such pretty arms,' my father often said.
Without him now she has no one to defend her from the
world and from herself. She gives everything away. I understand this thing about her because I am defenceless in the
same way.

My correspondence with my father started when I was
three months old. He did most of the writing then. I suppose
I always felt somehow that he would live for ever.

He really showed me how to look at the world, how to
feel the quality of the air, how to look at people and
why they say the things they say and how they are saying
them.

Sparks flew from under his boots when we walked into
town in the evenings. He liked to look in at the lighted shop
windows, he marvelled at the ways in which clothes, bread,
bicycles, tools and toys could be made to look so desirable.
In one shop cream satin cascaded, it was like a waterfall filling the shop and my father explained how he thought the
shop woman would have had to come backwards spreading
the material right up to the door, moving backwards out on
to the pavement. She would then have had to lock up the
shop without going back inside.

Back home he took off his boots and studied the soles of them carefully before placing them beside his chair.

'What shall I buy you for Christmas?' I asked my father.

'A lead pencil with a black point please,' he replied.

'What colour?'

'You choose,' he said.

'Red?'

'Yes, but remember the black point.'

And when he asked me what I wanted, 'I'd like some football boots,' I told him.

For the time being I have stopped working in my orchard to come indoors to try to write something from my childhood. It occurs to me that what I am about to write might be disgusting, not amusing and quite untrue. It's hard now to distinguish between the created and the remembered. I come from a household where people wept over Schubert Lieder one minute and tore up pictures of politicians the next. I'd like to be able to make a living picture from the half remembered by writing something from the inside and something from the outside. For me writing is an act of the will.

In this heat and this stillness all life seems withdrawn. This is the longed for and needed solitude.

I don't cry in the loneliness now but there were times when I did.

Between autumn-berried hedgerows I cried in the middle of a road which seemed to be leading nowhere. Brown ploughed fields sloped in all directions, there were no houses, shops, trams and there were no people, only the rooks gathering, unconcerned, in the leafless trees at the side of an empty lifeless barn. The anxious looks and little words of comfort from the other two girls only brought more fear and I screamed till all three of us stood howling there. And then we made our way back through our tears to what was left of our first boarding-school Sunday afternoon.

I didn't understand then what made me cry. It was only much later that I could put into words something of the shock of discovering the loneliness and uncertainty which is so much a part of living.

The tears of childhood are frequent and children sometimes know why they are crying but hesitate to explain. So when Edith and Amy said to me later in the cloakroom, 'Why are you crying again?', I couldn't tell them it was because there was something about the changing light at the end of the autumn afternoon which reminded of the time of day when my father would return, knock the carbide from his lamps on the doorstep and bring his bicycle into the safety of the scullery. How could I tell them of this longing for this particular time when he lifted his enamel plate off the hot saucepan and the smell of his pepper rose in the steam.

'It's my father and mother,' I whispered.

'Why what's wrong with them?' Edith asked.

'Oh,' I said, 'they have such dreadful fights.' I looked at my new wrist watch, 'It's just about now that my father comes home drunk and he beats my mother till she's black all over.'

Edith and Amy gazed at me with reverence. And I was so overcome with this new and interesting picture of my family life, I forgot for the time being this illness, this homesickness.

Later I learned more bitterly for myself this thing called homesickness. But I knew something about it when I was little.

When I lay in bed, long ago at home, I could hear my mother's voice like a stream running as she talked up and down to my father. And every now and then my father's voice was like a boulder in the way of the stream, and for a moment the water swirled and paused and waited and then rushed on round the boulder and I heard my mother talking on, up and down.

I thought I heard my mother crying in the night, her long sighs followed my father creaking on bent legs along the hall.

'What for is Mammy crying?' I called to him. He crawled flickering across the ceiling crouching doubled on the wardrobe where there was a fox.

'It is nothing,' he said in his soft voice. 'Go to sleep. It is nothing, she is homesick that is all.' Flickering and prancing he moved up and down the walls big and little and big. The eyes of the fox were amber and full of tears, tiny gold chains fastened its little feet. My hand reached into the soft scented fur touching the slippery silk underneath.

'Go to sleep,' my father folded and unfolded. 'I'm the engine down the mine,' he said, 'I'm the shaft I'm the steam laundry now I'm a yorkshire ham a cheese a cheshire cheese a pork pie I'm a mouse in the iron and steel works I'm a needle and thread I'm a cartwheel turning in the road turning over and over turning and turning I'm the horse the tired tired horse go to sleep go to sleep –'

I went in the dark after his candle had gone and fetched a cup of water. I took it to my mother.

'It's for your homesick,' I told her. 'Drink the water for your homesick.'

The tears of grown-up people seemed to come with such pain. Anti Daisy once sat a whole afternoon crying and my mother, not knowing enough English, tried to comfort her.

Anti Mote cried too. The police often called because of her. She stole the boards on which the tram conductors wrote numbers. These boards rested in slots.

'Very convenient,' Anti Mote said, 'for when I am getting off the tram.' She was brought home too for sunbathing naked in the East Park on cold grey November days. The English policemen wore their cloaks folded and pleated neatly over one shoulder, they had them to wrap round ladies who threw off all their clothes in public.

'Eat my little Duchess,' Anti Mote was on her knees beside my chair. She was knitting a wild cardigan. I turned my face away from the mess of egg, slimy brown, splashed over a silver tray.

'Eat my little Duchess!' she implored. 'It is only that I have scramble in mistaken for fryern, that is all. And in mistake I forget the plate!'

About Anti Mote's tears, she had deep furrows in both cheeks, and when she cried, she cried out of sight and she sounded like a man crying. She was homesick too my father said.

Like my mother Anti Mote was a baroness in her own right. They kept this shared misfortune a secret.

A few days before the move from Flowermead to Mount Pleasant my mother had a party. Her students brought their friends, they came in an old car with shingled heads and pink legs sticking out. They were from the technical college where my mother taught them enough German for their science exams, but she couldn't resist the poetry from her own language so they read Goethe and listened to Schubert with their scientific abstracts.

'*How do you feel when you marry your ideal,*' they sang, '*Ever so goosey goosey goosey.*' And they sang 'The Wedding of the Painted Doll'. My mother danced twirling her beads, strings of them, she danced kicking her feet out to the sides, heels up, toes down and turned in,

'*It's a holiday today! Today's the wedding of the painted doll,*' they sang. Together they all danced across the living room bending their knees and tapping their heads and knees and elbows. My mother had just had all her teeth out because of starving during the war and half starving before the war.

It was the fashion to have all new teeth then and to have the tonsils and the appendix removed. In some families these operations were given as presents at Christmas and birthdays.

In spite of having no teeth I could see by her eyes that my mother was enjoying her party.

They gathered round the piano and sang,

Am Brunnen vor dem Tore,
da steht ein Lindenbaum
ich träumt' in seinem Schatten
So manchen süssen Traum –

My father sat close by shading his eyes with one hand hiding his quiet tears.

I was learning the alphabet and was writing my own stories and poems in long lines of l's and f's and g's copying from a handwriting copybook into an old Boots diary. I loved the feel of the pencil on the smooth paper and as I filled the pages with the sloping letters I showed them to my father and he kissed them.

During the party Grandpa came in having walked all the way from Birmingham to Sutton Coldfield with hazel nuts in his boots. He reached into one boot and brought out some cracked nuts for the guests. To save expense he had carried a second-hand cot on his back. It was for Vera, the miner's child who was staying with us. A great many people were unemployed, it was very bad for the miners, their families had nothing to eat. It was the time of the hunger demonstrations before the great Hunger March which stretched all the way down to London.

My mother tried to feed Vera with a boiled egg but she didn't like it and the egg ran out of her mouth which was all square with her crying. My mother stuffed a toffee in with the egg but this only made it worse.

'Perhaps she's never had an egg,' one of the students said. Anti Mote said a little girl she knew wasted her eggs and I felt ashamed.

'Give her a piece,' the student suggested.

'I want a piecey too,' I said and then my sister wanted one and, in the end, Vera ate several.

As Vera had brought lice with her Grannie tied our heads up in rags dipped in paraffin and sat by us to stop us scratching.

Grandpa took my father on one side and told him if he tried to transplant the six cherry trees they would bleed to death.

All the same, on the day of the removal Grandpa walked over with his hazel nuts, his rupture and his shovel arriving at six in the morning and together they dug up the trees bandaging the roots and earth in sacks. I never saw any blood but, because of what Mount Pleasant was like, the trees died.

It was nearly Christmas and we were leaving. It was a world of jugs and basins and china chamber pots, of castor oil and mousetraps and earache and loose teeth and not knowing whether it would be Anti Mote coming into bed or Anti Daisy. And then there was the hot smell of the curling tongs and singed hair. It was a world of burned-out candles and gas mantles growing dim.

Grandpa always said it was only a matter of time before the horse manure, the great quantities of it, would block and even bury whole streets. Rapidly increasing motor traffic pushed aside the manure and repeatedly he began his conversations in an accusing voice, 'Do you know just how many people are run over and killed every week down there on the Stratford Road –'

When the removal men had finished my father asked, 'Where's Maud?' My mother and Anti Mote were to go in the van to arrive with the furniture. My sister and I were travelling with my father who drove a motor bike and sidecar.

'She was picking a bunch of flowers off the front-room wall paper,' my mother went through the empty house anxiously. But Anti Mote was nowhere to be found.

The removal was then held up by an official from the Tramways Department. A policeman was with him and Anti Mote, penitent but elated. She had for the last time outwitted the conductor on the number seven tram. In Mount Pleasant it was something called trolley buses and Anti Mote was looking forward to them.

'Don't you worry Mr Knight,' Missis Robbins, the neighbour woman said. She poured his tea for him. She gave us red jelly for our breakfast but she made us eat a piece with it.

'Just don't you worry Mr Knight,' she put his tea cup nearer to him.

'What for is Daddy crying?' I asked. Why should my father be crying these fast falling tears? He shaded his eyes with one hand as if to hide his tears. The other hand was clenched on the white table cloth.

Missis Robbins was banging with the iron, she tested it with her spit which flew sizzling across the kitchen. Why should Missis Robbins be telling him not to worry.

'What for is Daddy crying?' I asked. These mysterious tears. 'What for are we leaving Flowermead?' I asked.

'Eat your piecey there's a good girl,' Missis Robbins said. It was time to go.

'Just you mind how you go on the horseway!' Missis Robbins called from her gate and we were on the journey to Mount Pleasant.

In every place, however desolate, there will be some saving quality. Bricks, suddenly warm coloured, and corner stones made noble in an unexpected light from the passing and hesitant sun; perhaps a window catching tree tops in a distant park beyond steep roofs and smoking chimneys. Perhaps it is simply an undefined atmosphere of previous happiness caught and held in certain rooms.

To my mother there was nothing which could redeem the ugly house in Mount Pleasant.

'There is nothing pleasant here at all,' she said.

Grandpa had chosen the name Flowermead and he came there every few days to dig and plant. There was an apple tree, the six cherry trees, a pear tree, red and black currants, gooseberries, raspberries and roses, lawns and grassy banks and flower beds with Michaelmas daisies, larkspur, cornflowers and canterbury bells. The garden of the new house was a narrow strip of slag from the coal mine. A smouldering pit mound was at the end of the street. Other pit mounds covered with coarse grass and coltsfoot were beyond, and behind them the high wall of the fever hospital. There was a bone and glue factory near and across the street were the brick kilns. Framed on the sky were the wheels and the shaft of the coal mine. The noise of the cage coming up or going down the shaft and the smell of the bone and glue accompanied every action. The heave and roar of the blast furnaces and the nightly glow across the sky became my night light and my cradle song.

Grandpa couldn't think of a name for this house so it was called Barclay after the Bank.

In Flowermead there was a water pump bringing strange draughts from a well deep in the earth. My father was pleased with the new house. Water flowed from taps.

'It's nearer for me for the Central School,' he said, 'and we're the first people to live in it!'

'That's why there are no shelves,' my mother said.

'But electricity!' my father switched the lights on and off.

'And stairs to clean!' my mother was unable to accept the shining invitation from the new linoleum.

'The woodwork's cheap,' Anti Daisy came cream cloched with Grannie to see the new house.

'But look at the grain of the wood,' my father opened and closed the doors.

'There's knot holes,' Anti Daisy poked her finger through one in the pantry door. But Grandpa had arrived. To save the fare he'd walked with his hazel nuts, and his rupture and carrying two hens in a box.

'Come upstairs,' my father said to him, 'and see the W.C.'

Through the pantry-door knot hole lay another world, there was a lake of quiet milk, blue as dusk and fringed with the long fern fronds of carrot and celery, jewelled water drops hung sparkling in a cabbage and two apples promised a tub full of fruit.

It was Christmas Eve with frost flowers like lace curtains.

'Guess what I'm giving you for Christmas,' I said to my father.

'I hope it's a lead pencil?'

'Yes, Yes!'

'With a black point?'

'Yes. Now guess what colour it is.'

'Red?'

'Yes.' I couldn't wait to give him the pencil.

'I hope I'm getting some football boots,' I said to him.

'Nice little girls don't ever wear football boots,' Anti Daisy said.

My father suggested that Grannie and Anti Mote should

have a little ride in the side-car. There was just room for
them both.

'Come upstairs Grettell,' Anti Daisy never pronounced
my mother's name properly. She wanted to show my mother
the Christmas dolls. They had hair which could be combed,
we overheard her telling, and little shoes and socks.

'I still want the boots,' I called up after them. My sister
and I went out to look at the hens.

We found Grandpa lying across the cold grey slag, his
neck was all bulged over his collar and a terrible noise came
from him. I didn't know then that the noise was just his difficult breathing. In terror we rushed up the new stairs. Of
course Anti Daisy and my mother had locked themselves in
with the presents and wouldn't come out straight away.

Later we sat in the hearth with the dinner plates put to
warm. Grandpa sat in the armchair, his freshly combed white
hair looked like a bandage.

'Whatever made you have an attack out there!' Anti
Daisy came in twitching her dress angrily. 'Whatever made
you have an attack now!' she said to Grandpa. 'You frightened these two children,' she accused him. 'D'you hear me?'
she shouted at him. 'You frightened the children!'

When Anti Daisy had gone back to the kitchen Grandpa
shook his head slowly and tears rolled down to his white
moustache.

These mysterious tears? I wanted to put my arms round
his neck and kiss his wet cheek and tell him, 'Never mind.
Never mind.' But I was afraid of him and shyly I sat there
with my sister watching the old man weeping.

The Black Country was a mixture of coal mines, factories,
chain shops and brickworks and little farms in green triangles
huddled in the shadows of the slag heaps. Rows and rows
of mean little houses gave way suddenly to hawthorn hedges
and fields. Here, the air was suddenly fragrant.

Grannie enjoyed her side-car ride but couldn't understand
why they had stopped in a place where there was no view.

'I seemed to be looking straight into the hedge,' she said.
My father explained that the side-car had come off the

motor bike and had come to rest in a ditch. While he was fixing it Anti Mote had disappeared.

'I expect Maud is walking home,' he said, 'it's not very far.' His face was white in the dusk when he looked for her up and down the unknown streets. I didn't know then, as I do now, that it seems that a child, a person, has to look both ways and to look along and follow roads which often seem to be going nowhere.

Anti Mote was a little late for the present giving. The living-room door flew open at last, a breath of cold air came,

'*Guten Tag! Grüss Gott und fröhliche Weihnachten!*' she kissed all the anxious faces. 'On the trolley buses,' she announced, 'they have them too! Very neat and nicely made from metal,' and from somewhere in her skirt she brought out the conductor's board from trolley bus eleven.

'*Die mit Tränen säen, werden mit Freuden ernten,*' my father read aloud, 'They that sow in tears shall reap in joy.'

Grandpa and Grannie said, 'Amen! Amen!'

There were no football boots for me. I did get them years later on my ninth birthday. That was in June, by the autumn my feet couldn't squeeze into them.

'I only had time', Anti Mote said, 'for one Christmas knitting, it is for you!' She had knitted the cardigan for me. Unwillingly I put it on. She smiled happily.

'Is so wide and big,' she said, 'both children can wear it at the same time!'

Butter Butter Butter
for a Boat

We've had the outboard motor on the lounge cushions in the living room for some time now.

'The propeller's got to be higher than the rest of it,' my brother explained to mother. 'I don't think there's any oil likely to leak out,' he said. And mother said she hoped it wouldn't be there long as Milfords were coming to reclaim the lounge and the two chairs because of her defaulting on the payments.

'There really isn't space for that big furniture in this small room,' mother consoled, 'and though I liked the purple and green stripe when I bought it, I've really gone off it now. I'll be glad to see it go.'

I couldn't help remembering how pleased she'd been to really rest in comfort watching telly. Because of not being allowed to disturb the new outboard, we couldn't move the chairs to sit in them for telly or anything now.

'Better not have that engine in here when Milfords come,' she said. 'I wouldn't want them to think we've abused their stuff in any way.' She was having trouble with some corn-flakes my brother had spilled.

'Milk's a terrible thing to remove from fabric,' she said, 'unless you can pour a boiling kettle over it and I'm afraid to do that because of the purple, it's a dangerous colour.'

One night last week we had just come home from South Heights where I go with mother to help her clean the luxury flats. She says it's an education for me to go there and see the same *Mona Lisas* and *Laughing Cavaliers* in all the apartments, and the gorgeous rooms scattered with wigs and expensive boots and half-eaten pizzas. We had just come home and my brother was already there waiting for us.

'Butter, Butter, Butter,' he said as soon as we came in.

'What d'you want now!' mother said, she was tired out but started into the ironing straight away.

'Butter, Butter, Butter for a boat,' said my brother in his persuading voice. He'd tied the alarm clock on to a piece of string and he shuffled up to mother swinging the clock to and fro in front of her face.

'Where-do-you-keep-yor-ten-cent-bits?' he said in a monotonous voice. 'Where-do-you-keep-yor-ten-cent-bits?' I thought mother would die she laughed so much and all the time my brother kept on his monotonous voice, 'Where-do-you-keep-yor-ten-cent-bits?'

'You'll never hypnotize me!' mother managed to say at last. 'I'm too spiritual!' And we all roared our heads off.

'I've been arrested,' my brother said suddenly.

'Whatever next!' Mother calmed down at once but her nose went red, the way it does when she's excited or annoyed. I could tell she was upset because she let the iron stand on a pink dinner shirt and the iron went right through it and into the wood of the ironing board. The smell was terrible.

'It's the nylon,' mother explained. It stuck to the iron and it took her the whole evening to get it off and she had two baskets full of clothes to get done for South Heights.

My brother was arrested for being unlawfully on the premises of the Deep Blue Marine Co. The police didn't believe his explanation that he was looking for his boat which he said had been stolen from the jetty. So then my brother told the police that he was buying a boat from the Blue Marine and was just checking to see if she was all right. The police were doubtful about this too and said he was to report at the station first thing next day.

Mother understood at once and agreed he should call at the boat yard and put a deposit on a boat on the way to the police station. She lent him all her savings from the tin box under her bed. She doesn't believe in banks at this stage

in the economy. She says with governments going mad over
kinky coffee tables and the nude body you've got to look
after yourself.

'Always remember this,' she said to me. 'There's nothing
strange or new about the human body, it's been the same
since creation. Alive or dead the human body is just a body,
and if governments are going to waste our money promoting
something which belongs to us in any case, then it's the tin
box under the bed for me.'

Mother had my brother on her mind such a lot. 'Being
arrested,' she said to me, 'is better for him than just lying
around unemployed. Not being able to get a job is the same
as not being wanted in your life, it's a terrible thing. Perhaps
because of this new boat he'll get a job and stay in it.' She
tried not to nag him about being out of work because every
time she mentioned it he bought presents for her, chocolates
and roses and cosmetics and, as she said, she couldn't keep
on paying for them. The phosphorescent lipstick nearly
killed us all the same. I thought we'd never stop laughing
the day she plastered it on.

The next thing was this thin boat in the passage. It's silver
and new and looks as if it would tip over like a dainty little
doll in the first wave. And of course, there's the outboard
motor cuddled up on the cushions and propped between the
armchairs.

This is my brother's second boat. It'll take a while to pay
it off, it's new.

The first boat disappeared. He came in one night and we
knew something was wrong because of his white face.

'Someone's taken the boat,' he said straight out to
mother. I could see she was relieved. She was always afraid
he'd drown himself. She often wished he'd go for something
safe like being a vegetarian.

'Oh I am sorry,' she said managing to hide her relief. 'It's
probably sunk,' she said.

'It couldn't have!' My brother was indignant. When he
first got it he made us come down to the jetty to have a look.
He was so proud and pleased so neither of us said anything.

And, because of him wanting so much to take us out fishing, we didn't refuse though mother said she thought the river was looking a bit unpredictable.

'Oh it's not deep here anyway,' my brother said. 'You can walk to the shore from any part of the river.' But he had to admit later that he'd been wrong about this.

'What are the fence pickets for?' I asked him.

'You hold your face!' he said and made me sit in the wettest place.

'If you catch something give three pulls,' he said. Later I thought I *had* caught something but it was just my brother's line from the other side of the boat. For once he was quite nice about me being so stupid.

Mother laughed and laughed really enjoying her river trip.

'Just think,' she said, 'I never thought I'd be a member of the Blue Water Yacht Club!' Her nose was really red with excitement and fear.

'It's not a yacht,' my brother said, but he looked really happy.

'There's the South Heights!' mother exclaimed. 'Right on the river! It's such a pity that the people who pay all that money to live there can't actually see the river. There's no gardens or paths so they can't walk down to these pretty little beaches. When you're in South Heights,' she said, 'it's all basements, lift shafts and rubbish chutes, it's the way the place has been built, you have to get in the shower to see the view.'

It was just then the engine failed. My brother knew at once what it was.

'No fuel,' he said, 'we'll have to bring her in without the motor.'

'How?' I asked, but I should have known. There weren't any oars and I can tell you it was terrible trying to row that heavy old tub with fence pickets.

We were nearly at the jetty when the outboard motor slipped off and sank.

'Of course I'll lend you twenty dollars to hire a boat and a grappling iron,' mother said, as she helped my brother to struggle back into the boat, after he'd stepped out to reach down to where the outboard was quite beyond reach.

'It must be about thirty-five feet down,' he said and he couldn't stop shivering.

'Who would have thought the river could be that deep!' mother was amazed.

It was some days later that the police called. I fetched mother quickly, we could see who it was through the glass part of the door.

'Ask him to wait in the living room,' mother said. 'Tell him I'm busy writing cheques for the rent and the electricity.'

'What about the outboard?'

'That's all right,' she said, 'tell him to mind the propeller, they damage so easy.'

I could see she was wondering why the police had come.

'Is my nose red?' she asked me.

'Not very,' I said, not caring very much. I never liked answering the door. Mother quickly put on her good dress.

'Is Mr Morgan at home?' the policeman asked her.

'Oh No!' mother said, 'perhaps you don't know, he's doing life,' she dabbed her eye. 'You're new and you're young,' she said. 'I'm managing on my own with these two children.'

'We're all doing life in a manner of speaking Mrs Morgan. We're all doing life,' he said quite kindly.

'Ah yes! how wise you are. Yes, we *are* all doing life. But won't you sit down?' Mother remembered her good manners.

'It's young Mr Morgan I want,' the policeman said, still standing because of the outboard motor. 'Is he in?'

'Why, what's he done?' mother's voice changed.

'He reported the theft of his boat,' he consulted his book.

'Oh yes, the boat!'

'Did you ever see the boat?'

'Oh yes, he had it all right,' mother laughed, 'we went fishing in it didn't we Mary –'

'There's been a very old boat dragged up from the river,' the policeman interrupted mother, 'it doesn't fit his description, so I was wondering –'

'Well, it wasn't a new boat,' said mother.

'How long had he had it?'

'Oh, a few weeks only I'd say. He's spent a lot of time and money on her, he was doing her up himself. Then he had a bit of bad luck, he lost the engine, he knows just where it is –'

The policeman made a sympathetic noise, 'Is young Mr Morgan in?'

'No, he's gone after a job right across town,' mother said.

'I'd like to know if this is his boat –'

'There's nothing wrong I hope?' mother was anxious.

'It's just that it's so unlike what he described.'

'Oh I see!' said mother. 'I expect', she said, 'he saw the boat with different eyes from you if I might presume to explain. It's like this,' she said, 'he really cherished her. He got her from the firewood yard and spent all his time rubbing her down and fixing her leaks. He had a bit of trouble about the paint,' she explained, 'he couldn't make up his mind what colour he wanted her so that would explain something about her wouldn't it, all those dabs and streaks, then of course there's no engine, you wouldn't believe the river was so deep, he's spent hours trying with the grappling irons and can't reach it. What he's described to you is his boat. He's buying another –'

'So I notice.'

'He'll be in directly,' mother said.

'Tell him to call into the station first thing in the morning. Brown's Wood Yard have reported some thefts. We want to clear the matter up,' and he went off.

'They've found your boat,' mother told my brother when he came home. He seemed to fill the kitchen he was so pleased.

'They seem to think she's a wreck. They've pulled her out. I believe the wood yard's looking for her,' mother said. 'You better have a bit of a consideration about it before you say she's yours, and there might be something to pay too for a wreck 'specially if it's a stolen one!' she added.

The kitchen suddenly seemed really small for my brother. He looked as if he'd be able to lift the ceiling if he'd wanted to.

'If they've really found her I don't care how much the salvage costs,' he said. 'I'll go down right away.'

'What about Brown's yard?' mother asked. 'Your tea's ready,' she said, she always worried about what to get him for his tea.

'I don't want it,' he called, 'you have it.' And he edged by the silver dainty doll he'd never taken on the river, and we heard the door slam and his feet racing to get to the police station before it closed.

Woman in a Lampshade

One cold wet night in July Jasmine Tredwell took several
sheets of paper and her typewriter together with a quantity
of simple food and some respectable wine and, saying good-
night fondly to her dozing husband, she set off in search of
solitude.

'I'm going up to the farm,' she said, 'I'll be home first
thing on Monday morning,' she promised. But her husband,
Emeritus Professor of Neo Byzantine Art, was encased in
head-phones listening to Mahler and paid no attention to
the departure.

It was not her custom to give lifts to strangers. Indeed,
because of reported bashings and murders in lonely suburbs,
she had, in an impulsively tender moment, promised the elderly Professor that she would never pick up from the roadside any stranger however pathetic or harmless his appearance.

She saw the young man standing in the dark. He seemed
to be leaning rather than standing, the storm holding him
up in its force. He was an indistinct outline, blurred because
of the rain. It was as if he had come into existence simply
because someone, hopelessly lost among words, had created
him in thoughtful ink on the blotting paper. Immediately,
forgetting her promise, she stopped the car and, leaning
over, opened the door with some difficulty.

'Hop in quick young man, you're getting drowned!'

The grateful youth slipped quickly into the warm and
secure fragrance. He tried, without success, not to mark the

clean upholstery with the water as it ran off him in dirty
little streams. Jasmine took the hills noisily, the windscreen
wipers flying to and fro flinging off the splashings as if the
car boasted small fountains on either side.

'Thanks,' he said, 'thanks a lot.'

'Such a terrible night,' she said, 'are you going far?'

'As far as I can get.'

'Where shall I drop you?'

'Oh, anywhere. It'll do if you drop me off when you've
gone as far as you're going.' He gave a nervous little laugh.
'Tah very much,' he said. 'Thank you very much, tah!'

That the young man had no definite destination did not
cause Jasmine to wish that she had not stopped to offer him
a ride. They hardly spoke. Almost at once Jasmine was
touched to notice that her youthful travelling companion
had fallen asleep.

'He must have been exhausted,' she thought and she wondered about his ragged soaked clothes. 'He's probably
hungry too,' she said to herself.

Jasmine felt safe in the lamplight. And she felt safe in the
lampshade, pretty too. She was not a pretty woman, she
never pretended to be. But the lampshade, when she put
it on, made her feel pretty, softly so and feminine. It was
the colour of ripe peaches and made of soft pleats of silk.
It was light and it fitted her perfectly. It was like a garden-
party hat only more foolish because it was, after all, a
lampshade. To wear the lampshade suggested the dangerous
and the exotic while still sheltered under a cosy domesticity.

She never guessed the first time she placed it on her head
how she would feel. She had never experienced such a feeling before. It had taken her by surprise. After that first time
she had looked with shy curiosity at other women in shops
and at parties, at the hairdresser's and even while passing
them in the street, quietly noticing the private things about
them, the delicate shaping of the back of the neck or the
imaginative tilt of the ears. She wondered too about all the
tiny lines and folds and creases, all the secret things. So
recently having discovered something about herself, she

wondered what secret pleasures they had and whether they
had known them long before she had discovered hers.

She sang softly,

> *I love my little lampshade*
> *So frilly and warm*
> *If I wear my silky lampshade*
> *I'll come to no harm.*

'Are you awake?' she asked the young man later that night.
He was buried under a heap of old fur coats and several
spoiled pages.

'Are you awake? Hey! Are you awake? God? how soundly
you sleep! It's being young, I suppose, hey! wake up!'

'What's that? What the . . .?' he hardly moved.

'Young man, could you move over a bit, my typewriter's
falling off my knee, it's giving me the most awful cramp. Also
I'm getting a pain in my back. Ah! that's better. No, no
further or you'll fall out. That'll do beautifully. Hey!' she
laughed, pleased with the music of her own voice, 'don't roll
back! You know, if you lie on the edge of the bed, you'll
soon drop off!'

He drew the coats closer and made no sound.

'That was supposed to be a joke,' she said noisily rearrang-
ing the papers. 'But seriously,' she said, 'it's like this, I've got
a young man, he's a bit of a nuisance really. First he's in a
suburban post office in Australia. Can you imagine him
behind the counter with his pale offended eyes about to
burst into tears and all the little veins and capillaries flushed
on his crooked boyish face, or something like that?

'Then he turns up again in a depressing hotel in Calais
where two lesbians have gone to have a bit of privacy. The
younger one wants to get away from her husband and the
older one is the husband's secretary, a really boring stuffy old
maid. She's quite empty headed and very irritating to be
with for more than a few minutes as the younger one dis-
covers quite quickly. In addition, the secretary, the boring
one, drinks heavily and is not really very clean. An unfortu-

nate situation altogether. Anyway, my young man's there at
the hotel reception desk, in the night, being absolutely useless.'

'Who?' the voice muffled in furs could hardly be heard.

'My young man of course,' Jasmine, preening, fingered her
peach-ripe silk pleats lovingly. 'He's left the P.O. to be a
hotel receptionist in Calais,' she continued, 'And then, to
my surprise, he moves to a cheap hotel in India, Madras to
be exact, and I've got him there exactly the same, the pale
offended eyes filled with tears, the same blushing capillaries,
perhaps he's a bit thinner, more haunted looking and, as
usual, he's no earthly use,' Jasmine sighed sadly. 'He's absolutely unable to help the guests when they arrive exhausted
in the night. It's two more lesbians, younger than the others
and one is very uncomfortable with an unmentionable infection. Not a very nice subject really but, as a writer, I have
to look closely at *Life* and every aspect of it.' Jasmine sighed
again thoughtfully, her long fingers reaching up restlessly
plucked the folds of unexpected foolishness.

'*C'est un triste métier,*' she knew her pronunciation was
flawless. 'In all the stories,' she said, 'one of the women is
horrible to my young man. Absolutely horrible! I mean one
in all three. So that's three times he has a really bad time,
in all, he's despised, rejected and betrayed. But I'm glad to
say that on all occasions the awful unkind behaviour is
deeply regretted as soon as the resulting wretchedness is evi-
dent.'

'What's the trouble?' the young man sat up and yawned
almost dislocating his lower jaw.

Jasmine banged her typewriter.

'Can't you understand, I'm stuck! I'm stuck, stuck, stuck.'
She shuffled the papers across the bed. 'Oh by the way,' she
said as calmly as she could, 'would you mind not smoking
in bed. My husband can't stand it.'

'He's not here is he?' the young man began uneasily, 'you
said, I thought . . .'

'No of course not,' Jasmine said, 'but the smoke hangs
around and he's very sensitive, his nose I mean.' She laughed.
'But,' she said, 'whatever shall I do with them?'

'Who?'

'My characters of course. I suppose,' she paused, 'I suppose they could carry on in bed.' She began to type rapidly.

'Eh? Yeah!' He turned over.

'Mind the typewriter! Oops! I thought it was gone that time. That's better. You know I must tell you I've got a friend, Moira, well she's not a friend really, more of an enemy. Writers don't have any friends.' She settled comfortably against her mountain of pillows. 'Well Moira's trying to get a psychiatric musical off the ground. God! That woman's a Bore when she talks about her work. She never stops talking! All last week she was on about an official speech she'd been asked to write for the ceremonial opening of a deep sewerage system, I mean what is there in deep sewerage?'

'Quite a lot I should think,' he yawned again. 'Have you got going now?'

'No, not at all, it's awful!' she pulled another spoiled page from her typewriter. 'I'm afraid,' she said watching the paper as it floated to the floor, 'I'm afraid, well, you must feel so trapped and cheated. I mean, being here with me in this lonely place. Just think! I brought you all this way and then everything happening like that!'

'What d'you mean, happening,' he said patiently, 'I mean nothing has yet, has it?'

'I didn't expect my young man and the lesbians . . .'

'I thought they was in Madras,' he interrupted.

'Yes, yes that's right, so they should be, but my young man . . .'

'Well, where is he then? I thought the idea was we'd be having the place to ourselves and I'd work the farm and –' a note of disappointment replaced the impatience in his voice.

'It's such a nuisance,' Jasmine replied. 'Really I'm sorry. I was so looking forward, you know, to our getting to know each other and,' she paused, 'and there he is, stupid and useless!'

'Who? Where is he?' he sat up.

'In my brief-case. Would you mind awfully? I left it just outside in the porch, I'd be so grateful if you would.'

Reluctantly he looked at the cold floor.

'No stop!' Jasmine cried. 'Stay where you are in the warm. I must be mad! I'm the one who should go. It's my fault he's out there. I should go. I'm going out to get him. You stay in bed. I'm going!'

Jasmine slipped from the bed and pattered with quick bare feet over the boards. He heard the outside door open and slam shut. He heard the noise of plates and cups and cutlery, a plate dropped somewhere crashing and breaking.

'What's that? Who's there?' he called.

'It's nothing,' she replied through a mouthful of food, 'nothing at all to worry about. I'm just having a cheese sandwich.' She came to the bedside. 'Would you like some or are you the kind of person who doesn't like eating in bed? I've sliced up an onion and a hard-boiled egg. Do have some!'

'No thank you,' he said. 'I'm not hungry really no; no thank you, really not hungry thanks all the same.'

Jasmine ate ravenously.

'Have some Burgundy,' she said, 'or would you prefer a beer?' She poured a generous glass of wine for herself and opened a can for her guest.

'Just move over a bit,' she said with her mouth full, 'thanks.' She chewed and swallowed, 'I'm sorry, really I am,' she said, 'about these papers all over the bed. I'd like to be able to make it up to you in some way. You see I should never have picked you up. When I saw you at the side of the road absolutely drenched I simply couldn't help offering you a lift.' She studied the remains of the egg apparently lost in thoughts for which there were no words. 'Ever since I decided to become a writer,' she announced, 'I've been an absolute Pain! You hardly know me really. I mean, take tonight, I've been perfectly terrible. Please, please don't try to contradict me.'

In the silence of his obedience he hiccupped.

'Manners!' he apologized.

'Oh dear!' Jasmine was dismayed. 'Perhaps you shouldn't

drink beer in bed. My husband always gets hiccups if he drinks lying down. Try walking about.'

He was not inclined to leave the bed.

'Well,' Jasmine said, 'if you're shy put this old nighty on. You walk about and I'll think up a fright for you.'

Self-conscious and solemn in brushed nylon the young man paced to and fro on the creaking floor boards. He hiccupped at regular intervals. Every minute his thin body jerked.

'Manners!' he muttered, and one minute later, 'Manners!'

Suddenly she screamed, 'Help! Help!'

'What the, who's there? Where the hell are you?' he hiccupped. 'Manners!'

'Help! Hellup!'

He hiccupped, 'Manners! Where the hell are you?'

'Under the bed silly! Help me out there's not much space.' She was out of breath. 'Such a pity it didn't work.' In the brief silence he hiccupped again.

'Look out!' she whispered. 'Look out! There's a spider behind you. A great black spider. S.P.I.D.E.R. Look behind you!'

'Manners! What? I can't hear you. Manners!'

'Oh, it's no good. You'll simply have to wait till they wear off.' She was just the tiniest bit sulky. 'I really can't help it,' she said, adjusting the lampshade with one delicate finger, 'if He visits me in the middle of the night.'

'Who? Here? Who visits you?' He began to search through the heap of furs. 'Where's my clothes? I'd better be off. Look, I shouldn't be here.'

Jasmine laughed. 'Oh relax! The Muse of course,' she said, 'perhaps I should say My Muse.' She paused. 'It's very amusing really Oh!' Her laughter was like a shower of broken glass. 'Oh!' she said, 'I made a pun there. I wonder if I could use it somewhere in here, let me see.' She rearranged several of the papers. She laughed again. 'You look so serious walking up and down in that tatty old gown.' He turned to look at her seriously and steadily.

'I've been wondering what's that, I mean, what's that on your head?'

'It's a lampshade,' she replied.

'If you don't mind my arskin', why do you?'

'Always when I'm writing,' her voice was deep with reverence.

'But I thought we was going to have it away together.'

'Yes,' Jasmine said, 'I thought so too but it's my young man –'

'The one who was in all those places?'

'Yes.'

'Oh, I see,' he paused and said in a flat voice, 'praps I'd better go then.'

'Oh no,' Jasmine said, 'there's absolutely no need. I know,' she said, 'let's dance! My little transistor's here somewhere. I know it's here, somewhere here.' She rummaged among the bear skins and the ancient silver fox. 'Ah! here we are. If we danced, you never know, it might be better. I'll just see if I can get some music. Ah good! here's music. Listen there's a dancing teacher too. What a scream!'

The pulse of the music noticeably caused life to return and the dancing instructor's voice flowed quietly bringing shape and order into the disordered room.

'Now for the stylized step. Starting position,' the Irish voice was kind, 'beat one step up beat two step together beat three step back beat four step together up together back together and up together and back together arms loose relax and smile.'

'Come on!' Jasmine was laughing.

'I don't dance. Really, I don't dance.'

'Oh come on!'

'Not on beds. I don't dance on beds. It's too dangerous and, besides, it's rude.'

Jasmine laughing and breathless reached out and turned the volume on more.

There was a change in the music.

'Now the basic camel walk and step and kick and camel walk,' the instructor's patient voice continued. 'Beat one stub left beat two stub right beat three stub left beat four stub right beat five stub left beat six kick left beat seven stub right beat eight and kick and kick that's just fine you'll make it in time beat one stub left beat two stub right think happy and relax beat three stub left beat four stub right that's great you're great the greatest!'

Jasmine fell off the bed with a crash.

'And now the Latin Hustle,' the dancing instructor's persistent voice changed rhythm as the music changed. 'Touch and one and two and step back three and four forward five and six repeat touch and one and two and step and one and two and one.'

'Now you've properly done it!' The young man fell over the furniture. 'You've knocked over the light. Have you broke it? It's pitch dark!' He stumbled again, knocking over a chair. 'Where are you?' he shouted. 'It's pitch black dark. Yo' must 'ave broke the lamp.'

'Over here!' Jasmine sang, teasing through the music and the darkness.

'Where's the matches?' Panic made him angry.

'Yoo hoo! Here I am,' Jasmine was beside him, and then she was far away. 'I'm over here,' she called, and suddenly she was close again. Both were breathing heavily, gasping even, furniture fell and crockery crashed as if something was rocking the cottage. Jasmine was laughing and laughing, pleased and excited.

'Oh go on,' she cried. 'Don't stop!' she pleaded.

'Repeat these movements till you feel comfortable and confident in your performance,' the dancing instructor's voice, keeping time perfectly, penetrated above and below the sound of the music. 'Follow the beat sequence and turn and turn repeat and turn and repeat,' his patience was endless.

'I'm going outside,' the young man was polite and strained. 'If yo'll excuse me,' he said, 'I'll 'ave to go outside.'

'Yes, yes of course,' Jasmine said, 'Just through the yard and up the back you can't miss.'

'Thanks,' he let the door slam. 'Sorry!' he called.

'You'll make it in time,' the dancing master's voice consoled. 'Try once more beat one stub left beat two stub right.'

Jasmine switched off her tiny radio. She was laughing

softly, breathlessly. 'Now where's the other lamp and the matches? Ah! here they are.'

In the soft light she made herself comfortable with three pillows at her back. She began to type rapidly,

'My story just needs a bit of action,' she said.

A gun shot sounded close by, it was followed by a second shot.

'Splendid!' Jasmine said. 'That's just what I needed. Now I know what happens next.' She continued to type. 'He'd better do it at once. But not in Madras. He'd better get on a 'plane quickly.' Her typewriter rattled on. 'Oh well to save time he can do it at the airport.' She read aloud what she had written in the mincing tones reserved for her work. *Quietly he took the jewelled pistol from its silky case and held it to his pale crooked forehead. His eyes were full of tears ...*' She changed her voice. 'That's a nice touch, the crooked forehead, what exquisite writing. I've never written so well before.' She read again in the special voice, as she typed, *Closing his eyes, he pulled the trigger ...*'

The young man came in. He hiccupped.

'Oh my God!' said Jasmine. 'What happened?'

'I missed both times,' his voice was flat.

'Oh what a nuisance. So you're still here.' She pulled the page from her typewriter and crumpled it in her hand.

'Of course I'm still here. Where should I be?'

'But the shots,' Jasmine interrupted, 'I thought –'

'Oh that! I tried to get a rabbit but it was too quick,' he gave a shy laugh. 'I've never pointed a gun at anything before.'

'Useless, absolutely useless,' Jasmine was exasperated, 'you've muffed the whole thing. You muffed it. Can't you do anything properly.'

'I don't know,' he was almost tearful, 'I've never had the chance.'

'I suppose you've never tried for long enough,' she said.

'I would be able to if I stayed here. I –' he was eager. 'I've had a look out there. I like your place. It's just beginning to get light out there, I could see all the things that need doing. I'll fix the fence posts and paint the sheds. I think

I know what's up with the tractor, I'll be able to get it going. There's all the things I'd like to do out there.' He paused and then rushed on, 'on the way up here in the car you said I could stay and work the farm, you said you needed someone like me.'

'You never stay anywhere long enough, you said so yourself.' She put a fresh sheet in the typewriter.

'Well it's not my fault. Like I said, "I've had no chance." '

'What do you do?' Jasmine asked.

'What d'you mean?'

Outside a rooster crowed.

'Oh never mind!' Jasmine yawned. 'I suppose you're, how do they describe it,' she paused, 'discovering yourself.'

'I'm between jobs,' he shouted, 'That's where I've always been, between jobs. Between jobs. Between nothing!' he paused.

'But out there,' he was breathless and excited, 'I saw it all out there waiting to be done, there's everything to do out there. I'll fix everything, you'll see.'

'We like it as it is,' Jasmine said. 'My husband and I like it as it is, we don't want any change.'

'There's even a turkey yard,' he interrupted her, 'you'd like some turkeys wouldn't you, the yard only needs a bit of new wire netting. I'd have some fowls too.'

'But don't you understand,' Jasmine said, 'we only come here to get away from it all. We like the place as it is. It's only a weekender you know, we like it like this.'

'I'll measure up how much wire,' he ignored her, 'I'll need a bit of paper and a pencil. I'll work out how much paint.'

'Australia, Calais, Madras,' Jasmine said softly, 'what does it matter where I set him, London, New York, Bombay, Paris, Rome, it's all the same wherever he is. What does it matter where he pulls the trigger. First, I'll get him somewhere alone and then I'll kill him off.'

'What's that,' he said quickly, 'what did you say?'

Outside another rooster answered the first one.

'Oh, nothing,' she fussed through her papers. 'I think it's really quite light outside now. There's a bus down at the crossroads about five fifty. It should get you back to town around eight o'clock.' She paused and then said, 'I want you to know I feel really bad about the whole thing. I mean about bringing you all the way to the cottage like this,' she spoke rapidly, 'because of wasting your time like this, and I do feel bad about it, I'm going to give you this poem I've written. You can keep it. I have other copies.'

'Thank you,' he was only just polite, 'thank you very much.'

'Fourteen stanzas,' Jasmine crooned, 'fourteen stanzas all with fourteen lines and every one all about my adorable little black poodles.'

'What'll I do,' the young man said, 'when I get to the empty town at eight?'

'There's a little refrain,' Jasmine murmured, 'in the middle of every stanza.'

'What'll I do,' he said, 'when I get to the empty town at eight? I mean where will I go? What can I do there?'

'All the stanzas', she continued, 'have this little refrain to include every one of my little black dogs.'

'I mean,' he said, 'where will I go when I get there? I'd rather stay here and fix the fences. Where will I go? What's there to do in the empty town at eight?' He smiled a moment at his own thoughts. 'You know,' he said, 'there's something good about putting new paint on with a new brush. Dark glossy green, I can just see it out there,' he smiled in the direction of the yard.

'When I wrote the poem,' Jasmine said, 'I knew it was good. I was really pleased with it. It's a good poem. I love my poem.'

'Where will I go in the empty town?' he whined. 'I'll have nothing to eat and nowhere to sleep. Can't I stay and paint the shed? Please?'

'I want everyone to be pleased with the poem,' she said.

'Eight's early to reach town if you've no reason,' he shouted.

'There!' Jasmine smiled, 'I've just thought of a wonderful line for a new poem. I must get it down because I forget everything I think up if I don't get it down.' She began to type, made a mistake, and pulling the spoiled page out, started a fresh page.

'I mean,' the young man cried, 'where will I go when I get there? What's there in town for me to do?'

'I never realized before', Jasmine yawned, 'that my young man in Madras is an absolute Bore!'

He went to the door and opened it. 'Well, I'd better be on my way then,' he said in a quiet flat voice. He went out carefully closing the door behind him.

Jasmine sat in bed writing her autobiography. *My father*, she typed, *was the distinguished scientist who discovered heat and light.* She stopped typing to sing to herself,

> *I love my little lampshade*
> *So frilly and warm*
> *If I wear my silky lampshade*
> *I'll come to no harm.*

He wrote, she typed, *in his lifetime, two text books, the one on light was blue and for heat, he chose red.*

Wednesdays and Fridays

Wednesday 4 June
Dear Mr Morgan,

   You will be surprised to have a letter from me since we are living in the same house but I should like to remind you that you have not paid me board for last week.

Yours sincerely,
Mabel Doris Morgan
(landlady)

Wednesday 11 June
Dear Mr Morgan,

   This is to remind you that you are now owing two weeks' board and I should like to take the opportunity to ask you to remove the outboard motor from your room. There is an oil stain on the rug already and I'm afraid for my curtains and bedspread.

Yours sincerely,
Mabel Doris Morgan
(landlady)

Friday 13 June
Dear Mr Morgan,

   I know there isn't anything in the 'Rules of the House' to say outboard motors cannot be kept in bedrooms. I didn't think any one would want to. Since you mention the rules I would like to draw your attention first to rule number nine which refers to empty beer cans, female visitors and cigarette ends, and to point out that rule eleven states quite clearly the hour for breakfast. It is simply not possible, I am sorry, to serve breakfasts after twelve noon.

Yours sincerely,
Mabel D. Morgan
(landlady)

Wednesday 18 June
Dear Mr Morgan,

I am writing to remind you that you now owe three weeks' board and the price of one single bed sheet which is ruined. Please note that bed linen is not to be used for other purposes. Thank you for moving the outboard motor.

Yours sincerely,
Mabel Doris Morgan
(landlady)

Friday 20 June
Dear Mr Morgan,

No. Black oil and grease will not wash out of a sheet furthermore it's torn badly in places. I can't think how it's possible to damage a sheet as much as this one has been damaged.

I am afraid I shall have to ask you to move the outboard motor again as it is impossible for anyone to sit in the lounge room to watch TV the way you have the propellor balanced between the two easy chairs.

Yours sincerely,
Mabel D. Morgan
(landlady)

Wednesday 25 June
Dear Mr Morgan,

Thank you for the two dollars. I should like to remind you that you now owe four weeks' board less two dollars.

Yours sincerely,
Mabel D. Morgan
(landlady)

Friday 27 June
Dear Mr Morgan,

Leaving a note on the mantelpiece does not excuse any-one for taking two dollars which does not belong to them even if you are only borrowing it back as you say till next week. Board is at four weeks now. I'm sorry to have to tell you that the hall is too narrow for the storage of an outboard motor. And, would you please replace your bedspread and put up your curtains again as I am afraid they will spoil and they do not in any way help to prevent people from falling over the outboard as they go in and out of this house.

Yours sincerely,
Mabel D. Morgan
(landlady)

Wednesday 2 July
Dear Mr Morgan,

Board is up to five weeks. With respect, Mr Morgan, I'd like to suggest you try to get a job. I'd like to suggest the way to do this is to get up early and get the paper and read the *Situations Vacant, Men and Boys*, and go after something. I'd like to say this has to be done early and quick. Mr Morgan, five weeks' board is five weeks' board. And Mr Morgan what's been going on in the bathroom. I think I am entitled to an explanation.

Yours sincerely,
Mabel Doris Morgan
(landlady)

Friday 4 July
Dear Mr Morgan,

Thank you for your very kind thought. The chocolates really look very nice though, as you know, I don't eat sweet things as I have to watch my weight but as I said it's the thought that counts. Do you think it's possible you might be smoking a bit too much. Perhaps you could cut it down to say sixty a day for a start.

Yours sincerely,
Mabel Doris Morgan
(landlady)

Wednesday 9 July
Dear Mr Morgan

I'm still waiting for an explanation about the bathroom. I must remind you that you now owe me six weeks' board and the cost of one single bed sheet ruined plus the cost of one bottle carpet cleaning detergent plus the price of the four pounds of gift-wrapped confectionery charged to my account at the Highway General Store. Early payment would be appreciated.

Yours sincerely,
Mabel Doris Morgan
(landlady)

Friday 11 July
Mr Morgan,

Get a Job. And clean your room. I never saw such a mess of chocolate papers under anyone's bed, ever. In my whole life I never saw such a mess. Never. I must point out too that I do not intend to spend hours in the kitchen over the hot roast and two veg. for someone who is too full up with rubbish to eat what's good for them. I'd like to remind you how to get a job. You get up early to get a job. I see in the paper concrete hands are wanted, this should suit you, so GET UP EARLY as it's a question of being first on site.

Yours sincerely,
Mabel Doris Morgan
(landlady)

And Mr Morgan, Bathroom? Explanation? And Mr Morgan. Smoking!

Wednesday 16 July
Dear Mr Morgan,

I appreciate you have troubles. We all have our troubles and I do see you have yours and it was kind of you to think of sending me flowers when you have so much on your mind. Thank you for the thought.

Miss, I forget, if you said, what you said her name was, had no business to miss her last bus. In future no guests are to stay in this house without me. See that this does not hap-

pen again. You seem to have forgotten the outboard motor.
There simply is not room for it in the hall and it's all wet.
Please see that it is removed immediately. And please Mr
Morgan, Board seven weeks.

Yours sincerely,
Mabel D. Morgan
(landlady)

Friday 18 July
Dear Mr Morgan,
    First I must ask for an immediate explanation about the
bathroom please. And secondly, I must ask you to ask Miss
whatever her name is to leave. I suggest you ask her what
her name is if you didn't get it the first time.
    I hope you won't feel offended about this but there really
is not room for you to sleep in the hall, you know it has
always been too narrow. There simply is not room there for
you and the outboard motor. One of you will have to go.
And see that young Miss, leaves at once. And, Donald,
always make sure you know what a girl's name is beforehand.
You not knowing her name makes me feel I haven't brought
you up right.

Yours sincerely,
Mabel Doris Morgan
(landlady)

Wednesday 23 July
Dear Mr Morgan,
    I have to remind you Board eight weeks and Board one
week for Extra Person. Perhaps you could persuade Pearl to
go back to her lovely boarding school? Could you? I'm sure
she's a nice girl but I really can't do with the two of you
lazing round the house all day using up all my electricity and
hot water. And I don't need to tell you that there really isn't
enough space in the hall for your bed, her bicycle and her
extra cases and the outboard motor.
    Donald it's silly blocking up the hall with your bed. The
neighbours will talk in any case. They'll think immorality is
going on and what about young Mary? What ideas is she

going to get? Donald I'm warning you I'm putting my foot down furthermore the outboard motor is not to be used in the bath. Where can it get you? AND what about a Job?

Yours sincerely,
Mabel Doris Morgan
(landlady)

Friday 25 July
Donald, No more roses please. I haven't got vases. Besides how am I going to pay for them? You know me, I'd just as soon see a flower growing in someone's garden. Thank you all the same for your lovely thought.

Your loving landlady,
Mabel Doris Morgan

Wednesday 30 July
Mr Morgan, This is to remind you Board nine weeks and Board two weeks for one Extra Person. I must say young Pearl has a healthy appetite. I wish you would eat properly.

As I was saying. Board as above, also cost of one single bed sheet, one bottle carpet cleaning detergent plus the price of the four-pound box of assorted confectionery and four dozen red roses, two deliveries, long stalks extra, and to dry cleaning and dyeing one chenille bedspread (purple) and two pairs curtains (electric green). With dry cleaning the price it is it would have been better to consult me first and about the extraordinary choice of colours, especially as I don't think the oil and grease stains will be hidden at all.

Donald, I do seriously think a Job is a good thing. Get a Job. Do try to get a Job.

Yours sincerely,
Mabel Doris Morgan
(landlady)

Friday 1 August
Donald, No more presents please. You know I never use lip-sticks and certainly never a phosphorescent one. You must

be off your brain. Though I suppose there is always a first
time.

Your loving landlady,
Mabel Doris Morgan

Wednesday 6 August
Dear Donald,
   I'm pushing this note under your door since you won't
come out. I'm leaving a tray on the table outside. Do try
and eat something. I'm sorry I said what I said. I am sorry
too about the outboard motor. I suppose it wasn't fixed on
to the boat properly. You say it's about thirty-five feet
down? I didn't know the river was so deep there. Of course
I'll lend you twenty dollars to hire a boat and a grappling
iron. We'll simply add it onto the Board which is at ten
weeks now and three weeks for one Extra Person, plus the
cost of one single bed sheet, one bottle carpet cleaning detergent, one four-pound box assorted confectionery gift
wrapped, and four dozen red roses, two deliveries (long stalks
extra) and to the dry cleaning of one chenille bedspread and
two pairs of curtains and the dyeing of the above, purple and
electric green, respectively, plus the cost of one Midnight
Ecstasy lipstick (phosphorescent frosted ice). I do hope we
can find the outboard motor. I'm really looking forward to
going on the river in a row boat, it's years since I was in a
boat. We'll take Pearl and Mary with us and our lunch.

Your loving mother,
Mabel Doris Morgan
(landlady)

Dingle the Fool

'No one can tell what is taken up from the earth by a lemon tree,' Deirdre's mother said it didn't matter where the roots of the tree were, the lemons would take what they needed.

'What if they are in the drain?' Deirdre asked.

'What if they are,' her mother replied. 'Can you see drains on any of them lemons? Can you?'

Deirdre stood under the tree. It was fragrant with flower and fruit at the same time, she liked to be sent to fetch a lemon.

When Deirdre took off the cushion covers to wash them before Christmas, roses and peacocks from her childhood spilled out, frayed, from the worn covers underneath reminding her of the tranquillity in that expectation of happiness as she and her sister Joanna, years ago, sat on the back verandah twisting tinsel and making red and green paper chains.

Now Deirdre remembered her mother most around Christmas. At that time of the year the sisters stole mulberries from the tree in the garden next to theirs and their mother, approving, made pies.

'Take Dingle to the river while I'm baking,' Mother called them, so they took their brother out with them. They called him Dingle, it was his own name for himself. 'Dingle!' Mother called him softly, smiling at his gentle face. 'Always look after Dingle,' she told the girls. 'Remember people will say he is a fool and will try to take away anything he's got. And he will give them everything.'

He loved the river. He shouted on the shore and waded into the brackish water waving his thin arms and following the other children, he wanted to play with them. The other children swam and Dingle followed them, unable to swim. He waded deeper and the gentle waves slapped his knees and then caressed his waist and he held up his arms as he went deeper and then the water was round his neck and over his face and his round mouth gasped as the water closed and parted rippling over his shorn head.

'Dingle!' Deirdre shouted and ran into the river and grabbed him. She had to carry him home, her dress, sopping wet, embarrassed because she was big and her breasts showed up round and heavy under the wet clinging material.

After the death of their mother the three of them lived on in the old weatherboard and iron house. And, for the time being, after they were married the sisters continued to share the house. Dingle had the two attics in the gable of the house, a cramped spaciousness all his own. They could hear him moving about up there for he was a heavy man and they often could hear his thick voice mumbling to and fro as he talked to the secret people in his secret world in the roof.

The sisters spent their time looking after their babies which had been born within a few weeks of each other. Every day when they had bathed the babies and were washed themselves and dressed in freshly ironed clothes – they were always washing and ironing – they went out from the dark ring of trees around the house into the sunshine and, crossing the road, they walked, brushing against hibiscus and lantana with their hips and thighs up the hill to the shops. Joanna had a little pram but Deirdre carried her son, his dark fuzzy head nestled against the creamy skin of her plump neck. The sisters gazed at the things in the shops and they met people they had known all their lives and they showed off their lovely babies.

Everything was peaceful in the household except when the conversation turned as it often did, to land prices and whether they should sell the house and the land. All round them the old houses had been sold and blocks of flats and

two-storey townhouses with car parks instead of gardens
were being built. Joanna longed for a modern house on one
of the estates, she had magazines full of glossy pictures and
often sat looking at them.

'Look at this all electric kitchen Deirdre,' she would say.
'Just look at all these cupboards fitting in to the walls!' But
Deirdre wanted to stay in the house; as well as being fond
of the place where she had always lived, she had a deep wish
to go on with a continuation of something started years ago.
Sometimes she pictured to herself the people who first built
the house and she thought of them planting trees and
making paths and as she trod the paths she rested on these
thoughts. And of course the house with the big tangled
garden was the only world Dingle could have. And the house
did belong to all three of them.

'The value of the land's gone up again!' Joanna said at
breakfast. 'Why don't we sell now and build? Oh do let's!'
Deirdre moved the milk jug and pushed aside the bread. 'I
want to stay here,' she said.

How would Dingle be on a new housing estate where no
one knew or understood him? She imagined him pressing the
old tennis ball, which he thought contained happiness, on
complete strangers. It was all right at the bowling club where
he went sometimes to trim the lawns, they knew him there
and would take the dirty old ball and thank him and then
give it back. Sometimes Dingle lost his ball and Deirdre and
Joanna, scolding, had to leave their house work and help him
search for it in the fallen leaves beneath the overgrown
pomegranates, and, in the fragrance of the long white bells
of the datura, they parted stems and flowers searching for
happiness for Dingle.

'What about Dingle?' Deirdre asked, her voice trembled.
She was afraid Freddy, Joanna's neat quick husband, would
insist they have a place of their own. Freddy and Joanna had
more money, and in any case, Joanna was entitled to her
share of the house and land.

'There would be enough from the sale,' Spiro, Deirdre's
husband said, he spoke slowly with a good-natured heavi-
ness. They had to wait while he slowly chewed another

mouthful, 'With his share, your fool of a brother could be very comfortable in some nice home.' Spiro did not mean to be unkind, Deirdre knew this, but she could not bear what he said. She felt they were all against her. More than anything she wanted to stay in the house and she wanted for Dingle to be able to stay but she and Spiro had no money with which to pay Joanna and Freddy their share. So Deirdre said nothing, she got up from the table and started to go about her work and the talk was dropped for the time being.

Their lives went on as usual and the two sisters were kept busy with their babies.

One day Spiro came home in the middle of the afternoon. He walked straight through the kitchen and into the room which was their bedroom and he shut the door. The two sisters looked at each other and Deirdre put her baby down in his basket and went after her husband.

'He's not feeling well,' she said, coming back after a few minutes.

'Why? What's wrong?'

'Nothing much, but I think he's had words with the Boss. He's going to have a sleep.'

Joanna shrugged.

'There's nothing like a good sleep,' she said. 'We'd better keep quiet.'

'Yes a good sleep,' Deirdre agreed. Mostly the two sisters agreed. Their mother too had been an agreeable woman hard working and thrifty, she had wisdom too.

'Sisters give things to each-other,' she said when Joanna wanted to sell her sequined party bag to Deirdre.

'Give the bag,' Mother said. 'Sisters don't buy and sell with each other. They share things. Sisters share.'

And she had left them the house to share, Dingle included of course. But when Deirdre thought about it, how could she expect Joanna to give her her share of the house.

Deirdre's husband continued to stay at home. He seemed to step on plastic toys and lemons and he was bored with all the washing and ironing and the disorder brought about by the two babies. For though the sisters kept the shabby house clean, there was a certain untidiness which was comfortable but Deirdre, as Spiro stumbled crossly, began to see squalor everywhere. The verandahs needed sweeping every day, paint peeled and fell in flakes and there were rusty marks. For some reason wheat was growing wild in the rough laundry tubs and they had to wash clothes in the bathroom. Joanna worked hard too but she complained and kept on wishing for a modern house. She reproached Deirdre.

Deirdre felt annoyed with Spiro for being at home all the time when she wanted to clean the house. As well as being annoyed she was worried that he might not have any work, and then how would they manage. She avoided her husband.

And then the two sisters began to quarrel over small things.

'If you don't want to make your bed,' Deirdre shouted at Joanna, 'at least close your door so the whole world needn't see what a pig sty your room is!'

'Who cares! Bossy Boots!' Joanna tossed her head, and their voices rose as they flung sharp words at each other. They moved saucepans noisily and scraped chairs and there was no harmony in their movements when they prepared the dinner.

Joanna began to do things for Deirdre's husband. She made tea for him in the middle of the long hot afternoon, she sat talking to him, her pretty head turned to one side as she gazed attentively while he replied in his slow speech. Deirdre saw that she sat there with her blouse still unfastened after feeding her baby. And it seemed to Deirdre that Spiro was watching Joanna and looking with admiration at her small white breasts which were delicately veined and firm with the fullness of milk.

Deirdre went out shopping alone.

'I'm leaving Robbie,' she called out to her husband. 'Watch him when he wakes will you.'

She had several things to buy from the supermarket. It would have been wiser to ask Spiro to go with her. She took upon herself the burden of the shopping and in her present unhappiness she thought she wouldn't buy a Christmas tree.

The two sisters had taken some time to find husbands. Deirdre, nine years older than Joanna and with her straight

cut dull hair and sullen expression, had taken somewhat
longer. Spiro had come just in time into Deirdre's life for
the two sisters to be married on the same day.

Deirdre wished she could be alone with Spiro and persuade him to go back to his work before Christmas even if
only for half a day to make everything all right for after the
holiday. But she knew he was a quiet man and proud, and
besides, he was enjoying a kind of new discovery in her sister.
Nothing like this had ever happened in the household
before. Joanna's husband was deeply in love with his wife.
He was always kind to Dingle and roguishly polite to
Deirdre, admired her baby and her cooking, but really he
only cared about Joanna and their own baby daughter.
Joanna took all his love, basking, cherished, she seemed to
glow more every day with the love she had from Freddy and
now here she was trying to attract her own sister's husband,
as if she wanted both men to pay every attention to her.

Unhappiness and jealousy rose in Deirdre and she
trembled as she put packages in her bag and she thought
again she wouldn't bother to have a tree this year. But on
the way home she passed a watered heap of Christmas trees
sheltered from the sun by a canvas screen.

'How much are the trees?' she asked the boy.

'Dollar fifty,' he looked at her hopefully.

'I'll take one,' she said, sparing the money from her purse,
wondering whether she should.

'Which'll you want?' he reached into the heap and shook
out one tree after another till she chose one with a long
enough stem. Slowly she dragged it home.

They put the tree in the hall, it seemed the best place for
it though they had to squeeze by. It seemed to Deirdre when
the tree was decorated with the little glittering treasures
saved from their childhood that there was an atmosphere of
peace in the tranquil depths of the branches, and, as she
brushed against it, a fragrance which seemed to come from
previous years soothed her. The corners of the rooms and the
woodwork seemed as if smoothed and rounded, the brown
linoleum and the furniture, polished for so many years, were
mellow and pleasant to look upon because of this fragrance

from the tree. She felt better and wondered why she had been so unhappy.

'I think I can smell rain,' she said smiling as she stepped on to the back verandah. 'It must be raining somewhere.'

'Yes, there's weather coming up,' Freddy agreed and they paused to breathe in the sharp fragrance of rain-laden air. Later they played table tennis; the old boards creaked and the house seemed to shake but the contented babies and Dingle the Fool slept in spite of the noise.

For some reason Joanna had put on a stupid frock. It had no shoulder straps or sleeves and she kept missing the ball and spoiling the game because she kept tugging up her frock saying it was slipping down. And every time she missed the ball she dissolved into laughter and the two men laughed too and Deirdre noticed how her husband only looked at Joanna. Usually he was impatient if any one played badly but tonight he was laughing with Joanna.

'Oh I'm too tired to play any more,' Deirdre put her bat down suddenly.

'I'll take on the two men then,' Joanna cried. Deirdre wanted to shake Joanna, but she tried to control her anger, her voice trembled.

'No Joanna,' she said as quietly as she could. 'I want to talk about the house.'

'Oh Deirdre!' Joanna said. 'The agent was here again this morning while you were out, they're going to start building on the block next door quite soon. He promised us a really good price if only we'll sell!'

'Be quiet Joanna!' Deirdre said. 'I want to say how a house has such history, such meaning. Places, especially houses are important, they matter,' somehow she couldn't go on, she kept thinking about Dingle.

They had to wait, Spiro was speaking, his broken English more noticeable.

'It's what a person really wants that has meaning,' Spiro said slowly. 'For you Deirdre, this house. For Joanna it is a new house,' he shrugged his shoulders lazily, 'It is the wanting that matters,' he said. Deirdre's sallow face flushed a dull red.

'I know you and Freddy want a modern home of your own,' she said. 'We'll sell this place,' she forced out the words; she had been preparing them all evening.

'Oh Deirdre!' Joanna hugged her sister 'Shall we really!' she was shrill with excitement. 'Mr Rusk, you know, the agent, said our two acres could be a gold mine if only we'd sell now!'

'Oh be quiet Joanna!' Deirdre said, she couldn't stop thinking of Dingle. 'There's no more to be said,' she snapped. 'Sisters share,' her mother had said. Deirdre couldn't share Spiro with Joanna.

'We'll sell,' she made herself say it again.

'Oh Deirdre!' Joanna hitched up her frock. 'Oh we'll go on Sunday and look at the show houses on the Greenlawns Estate. Do let's!'

'Perhaps,' Deirdre said shortly. Joanna got out her magazines. 'Look at these kitchens.' She was showing her treasures to the two men long after Deirdre had gone, sleepless, to bed.

The two sisters sat together in the humid heat.

'I hope it'll be cooler on Christmas Day,' Joanna said. They fed their babies and drank cold water greedily taking turns to drink from a big white jug while their babies sucked.

Spiro was out. Deirdre felt comforted. He was driving a load of baled lucerne hay, it was only work for one day, but it was something. She leaned over to smile at Joanna's baby.

The air was heavy with the over ripe mulberries fermenting and dropping, replenishing the earth. Soon the tree next door would be gone, the house had already been pulled down.

Dingle the Fool came in, his hands and face stained red.

'Oh let us get some mulberries too!' Joanna laid her baby in her basket and Deirdre put her little son down quickly.

Soon the three of them were lost and laughing in the great tree, it was as big as a house itself.

They pushed in between the gnarled branches and twigs climbing higher and deeper into the tree, pausing one after the other on the big forked branch where Dingle often slept on hot nights. All round them were green leaves, green light and green shade. For every ripe berry Deirdre picked three more fell through her fingers splashing her face and shoulders, they dropped, lost to the earth. She felt restored in the tree, as if she could go on through the thick leaves and emerge suddenly in some magic place beyond. And, as she picked and ate the berries one after the other, she wondered why she had let things worry her so much.

'Here's a beauty!' Joanna cried. 'If only I could get it,' she leaned, cracking twigs, 'Oh I missed it! Here's another. Oh Beauty!' The tree was full of their voices.

'Here's another!' Deirdre heard Joanna just above her and then Dingle slithered laughing beside her smearing her white bare legs with the red juice. From above Joanna showered them both with berries and soon they were having a mulberry fight as they did when they were children together. Dingle could lose what little wits he had for joy.

Breathless and laughing they stood at last on the ground stained all over with the stolen fruit.

'Anyone for a swim?' Spiro was back, he had the truck till the next day. His face widened with his good natured smile as he saw them.

'Oh I can't' Deirdre said. And he remembered the mysterious things about the women after their childbirths and he was about to go off on his own.

'Wait for me! I'll come!' Joanna cried. 'Watch Angela for me, Deirdre, we'll not be long. Wait Spiro! I'm coming!'

In the kitchen Deirdre stuck cloves into an onion and an orange. Slowly and heavily she began preparations for the Christmas cooking tomorrow. Reluctantly she greased a pudding basin. Sadness began again to envelop her. Joanna had scrambled up so quickly beside Spiro in the cabin of the truck. Deirdre tried to think of the mulberry fight instead.

Dingle came in, he had washed himself and flattened his colourless hair with water. He picked things up from the table and put them down, he examined the orange and the onion, he pulled out a clove and chewed it noisily.

'Oh Dingle don't!' Impatiently Deirdre snatched them from him.

So then he began striking matches, one match after another. He watched the brief little flame with pleasure.

'Oh Dingle don't keep on wasting matches. Stop it!' Deirdre spoke sharply and then she tried to explain to him about the house being sold but he didn't seem to understand.

'You'll sleep in the Doctor's nice bed,' she told him and tears came into her eyes as she spoke. Dingle came over to the table.

'Here,' he said to Deirdre. 'You have this,' he held out the old tennis ball to his sister.

'No No Dingle,' Deirdre was impatient. 'Try and listen, we are selling the house – No! I don't want your old ball!'

'Go on!' Dingle interrupted. 'You have it, there's happiness inside.' He bounced the ball and gave it to her. She took it, her hand covered in flour.

'Thank you,' and she tried to give it back to him.

'No, you have it, keep it,' he insisted, his voice was thick and indistinct but Deirdre always knew what he said. She refused to keep the ball. Flour fell on the floor.

Dingle drew a chair up to the table close to where she was working, he took her vegetable knife and began to cut the ball in half.

'No Dingle you Fool. Don't!' Deirdre cried out and she tried to take the knife, but Dingle had strength and he held on to the knife and began working it right into the ball.

'Dingle, you don't understand!'

'I understand,' he muttered, 'I understand, half each, you have half.'

He cut the ball and stared at the two empty halves of it. He looked at Deirdre and he looked at the two halves and, perplexed, he shook his head. He sat shaking his head and, as he realized the emptiness of the ball, his face crumpled and he cried, sobbing like a child except that he had white hair and a man's voice.

Deirdre had not seen him cry for years, she saw his mouth all square as he cried and it reminded her of Joanna's mouth when she cried and she could hardly bear to be reminded like this.

'Don't cry Dingle. Please don't cry,' she spoke softly trying to comfort him. But it seemed there was nothing she could do.

In the night Joanna was thirsty and she got up to go for water. The hall was full of smoke.

'There's a fire!' she called, terrified in the smoke-filled darkness. 'The Christmas tree's burning! Deirdre! Quick! The house is on fire. Freddy! Spiro!'

The whole house seemed full of smoke and they couldn't tell which part was burning the most. They saved their babies and most of their clothes.

'Where is Dingle?' Deirdre hardly had breath to call out. Her eyes were blind with pain from the smoke.

Spiro tried to rush up to the attic but the heat and the burning timber falling forced him back out into the garden.

There was nothing any one could do to save Dingle and nothing to do to save the house. They stood in the ring of trees. The Norfolk pines, the cape lilacs, the jacarandas and the kurrajong and the great mulberry tree in the next garden were all lit up in the hot light of the flames. The noise of the fire seemed to make a storm in the trees. They stood, helpless little people, beside the big fire, their bare feet seeking out the coolness of fallen hibiscus flowers which had curled up slowly in their damp sad ragged dying on the grass.

There was nothing they could do to save Dingle. 'He will have suffocated from the smoke before the fire could reach him,' Spiro spoke slowly, he tried to comfort them. Deirdre saw his hands bursting with the burns he had received and she saw how he was hardly able to bear the pain of them and she persuaded him to go with a neighbour to have them bandaged. They all allowed themselves to be looked after, quietly, as if they couldn't understand what had happened.

And later, Deirdre, wandering in the half light of dawn while the others slept on the vinyl cushions in the lounge of the bowling club, went back to the smouldering soaked remains of the house. She half hoped her brother would be dead but how could she hope for him to be burned to death. In her unhappiness she felt the burden of his life. His life

was too much for her but the pain of wishing him burned
in the fire was even worse. She felt she must search in the
remains of the house and was afraid of what she might find.
It would be easier if he had slept on and on in the smoke
as Spiro said he had.

She thought she saw him in the forked branch of the mulberry tree. She paused, shivering and hoped it was only his
old washed-out shirt that was there, left behind after the
mulberry fight. Dingle sometimes forgot his clothes and
Deirdre often went about last thing at night gathering up
his shoes and things.

She stood now and tried to see what was in the fork of
the tree. She began, with hope and with fear to climb into
the quiet branches, the cool damp leaves brushed her face
and her arms and legs.

It was not just his shirt up there. Gently she woke him,
empty match boxes fell as she shook him.

'Dingle, wake up!' He was asleep in the tree after all.
Dingle the Fool stretched himself along the friendly branch.
His face was as if stained with red tears. Deirdre hugged her
brother clumsily, crying and kissing him. How could she have
wished him dead?

'Another mulberry fight?' Dingle asked in his strange
thick voice and he made a noise and Deirdre was unable to
tell whether he was laughing or crying.

They thought they might as well choose a motel right on
the sea front. They had only a short time to wait for their
new houses to be ready. So every day they lay on the sand,
even the babies sunbathed in their baskets.

'The quick brown fox,' Deirdre thought to herself as she
watched Freddy put up the beach umbrella to make the best
shade for Spiro who was still unwell after his burns.

Lazily they spent the days talking about nothing in particular and swimming and eating. They bought fried chicken
and hamburgers to eat while watching television in the
motel. There wasn't any point in wondering about the fire
so they didn't talk about it.

Deirdre couldn't help thinking about Dingle. When she

took him to the hospital he sat so awkwardly on the edge
of the white bed. She wondered whatever could he do there.
She went to the window.

'You can watch the road from here,' she said. Dingle got
up and came to the window and obediently looked out at
the corner of the road. There were no grass plots, Deirdre
wished there was some grass and she could have asked if he
could trim the edges. It was something he always enjoyed.
She thought about him watching the empty street. What
would he be doing now, Deirdre wondered. She watched
Joanna and Freddy laughing in the sea. Joanna looked so
happy, the green water curled handsomely round her lovely
body. Deirdre envied Joanna, she envied her sister's innocence.

'The land's more valuable than ever with the house and
sheds gone and on top there's all the insurance!' Deirdre
seemed to hear Joanna's excited voice ringing, she envied her
happiness but more enviable was her innocence. Joanna had
never wished her brother burned to death.

'Where's that Fool of a brother of yours?' Spiro often
asked this question when he came in, sometimes he had
something for Dingle, a cake or some apples, sometimes he
wanted Dingle to help him move a heavy box or shift the
load in his truck with him.

Everyone called Dingle a fool, their mother said he would
give everything he had and people would take it.

Deirdre had taken everything from him, she had made
him give everything. Freddy and Joanna seemed hilarious in
the water and Spiro, sitting with both hands bandaged, was
laughing and laughing and all the time he watched Joanna.

'It's the wanting that really matters,' Spiro had said it himself.

Deirdre longed to talk about Dingle. She wanted to ask
Spiro if he thought Dingle would be all right. She wanted
comfort and reassurance but did not ask.

Near them on the beach was a bread carter woman eating
her lunch. She looked so carefree and sunburned and strong,
Deirdre almost spoke to her.

'I have a brother –' but she didn't. In a little while the

bread carter would eat her last mouthful and be gone, taking
with her her strength and vitality.

Deirdre lay back, she heard the sea come up the sand with
a little sigh. Tears welled up under her closed eyelids. Joanna
and Freddy came running from the water and Deirdre
turned her face away so that they shouldn't see the tears spill
over her cheeks.

The Representative

Strange regions there are, strange minds, strange realms of the spirit, lofty and spare.

Thomas Mann

'How can it be opened to me if I do not knock?' Uncle Bernard said when the woman asked him.

'Is that you knocking at these gates?'

'How can a man enter if he does not knock?' Uncle Bernard replied. He waited while the small woman sorted the keys with her busy hands. He looked at her smooth grey hair and at her sensible shoes and he smiled at her.

'Greedings from the modderlaand,' he said.

'I'm sorry our Secretary, who is our interpreter too, is away just now, it's this oecumenical movement, he's planting the seed –' she selected keys one after the other at random.

'Ha! No worries,' Uncle Bernard interrupted, 'Enklisch spoken suit me better. I am away so long I forget everyding from mine own country.' His smile deepened the creases in his face, and his white hair fringed round his head was like a halo.

'I'm sorry, our Gate Keeper is at –'

'Ach Ja! I come at inconvenient time, but there is never a suitable time is there,' he paused while she cautiously unlocked and opened the ornamental gate and, remembering his good manners, he asked, 'Gut Evenink Madam, how is your health? It is to be hoped a ball o' dash, isn't it?'

'If you put it that way, yes I suppose I am quite well, thank you,' she replied. 'I'm rather busy as Everything is left for me to do, Spring Cleaning,' she said and gave a careworn little laugh.

'Madam,' Uncle Bernard bowed. 'May I rest my cases on

171

your table please?' He stopped to pick up the heavy suitcases
which stood one on either side of him. 'I shall not take up
too much of your time. I have come to demonstrate the soil.
In my cases here I have example and sample of the soil. On
this side is for clay brick, but first let me show you soil for
vineyard.' His voice deepened. 'You know soil for the grape,
listen to the poem of the grape, Tokay, Shiraz, Grenache,
Pedro, Muscat and Frontignac but first the soil, listen to the
soil! In this peckage is a deep alluvial sandy loam and here
in this –'

'Yes yes, very interesting –' the bustling busy little woman
interrupted him. 'I'll tell the Director you're here. You'd
better see Him. At present He's rewriting the Miracles. He's
adapting them for colour TV, animated comic strip, very
popular these days. He intends to do the same with the Parables and submit them. They are always arguing about
them, I do so love an argument about parables don't you!
And, we're in the middle of a world-wide conference on
clouds and on top of that there's the spring cleaning,' she
sighed. 'I'll clear a corner so that you can sit down.'

'No worries!' Uncle Bernard said.

'I really am sorry there's such a mess everywhere. By the
way, my name's Martha. I'm the Matron here.'

'Gut Evenink Frau Martha. And I, I am Bernard Oons,
Representative of the Outworks of the Kingdom, Madam.
I represent the Earth! It give me pleasure to shake you by
the hand. As for the mess, you have prepared for me *the best
place in your house.*'

'Oh, in this House are Many Mansions,' Martha
explained, 'and none of them belong to me, I only work here
– oh just a moment, I almost forgot the ten o'clock feeds!
Good Heavens! there's so much to remember.'

She opened another door and a noisy chattering group of
young women passed through the airy hall. All had oval faces
and tender expressions and their clothes were richly blue and
flowing. Some cloth was delicately embroidered and some
was trimmed with soft white fur and yet others wore dresses
decorated with wide bands of gold and silver. And a few of
the women, Bernard noticed, though they were dignified in

their youthful maternity, were dressed in rags. They disappeared singing and laughing and joking together through a far off door beyond which could be heard distinctly the crying of several hungry babies.

Uncle Bernard found himself thinking of all young creatures. 'Little lambs,' he said, 'baby birds, baby peoples all cry. We do Everyding we can think of for them and always they cry. Why is this –' But Martha was not listening to him, impatiently she jangled her keys, she jerked her head in the direction of the noisy procession.

'The Madonnas,' she said, her lips looking as if she had just tasted a lemon. 'We have so many of them – for every country and for every state, a madonna. All nationalities, all races, all colours. The People, you know, like to have their very own Madonna. Though, as you see by our notices up there, we like them all to learn English. We really feel it's such a good mother tongue.'

At that moment a door opened and a voice called, 'Matron! Matron!'

'Oh,' said Martha, 'That's the Director Himself. I wonder what He wants.'

'Matron!' the Director called again. 'Oh there you are Matron. I've just thought up this splendid slogan. It's an inspiration for Weeties Week. Listen. "Is not the Body more than Raiment".'

'Why Director! You certainly *have* been inspired,' she smiled impishly. 'I'm not sure everyone will agree with you. Oh by the way, Director, this is Mr Bernard Oons, the representative of –'

The Director interrupted her, 'Oh Jully Good! Jully Good Show! Just arrived? We've been expecting you. Matron get him fitted will you, there's a dear. I'll catch up with you later Mr ahem – I'm just off to dig out irrigation canals with the unemployed. Never a dull moment! Back in five minutes. Matron you'll show Mr Ahem – round our little place? It's not such a bad little spot. Actually, we're quite proud of it. A place is what you make it isn't it? Heaven on Earth, Earth in Heaven, Heaven within Heaven and all that jazz – I think that's the word. Matron! where's my bucket and spade? Oh on second thoughts I'll not be needing them, I think today I'm making a tour of Disaster Areas and conveying deep sympathy and after that I'm just giving a talk on "Digging with the unemployed".'

Martha muttered to herself, ' "Is not the Body more than Raiment" I'm sure T. S. Eliot wrote that or Tolkien or is it in Hansard? I'll query it at our next meeting if I have the chance. As I said, at present we're so involved with the clouds. There are complaints from many places that they are too thin to be rain bearing. It's simply no use sending out the Word about the Sabbath of the Land. They, Those People, persist in regarding it as a drought and all the promises of better years to come do not compensate. My own opinion, for what it's worth, is that you can't get the same good old material any longer, take these old curtains, for example, cumulus. I ran up them myself years ago, you just do not get the good stuff these days.' She smiled with that brightness which so often hides a lack of intelligenee and memory.

Droning music came from somewhere close by, it was dreary and halting, stopping and starting, very ragged with a lot of coughing.

'We're trying something entirely new,' Martha said, 'we're recycling the Christian Brothers. That's them you can hear trying to learn a song from the top of the charts. They're trying to learn the guitar too, but they're hopeless and hopeless on the drums and, as for their voices, quite unsuitable! But I shouldn't be saying all this. Come along I'll show you the places of interest.' She paused under the blue vaults. 'In here,' she said, 'we're promoting the World Resorts.' She showed him the weatherboard and iron, the pruning hooks and the ancient plough-shares, the mangles with heavy wooden rollers, rusty old chip heaters and boilers and various household articles made from flour sacks and sugar bags.

'This particular promotion', she said, 'is the ghost towns.' She gave him an inquisitive look. 'Isn't that part of the place where you've been?'

'Well, Madam,' Uncle Bernard said, 'I had much experience in far off places but you know one man in his life cannot see and do everything even if he come quite near it. I could describe for you the songs of strange birds and I could tell you how the sun wraps colour round the burned bark of unfamiliar trees, and I know the soil –'

'Yes, yes, of course,' she hurried on, not listening. Her neat feet seemed so comfortable Bernard could not help remarking on them.

'Yes,' Martha said. 'It all comes down to physical culture in the end. In fact the Director Himself, if he wore shoes, would choose these,' she sighed. 'If He would wear shoes it would save us all the trouble of washing His feet all the time and, of course, we'd save on the oil too. You know how expensive oil is these days and how those dreadful people sit on the world's natural resources,' she shuddered insincerely.

'They have such ugly heads you know,' she said in a low voice, 'those people you know, oh! naughty little old me I shouldn't be saying those things! And you must be tired too. I'll pop into the linen room and get you a clean shroud. Let me see what size would you be, quite small really.' She kept on talking and talking, 'people are always so much smaller than they think. There's no such thing as larger than life, that's what I always say.'

Just then a young woman, carrying a fat baby, hurried by towards the nurseries from which the soft contented noises of Mother and Child could now be heard.

'Hurry up Mary, do!' Martha called. 'You're late again! This will never do. Hurry!' She wagged a finger reprovingly and showed her bottom teeth with a suggestion of insincerity in her smile. 'Sitting for Raphael is no excuse at all.'

It seemed to Bernard that the young woman had the sweetest expression he had ever seen. As she passed him, she smiled with a shy tender hopefulness.

Martha looked after her sourly and, when she had gone, she said, 'Of course these girls all get away with their pregnancies. I never heard of so many immaculate conceptions in my life. To hear them talk you'd think they'd spent their entire lives on desert islands. It's the Secretary, I'm sure of it, he's going too far too often. We simply won't be able to

afford it *and* there'll have to be retrenchments among the
carpenters and you know what troubles can accompany one
carpenter let alone several! The whole thing'll have to stop.
It's not that I'm against the concept of the oecumenical
movement, but all things in moderation, I say, after all that's
what life's all about isn't it.' She gave a little laugh, 'they
tell me that's a cliché but clichés are so often true aren't
they, as I was saying, we'll have to send out a circular to those
concerned. But here we are on the edge, we usually bring
our guests here first. How do you like our view?' She turned
to him quite eagerly, her nylon pleated skirt was knee length
and she stood with her bandy legs apart like a land agent
who is trying to sell a steep rocky outcrop, a piece of land
with its feet in a salt swamp and its head over a precipice.

'Holy Schmoking vot is that bleck schmoke!' Uncle Bernard exclaimed, 'Looks like Mitzi is having some sort of pic-
nics down here. Hullo Mitzi!' he called. 'How are things
down there Mitzi! How are you down there? You havink one
of your little cookinks?' he called, and then he laughed softly
and sighed, he was very tired.

'It's called the Bonfires of the Widows,' Martha
explained.

'Ah So!' Uncle Bernard nodded his head. 'Mitzi is burning
up all my clothes to tidy up, I see.' He put down the heavy
cases and turned to Martha.

'You have it very fine up here,' he said. 'Is like seeink the
whole world from that wonderful restaurant on the top floor
of that tall building back home. The whole floor turns round
so slowly and all the time is an ever changing view.' He
remembered it with pleasure.

'I'll have to take down your particulars,' Martha interrupted his thoughts. 'You know, Age, Sex, Religion, Next
of Kin, Diseases curable and incurable, Country of Birth,
Country of Death–Blast! I've left my biro by the Gates.
While you change, I'll go and get it.'

Washed and clean and neat in the new garment which
covered him down to his feet Uncle Bernard sat alone. He
felt a great peace, it was a feeling he had sometimes in the
evenings. He seemed to be sitting at the edge of a long green

paddock, it flowed back from him like a river, so wide that the banks were invisible. There was a pleasant quality in the evening and the wish to prolong, perhaps for ever, that quality of tranquillity and half-faded gentleness. Lower down the slopes on either side the trunks of trees and foliage merged in a tremulous movement like the rocking of a cradle. And there was a certain warmth lingering on, just enough warmth.

Down there the ashes of Mitzi's fire were whitening. Uncle Bernard felt it was a shame no one had thought to warm a saucepan in the ashes. But it didn't really matter, he could go on sitting in that softness and in that feeling of complete rest. It was something he had never really known before.

Martha returned, she was now wearing a flowing cap on her head and she carried an enamel bowl containing a small syringe.

'Oh I do not need any medicine,' Uncle Bernard began.

'Just a little prick in your arm,' she said. 'It's the Peace that Passeth all Understanding,' she said, 'an old-fashioned remedy which we still hang on to up here.' She rubbed his thin arm with a swab of cotton wool. 'I'll be back soon to show you where you'll sleep,' she said, 'and tomorrow you'll meet our multitude.' And before he could answer she was gone.

From nearby he heard someone singing, it was the young Madonna with her child, the one who was late. Bernard thought he knew the tune, even the words in English.

'*Every year returning –*' he tried to remember the hymn. The young woman with a smile which combined tenderness and care with a certain provocation exchanged a look with him as she came.

'*Comes the Christ child down,*' she sang.

'What is a man's life if he does not struggle for something,' Bernard said. Together they looked down and saw the trams going from the crowded squares where fashionable hotels faced each other, to the quiet places where there were lawns made of water, these water lawns were light and smooth and enclosed in low walls.

'Water is the last thing to get dark,' Bernard said.

'What long journeys the trams make from the old part of the city to the broad streets full of new clean houses,' Mary said and Bernard agreed. They could see the shining canals and rivers below them and then the wild colours of the fairgrounds and the markets and then the dark mysterious railway stations and, beyond all this, all the various lights and shadows of all the cities turning slowly like great wheels spoked brilliantly with lives and thoughts and hopes, all the things people wish for and all the things they dread.

They saw mountains and mountains and more mountains and there were oceans and floods and deserts and, suddenly, in the half light, as well as all the solid things of the world, they saw all that was transparent too. The greatness of the world and its shabbiness were revealed to them simultaneously. They looked slowly into each other with that particular love which penetrates and gives the undistinguished that distinction which allows the real character to emerge. After this exchange there were only certain things which could be said.

The moon rose up swiftly from the long arms of a smoky sunset.

'Men long for poetry,' Bernard said, 'men long for the poem of the earth, for an explanation from the earth, but so often they never say what they long for. Is the same with the poem of the vineyard. Let me show you –', he pointed to the long slopes where the shadows gathered as the sun left the earth. The vines grew in patterns, with the neatness of ribs across the flat land and over the low hills. It was as if they were kneeling on the earth to pray.

'Perhaps they pray for kind owner,' Bernard said. Longer shadows crept over the distant orchards and crops. In some places the last light from the setting sun caught the new leaves as they burst from the twisted black vines and edged the fresh green with gold. 'I am denking very much of the early mornings,' Bernard continued. 'There was so much I could do in a new day.' He laughed. 'I liked to watch the mist rise slowly like a lazy girl, and the spiders' webs would sparkle and stretch so delicately from one prickly bush to

another. I'll tell you, it was like this, I and my nephews
bought some land in that far off place,' he shrugged his
shoulders, 'it was no use for vineyard so I make clay bricks,'
he paused and then he said, 'Madam I have proposal to
make. Sometimes a man himself is a waste. My proposal will
bring great personal gain on both sides. Our two worlds
adjoin one another and there are no boundaries. What you
say Madam, Mary? Would you come back there with me?
I know a place where there is small house under a fig tree,
the vines come in to the windows of the house! *That* would
be our place. Will you come Mary?'

'My son sleeps,' Mary said. 'What about my son?'

'Ja!' Bernard laughed. 'He sleeps. He represents all the
strength which is needed, all that is loving and useful and
necessary. Did you know,' he continued, 'if you look at a
sleeping child too long, he will wake up!'

Bernard opened his other case. 'All my life I want to grow
grapes and make good wine,' he said, 'so I design wine labels,
here are my labels.'

'Oh!' Mary said, 'the ladies haven't any clothes on and
they're very fat!'

'Ladies on wine labels should be curved,' Bernard
explained, 'and you will see I have drawn red and blue vine
leaves which clothe them sufficiently.' And then he had an
idea. 'Liebfraumilch!' he exclaimed. 'Why didn't I think of
it before! Liebfraumilch! I must take another label. What
do you think?'

'What if the grapes don't grow?' Mary asked.

'All crops, if they come, are certain crops,' Bernard replied.
He went on, 'From what I have seen here I have no wish
to remain. In that other place a man has the chance to discover what he is himself. In this system which I see here,
there can be no such discovery. Will you come with me?'

Mary thought for a few moments.

'I suppose I'll miss the other Madonnas,' she said, 'but I'll
tell you something, I'd like to get away from that Martha.
I feel I can't stand her. I'd like to shake her!'

'Best to shake her, josst by the hand,' Bernard said. They

sat close together side by side. It was as if everything lay
before them.

'Till I met you,' Mary said softly, 'there were no seasons.
And –' she said, laughing, 'I never saw Martha the way I'm
seeing her now. Stuffy old maid! She smells like a stuffy old
maid, the cheap soap she uses only makes the stuffiness
worse! What's more, she's a fraud! She doesn't know the difference between a real person and something that's just
made up.'

'She is only doing her best in the only way she knows how,'
Bernard said gently. 'Is not her fault! Is only way she knows.
If you begin to feel hate try to change to pity. Is better so.'
He got up. 'All we do now, is explain that we would like to
go from here.'

'Yes you're right,' Mary said. 'How kind you are too! Let's
go at once. I don't think we need to explain, it's enough if
we want to go. Won't our action explain itself?'

'Yes is right that way. You are right!' he paused a moment.
'There is josst one thing though, as you know we cannot
bring our worldly possessions with us here. I had to leave
everyding with Mitzi. I tell you, *she* is my first wife but is
remarried since many years with great comforts of course to
a man with a good failed business which she build up, no
worries for Mitzi, but I, I have nodding of my own except
my two cases here and my head.'

'I have some heavenly currency,' Mary said, 'but it's been
horribly devalued lately, it's only suitable now for decorating
Christmas trees. But you know, I think we'll manage.'

'No worries!' Bernard said. 'To start, I travel in macaroni.
Every day while you nurse the child, I go out with my two
cases, you will see, with macaroni, noodles and ravioli. Some
are thick strips and some are thin, some long spaghetti tubes
and some short fat ones, some are shaped like shells and
others are flavoured with caraway seeds and yet others are
reinforced with an egg. I shall describe all to my customers.
For ourselves? Mostly we shall eat plain macaroni which I
boil in salty water, is quite good. You will see! I use the
broken or shabby packages from my display case, but for the
child, your son, there will be noodles with egg. He will

become strong to bear all the cares of the world. We'll save and save and you will choose a vineyard and plant it.'

'With my own hands!' Mary interrupted him.

'Is right,' Bernard said. 'And we shall get up early and go into the vineyard, we shall see whether the vine has budded and we shall watch for the tender grape to appear.' He paused. 'But we mosst leave at once,' he said. 'The place I am denking of you will like very much, there is a fig tree, golden light drops through the leaves, under this tree is a table piled with grapes and, behind this, is small house, I know you will like! But time goes so quick! We mosst leave at once.' They moved towards the Gates.

'Come my Beloved let us go forth into the field, Is quotation!' Bernard laughed.

'Come my Beloved,' Martha muttered to herself. 'Now *that's* a quotation I'm sure. I wonder if T. S. Eliot wrote that or was it Tolkien? Could be in Hansard I suppose or even Shakespeare, Shakespeare's full of quotations!'

She stood watching the two people going out through the Gates, this in itself was unusual, people mostly came in through the Gates. She thought to herself that the woman, if she had been dressed properly, looked like a bride. Being a little short sighted she thought the bride was carrying either a baby or a kitchen sink. People did all sorts of queer things these days. The man was entirely ordinary, she thought, he must be a representative of some sort.

'I can't make them out at all,' Martha said to herself. 'I am getting more short sighted than ever, but to risk another cliché, it takes all sorts to make the world go round, and that reminds me, the cancellations, I'll have to send out a circular to cancel all those conceptions.'

Clever and Pretty

There were rats in the shed. The father took a seed potato from the sack and the children saw the tooth marks, like a human bite, except that a human would not bite a raw potato.

'He might if he had to,' Clever said.

'Yes he might.'

Because of the rats the father brought home a cat. A rat, he explained, if cornered would fly at a man's throat, but Nature had given cats the quality of being able to deal with rats.

'The cat sat on the mat to catch a rat,' Clever wrote in her book in curly writing and the father praised the page with a kiss.

The policeman who brought the children home later that day, asked the mother if she had pinafores for them. He showed her how to tie the strings with double bows at the sides so that they could not take them off and wander again naked down Market Street Hill. Gratefully, through her tears, she invited him to stay for tea and offered him bread and butter and soft, red jelly in a soup plate. He stood to have his tea explaining that he was on duty and that, because of this, he could not sit down neither could he take his helmet off.

Anti Mote offered him a lady's bicycle and a tin of white paint.

'In order to disguise,' she said, 'then the real owner of the machine will no longer recognize.' She laid one finger know-

ingly alongside her kind nose. 'After certain age is too hard
to learn to ride happily.' She had four tins of red salmon she
explained after the policeman had gone, hidden in her
pockets. She gave one to each of the children and one to the
mother and, opening the fourth, she presented it to the cat
on a newspaper.

'Anti Mote,' the mother called later, 'come quick, something has happened to the cat.' There was a rattling and a
banging in the brick yard outside the scullery.

'He has no head,' the mother said.

'It is in the tin,' Anti Mote said. 'It is on his body still
and he is trying to get it off banging like that everywhere.
He has his head,' she said, 'there is nothing to worry about,
simply his head is in the tin.' She went back to winding her
wool. In all colours it was over the backs of chairs and, with
several different balls in her hands she, like the ribbons from
a maypole, streamed round the room winding, egg shaped,
for wasn't that better, egg shaped, for the knitting.

'Egg shaped makes even.'

The mother caught the cat by the tail and, after only a
few moments, the tin rattled away by itself across the blue
bricks. The cat, released between the legs of the children,
made a quick tour of the house and plunged into the lavatory. The father, recently returned, was washing his hands
at the hand basin; he pulled out the animal and held it head
down and dripping as calmly he walked through the house.

'Where is Maud's bicycle!' he asked the mother.

'At the police station.'

The children tried to climb all over him.

'Daddy am I ugly?' asked Clever one.

'There's no such thing as an ugly little girl.'

'I mean, why aren't I the Pretty one?'

'There are some tins of salmon also,' the mother said. The
father put aside the children. He told the mother he would
go to the police station to see about the bicycle and, on the
way, he would explain about the tins of fish and pay for
them. He would not be long, he said, perhaps she should get
dressed.

The sweet scent of the fox shadowed silk sat on the

mother's sloping shoulders and her veil kissed the children's bright hair. Gently she disentangled the foxy gold chain from Clever's fingers. Behind the veil the mother's eyes were dark and mysterious with the happiness of going to the concert.

'Be good children while we are out,' she said. Anti Mote, prepared to be amusing, wore a paper hat.

'What will my Princess choose for her little supper?' She lifted Pretty, who had on the wrong night gown, on to the table.

'Say you'll have a cocoa sandwich,' Clever danced from one arm chair to the next. 'Say you'll have banana peels, say you'll have, say you'll have . . .' Clever began to throw the animals at Anti Mote.

'Children! Children Stop!' Anti Mote held up both hands to ward off the knitted dog and the knitted cat. Her three-cornered, cockaded, paper hat was knocked over her eyes. The stuffed rabbits followed the cat and the dog.

'Come under the table,' Clever said to Pretty, and hidden in the green fringes, Clever cut Pretty's hair till there was only a tuft on top like a turnip.

'Don't cry!' Clever said to Pretty. 'You can be the Kitty on the newspaper and sleep all night downstairs by the fire. Don't cry.'

Anti Mote tried to tidy up the animals and the scattered curls and the newspapers.

'I shall go now,' she said to the children. 'I shall go now to my room and practise my bassoon. Und later, when you hev finished your game I make an evening soup for you.'

Anti Mote, when she cried, did not show herself. She sounded like a man when she cried.

'Anti Mote won't want us to see her crying,' Clever explained to Pretty. 'She is crying because she is a baroness and she cannot help it. Also, same with our mammy. They are both homesick for their country, that is all. Clever drew in her breath importantly and began to shape R's and A's and T's on a fresh page in her book.

'No, Pretty!' she said. 'No, Pretty! You can't write in my book. Only I can write in my book.'

Clever went alone, lonely, to bed. She went to bed without the promised evening soup and without the soft, fragrant cheeks and the gentle hands of the mother. She lay in bed in the tight night gown thinking of these things. Downstairs, Pretty, dressed in the concert scented fur of the fox, played with necklaces and pendants and jewelled rings warm and happy in the fire glow. She could, if she chose, sleep on the newspaper all night like a little kitten. She could choose.

For the holiday Pretty had a new costume, a skirt with a matching jacket. The jacket had a narrow leather belt. 'Elegant,' the mother said. With the costume Pretty wore a halo hat. Clever, after her first year at boarding school was independent. She carried a rucksack over one shoulder and a buckle had come off her sandal. When she walked, because of the sandal not being fastened, she gave the impression that she was limping.

There was not much room in the compartment, the whole train was filled with soldiers. Though the corridor was packed with soldiers, the father said he would stand there for the journey. Because of all the soldiers and the thick uniforms and the kit bags, it was not easy to see the mother and Anti Mote who were on the platform.

'Did you manage to wave to mother and Aunti Maud?' the father stuck his head in through the crowded doorway of the compartment as the train moved slowly off alongside the platform leaving behind the people who were waving to the masses of bodies. Some, with cramped arms, attempted to wave back.

The first night of the holiday they saw the horseman riding along at the edge of the sea, far out, a long way off. He galloped where there were no waves to be seen only a flat fast-running tide. The water came flowing round unseen making the sands into islands. The water spread, running so quickly, that the sands were cut off from the land. Soon the sea would be on all sides of the sands and the horseman, as fast as he could, sent people back from the edge of the sea.

He galloped and galloped waving to the few people who had not noticed, to go back, to hurry back.

Low at the edge of the sands, in the shadow of the mountain, was the holiday house. It was a house standing all by itself in a garden hedged in from the sands. All night it would be possible to hear the sea, the father was pleased but, at the same time, he was afraid that it would be damp. The house had a narrow front door, the narrow hall beyond was badly washed, the dirty linoleum was spread with newspapers, diamond shaped, leading to the back part of the house.

'Scree,' the father said on the mountain. He made a lesson out of everything, especially out of the holiday. Scree, it was blue all down the mountain, sharp some of it and loose, and if you were not careful, you could fall to your death.

On the first night they found a purse at the edge of the path as they were coming down. It was almost dark, almost night. They had stayed out too long in the strange place. Ronnie from the holiday house was with them. He said his name was Ronnie but his mother, who kept the holiday house, called him Daffyd. He had a red face and his black patent leather shoes had pointed toes and were quite unsuitable for the mountain path.

'I'll lead you the way,' he told them. The scree slipped away from under their feet. They slipped, the father in his new boots, Ronnie in his shiny shoes and Clever with her broken sandal but Pretty did not slip even though she had on her high heels.

Ronnie saw the purse first and laughing, with his broken teeth showing, he poked at the tuft of grass where the purse lay, with the stick he had.

Pretty pounced on the purse.

'Finders keepers, but you can have it,' he said to her in his good-natured way.

'Open it,' Clever said, 'let's see, there might be a fortune inside.'

There was nothing in the purse.

'We'll have to take it to the police station,' Clever said with a wise nod.

'No, not the police!' Ronnie started to speak but Clever was reading the inscription on the purse, it had gold lettering. She read aloud, ' "And I oft have heard defended Little said is soonest mended." It's lovely,' Clever said. The sight of it made Clever long for a paper and a pencil to copy out the words in her best writing.

Ronnie, agitated, urged them, 'Hurry now! Your Dadda's a long ways down the path. Hurry now!' The girls nudged each other. Funny to call him Dadda.

'Scree is the loose stones on a slope,' the father went on telling them. In old Norse it meant a landslide. You could fall to your death or the land could move suddenly and slide down the steep mountain taking people, houses, sheep and cattle into the sea.

The gravel pits, the weathered hills, the water shed and the catchment, the castle keep and the mound which had the water well going down from the top where the enemy could not reach it. The castle had a moat and ramparts and a portcullis. He spelled portcullis for them. The castle was the home and the protection but the enemy would try to capture and destroy. So the father made his lessons and, even now when Ronnie was talking, the father helped him correcting his words now and then because he, the father, knew all the words.

Near the bottom of the mountain the path was narrow. Pretty walked in front, her childish hips twisting from side to side in the tight skirt of her costume. Clever limped at the end of the little procession. The path wound down through thick undergrowth and bushes. The father said he was glad Mr Hughes had accompanied them since he knew the way so well. And Ronnie, red with pleasure, broke some sticks from the hedge for them.

'Pick your choice,' he said smiling as if his cheeks would burst, 'what'll you have, choose your pick!'

The girls nudged each other. Funny to have pick and choose together like that. Clever chose first. The stick slashed with a whipping sound. The sound seemed to sting the night. She held the long stick high again and brought it down with the whip sound once more. She let the slender stick sing and sing in her hand as she ran and ran across the sands, her dress like a cloak flying. She too could be on horseback.

'Too much imagination and not enough application,'Miss Salmon had written on her report. Sammy, the girls called her, at least the ones with the right accent did. Sammy was a wonderful person everyone said so. She could do anything and it would be all right. If Sammy should decide to wear an old lace curtain for Speech Day she would look well dressed, they said. But of course she never did. Anti Mote often wrapped herself in the curtains on the way down to breakfast. Naturally, Clever did not talk about this at school.

Miss Salmon understood all the poems in *The Golden Treasury of Songs and Lyrics Book Fifth*. Perhaps next term Clever herself would be able to say, in that special voice, 'But Sammy!' like the other girls did. 'But Sammy!' The wand whipping, sang. Clever out of breath, practised, 'But Sammy!' and urged her legs; 'Faster! Faster my immortal and worthy steed!' It was a singing wand and its song was both joyful and plaintive in her hand.

Pretty could not make up her little mind. She held the ends of two sticks and Ronnie did not let go of either. His smiling red face was peeling, it peeled all the time as if he must shed his outside skin to get to a better one which was never there. His face was bursting with a happy grin and his eyes were overflowing, blue with tears.

'Pick your choice,' he said again. Pretty couldn't choose and Ronnie, bending the wands, leaned down close and kissed her.

The night was now excitingly dark. The father stopped by the door of the holiday house and turned his face towards the stars as if to breathe as much of the fresh air from the sea as he could. He pointed out the waggon and horses, sometimes called the plough, in the sky.

'Four stars to the waggon and three for the horses and that's the pole star. He made another lesson. They could hear the restless sighing of the flat sea as it was turning and leaving the sands.

The house really was the nearest place to the sea. Mrs

Hughes came to let them in. She laughed the nervous laugh of a landlady and pushed her hair back from her face frequently. She ushered them into their sitting room where the table was laid for supper.

'Daffydd!' it sounded like Daffydd, 'Daffydd!' she called down the passage. 'Yours is out in the back kitchen.' There was no sound from the rest of the house while Mrs Hughes hovered and poured tea for them. 'I hope he wasn't a nuisance to you Sir,' she said to the father, 'it's the company,' she said. 'He loves company, that's what it is.'

Clever thought she heard someone crying in the night.

'What is that crying?' Clever called.

'Go to sleep,' the father said. 'Go to sleep. Everything is all right. Go to sleep, clever one.

Clever sat up. There was Pretty asleep tucked in right close up to the wall and the father was in the low bed over by the window. He had pulled back the curtain so that he could see the stars. The holiday house had only one bedroom and one sitting room for holiday guests, that was all.

'I thought I heard someone crying,' Clever said.

'You were dreaming,' the father said.

Far out across the empty sands the tide was running and whispering and sighing and somewhere down in the narrow part of the house someone was crying.

'It's the sea,' the father said. He blew out the candle. 'Go to sleep!'

> *Morning has broken like the first morning,*
> *Blackbird has spoken like the first bird . . .*

Clever sang in the high piping voice of someone who is unable to sing. She felt sure, always, that Pretty liked to hear the hymns they sang at the boarding school.

> *Sweet the rain's new fall, sunlit from heaven*
> *Like the first dewfall, on the first grass . . .*

They ran together towards the foot of the mountain. It had

always a silence and a shadow, even during the day time when holiday makers climbed, and even when the sun was shining.

'*Mine is the sunlight, mine is the morning,*' Clever screeched. Mrs Hughes had noticed the missing buckle and had offered to sew on another. And so well shod, Clever felt that she flew across the sands; so firmly her foot and her sandal were one. Her voice rose, '*Mine is the sunlight, mine is the morning . . .*'

Lying on his back in the entrance to the path was Ronnie.

'The mountain's falling over me,' he said still lying down, his blue eyes bright in the peeling red face. 'Try it,' he said, still gazing upwards. Clever and Pretty lay down beside Ronnie, feet towards the mountain as he was lying.

'I thought as how it was them sea gulls coming after me,' he said, 'all that noise!' He had on a great coat with the collar turned up round his red ears.

'Have you been out all night?' Clever knew that some grown up people had strange habits.

'The mountain's falling,' Ronnie said.

High white clouds slipped across the sky, and the mountain hung over, the blunt peaks always moving towards the sea. As the white ripples of cloud raced overhead towards the town the mountain leaned and leaned slowly to fall over, to be forever falling.

'The mountain's falling,' Clever said happily. It seemed as if the earth rocked below the mountain and under them where they lay.

'I'll show youse somethink,' Ronnie said scrambling to his feet. Quickly they followed him bending double as he did through the bushes.

'Mind the bramblies,' he held the thorny stems to one side and they crawled through.

'It's not far away,' he said laughing as if to himself. He seemed excited and pleased about something. 'Mind the bramblies! Mind the pricklies!'

'What is it?' Clever wanted to know.

'Wait an' see. Just you wait an' see.'

The damp earth and stones were undisturbed and the

briars and small bushy branches sprang together after being
parted briefly.

'Here!' his red face bursting in the cold morning, he
showed them his secret abruptly.

'It's a little cave,' Clever understood with delight, 'it's a
real hidey hole!' They all crawled in to the cramped space.
They examined the little parcel of bread and the shelf with
the matches and the water bottle, and Ronnie lit the candle
which was hidden in a tin box. Under the shelf was a space
like a nest.

'This where you sleep on these newspapers?'

'Sometimes.'

'Just now? Now? Do you sleep here now? Is it comfy?'

'Yess and Yess and Yess.'

The father was whistling for them, they ran down and were
suddenly near him on the path.

'It's the breakfast is it?' Ronnie said but he did not go with
them into the holiday house.

On the white cloth there was a glass dish with slices of
beetroot in red vinegar. The father explained it would
always be on the table. Without disdaining the small offerings of the house he said they need not eat any. To show
his appreciation he ate some of the beetroot, but being unaccustomed, he took only a little.

They could hear Ronnie's mother calling him. She called
and called, 'Daffty!' It sounded like Daffty.

'Daffty that's what he is.' Clever dipped fingers of bread
and butter into an egg. 'Daffty', she said, 'is right'.

'Be kind,' the father said, 'always be kind.'

'Daffty!' they could hear the landlady calling across the
deserted, early morning sands. 'Daffty come along home,'
she called and called, 'Daffty! It won't be half so bad, you'll
see,' she called, 'you'll get used to it. If you go back now,'
she called, 'it'll not be so bad. But if you don't go. Oh Daffty!
Come home Daffty.'

As he ate his breakfast, the father seemed to listen to the
woman's voice calling from the hedge. There was no sound
of Ronnie coming home.

'Oh Sir,' the landlady said later as she stood by the smooth clean table, 'if you could just have a word with him. Maybe he'd listen to you, you being such a gentleman and a school teacher too.' She turned to Clever and Pretty, her blue eyes which were like Ronnie's bright with tears. 'Your Dadda's a lovely kind man,' she said, and then she spoke again to the father, 'See, I've pressed out his uniform, there it is.' The khaki battle dress, rough and awkward on a coat hanger, hung on the back of their sitting-room door. 'He's shy,' she went on, 'he's shy and strange, that's all it is, he's not used to going away from his home. But he'll have to go back. You see they'll come here for him. You can't get out once you've gone in.' The tears overfilled her eyes and ran steadily down both cheeks. She cried quietly as if grief simply overflowed from her because there was too much. 'It's not in his nature to kill. He wanted to join up,' she said. 'I told him "Think Daffty!" but he said he should go, he said he ought to go, and then straight away he couldn't stand it, couldn't stand any of it, the men, the camp, the strangeness. The Redcaps have been here asking for him. You do see Sir, don't you, you do see, the Redcaps will be back?'

The father, looking at her, stood up almost touching her shoulder as if to caress her with his outstretched hand.

'Yes,' he said, 'I do see.' His face was tired looking and grey and, after she had left the room, he sat for some time at the table shaking his head and sometimes resting his head in his hands.

In the house too there was a little girl and a white-faced baby with swellings in his neck. He cried with a tiny voice and the little girl carried him everywhere, all the time, rocking him in her thin arms. And his large pale head rolled from side to side on top of the swellings. The father was obliged to turn his head away and the landlady, noticing, sent her little girl to walk round and round the damp garden with the baby.

The father, agreeing to speak to Ronnie before they left, asked if the bill could be reckoned up.

Why were they leaving so soon Mrs Hughes wanted to know, they had had only one night of the holiday. Was it because the beds were not comfortable or the breakfast not to his liking, she wanted to know. The beds were not damp, she knew that, for she had aired everything herself so carefully. Was there something else they needed? She would get anything they needed for their holiday. She asked him to say outright if something was wrong and she was exceedingly sorry she said if she had burdened him with her own troubles. He was to forget everything she had said and she would see that the rest of their stay would be quiet and happy.

Again the father reached one hand towards her shoulder.

'No,' he said, 'everything you have done for us is very nice and the beds are nice too.' He told her that they would stay longer after all, he had changed his mind, he said she was not to be upset any more, he would do all he could to help Ronnie.

'See, his uniform's all ready.' Mrs Hughes stroked the battle dress. 'Tell him all he has to do is to go back,' she said.

'Hallo little miss, you playing all alone?' the soldier said laughing to Clever.

'You can't play hide and seek by yourself,' Clever replied. 'Actually, I'm playing with my sister and my Boy Friend,' she added making her mouth small and prim.

There were two soldiers, there would be one each when Pretty was found. They climbed with Clever up the mountain. All the way up they were asking and Clever answered.

'Yes, that's the house, down there, where I'm staying. Yes, my sister's staying there too,' and, 'Yes, that's where my friend lives.' The holiday house from just a part of the way up the mountain looked small and narrow inside the hedged off narrow garden.

'No, I've not known him long. He's awfully nice.' Clever, stiff faced with keeping up her boarding-school voice, sighed, 'But Sammy says I'm to consider a career before marriage.'

'Gawd! And who's Sammy when he's at home?'

'The Head, you know, my Headmistress.'

'Aw! Go on with you! She must be joking. She's an old maid. I'll bet.'

'Oh No! She's a jolly good sport. Awfully jolly.' Clever

parted the bushes and the soldiers, bending double as she did, followed her.

'Mind the bramblies! Mind the pricklies!' Clever said in her own voice with only a hint of Ronnie's. The soldiers pushed the thorny stems aside.

'It's not far away now.' Clever was excited and pleased. 'Just wait and see, it's the perfect hiding place. I didn't go straight to it though I guessed they would choose the obvious. I gave them more time, pretending to look somewhere else first.'

The small branches sprang together after being parted. Close in the game Clever could feel the soldiers' uniforms moving closer. It was as if their bodies were made of the rough cloth and their hearts were beating wildly like one excited heart on the outside of the material which alternately pressed and rubbed against her.

'Here!' Clever said showing her secret abruptly. They all crawled in.

Suddenly there was not enough room. Disbelief and terror changed Ronnie's face. Crouched in the corner under the little shelf of rock with Pretty tucked and cuddled in beside him like a kitten, he made no sound.

'Ha! so you two did choose the obvious,' Clever started to speak. 'I thought you would hide here ...' Ronnie did not seem to see her.

'Blimey! Molester! As well as deserter! Gotcha!' The soldier's open mouth did not close again. In the small space Ronnie, at eye level, seemed to spring forward. All three men were too close. The soldiers grabbed at the shiny blue serge as Ronnie brought both his hands balled into fists into their faces. And then, still crouching, rolling from his heels to his toes he rocked to and fro leaning over grunting and spreading his hands. He rocked back on the balls of his feet and forward once more, and with more exertion, he was moving forward faster. Springing, he grasped one of the soldiers round the neck. His fingers, squeezing, sank like teeth deeper into the soft pink throat. The other soldier tried to thump Ronnie's shoulders but there was not enough room.

They all rolled out together blood stained and gasping into the tunnel of the path.

'You dirty rat!' but the other soldier's sobbing was not heard by Ronnie, neither did he seem to feel the beating. Fingers like teeth still locked into the pink neck, they rolled over together through the bushes at the edge of the path. And, like a human ball, the two men went on rolling over and over sliding down the scree.

'Rat! Murderer!' the other soldier cried.

Clever, pulling Pretty by the hand, slipped quickly away from the little cave.

'The soldier won't want us to see him crying,' she said. Bending double, crawling quickly almost on hands and knees, she led the way down the narrow twisting path and soon they were walking out towards the sea. A cold change in the weather had scattered the holiday makers so they had the sands to themselves. Both were demure and, as they walked hand in hand, mincing, they played at elocution.

'Let's buy the little girl a dolly,' Clever suggested later when they walked into town to leave the purse at the police station.

'And I oft have heard defended, Little said is soonest mended.' The police officer read aloud the golden message on the purse and agreed that it was indeed a nice article and if they left their address he would send it to them if no one claimed it.

They found a toy shop easily in the holiday town and Clever chose a celluloid baby doll. As it was naked she bought a yellow duster from another shop to wrap round it like a shawl.

Everywhere there were soldiers in little groups of two or three and sometimes a lorry load of cheering singing soldiers drove through the winding street.

'Is there going to be a war?' Clever asked.

'I don't think so. I don't think so.' The father said he hoped there would not be another war.

'What's a war like?' Clever asked, knowing how he would describe it.

'It's wrong for men to have to kill each other,' the father said. 'If a man kills another man he is put in prison for the rest of his life. But in a war men are made to kill other men and it's considered honourable.' His boots, suffering, struck sparks from the cobbles of the footpath. Clever and Pretty ran to keep up with him.

'I like the Dolly,' Clever said, and telling Pretty it was her turn, she took the new doll and carried it.

They ate bread and raw carrots on the mountain and stayed there all afternoon. The sun was hidden by the clouds and the mountain seemed strange and cold and unfriendly. Down below, the holiday house looked dark and lonely on the sands. Far out, the horseman had set off on his wild ride, for though the grey shining sea was flat and calm, it would soon, from an underlying force and strength, come flowing in faster than the man on his horse; it would come running steadily round cutting off, treacherously, an island of sand from the land.

'Race you!' Clever challenged Pretty and they ran off one behind the other across the hard rippled sands. The sea gleamed, catching near the horizon a last light from behind the bank of cloud.

'Race you to the sea and back!' Clever shouted. The excitement of being in the place where land and sea meet caught Clever once more, just as it always did on that part of the train journey when there were the first glimpses of the sea before the train left the coast as quickly as it had come to it on the way to the holiday towns. She ran and ran towards the calm but fast-flowing water. The horseman had turned, a tiny figure on a toy horse, his little arms, like matches, waving and his unheard bugle too far away. Closer to the sea, the horseman was bigger but not much. All round them the water was running and Clever and Pretty were running back now to race the water as it flowed swiftly between them and the land. The expanse of water widened and deepened. The horseman, leaping in his saddle, was coming back to them but was still far away. Suddenly, Clever felt herself half lifted and half dragged. It was the water. She thought she heard Pretty crying. Again Clever felt herself lifted,

pushed and dragged. Her feet trying to touch firmness found
nothing beneath them.

'Don't youse cry now,' it was Ronnie, wet even to his hair
which was flattened making his head look like a seal's. 'Don't
youse cry now. Hold your noise. Save your breath. Now come
on with me. Both together now. Mind the water, just come
on with me. Get your breath and force your legs.'

The water was flowing so quickly, up to the waist and up
to the chest and up to the neck.

'Save your breath don't use it cryin',' Clever could hear
Ronnie. She felt his hand and arm. 'Come on!' he urged.
'Hold yer noise, don't cry! Save your breath! There's yor
Dadda comin'. My! he's as wet as uss. There's yor Dadda
comin'. Keep on with your legs. I've got a holt of you.'

'I seen them from the mountain,' Ronnie said in the
kitchen. They were all in dry things. Ronnie towelled his
head, his smile bursting his red face, peeling. 'I seen them
nearly drownding.'

Mrs Hughes, when she had helped them to get dry said
that she hoped they would be comfortable for their teas in
the kitchen as it was warmer there. Clever could see that Mrs
Hughes was pleased to be piling food on to a plate for Ronnie.

'It's a bit of a squash, this kitchen's too narrow', she
laughed the nervous little laugh of the landlady. She poured
a cup of tea for the father and put slices of bread and butter
on the cloth next to their plates. 'Eat up!' she said. 'There's
quite a storm blowing outside.'

'Dumplings,' Ronnie said. 'You like dumplings?' he asked
them.

The little girl sat a little way off with her slice. She was
nursing the pale baby. Awkwardly she managed to partly
hold the naked doll in her already filled arms. The yellow
duster was folded neatly on the mantelpiece.

The father, in the deep voice he used for teaching the boys
at the Central School, thanked Ronnie for rescuing his
daughters. He said he had never, in his whole life, seen such
bravery and he was sure his girls would remember what he

had done for them for the rest of their lives. Mr Hughes, he said, had acted very quickly and had shown great courage.

'I seen them from the mountain,' Ronnie said. He ducked over his plate and his ears were bright red. 'You like dumplings?' he asked them again.

From the front of the house came the sound of a loud knocking.

'There's someone at the front door,' Mrs Hughes looked up anxiously, her face quite white. The knocking went on and on and then there were footsteps, boots, in the hall. And all at once they were there in the kitchen. Suddenly there was not enough room. Disbelief and terror changed Ronnie's face. All the faces changed.

'The Redcaps,' Mrs Hughes whispered, trembling. She stood, well mannered, with the ladle in her hand. 'Won't you sit down?' she said to the two visitors. 'Can you do anything?' she whispered to the father. She turned to her visitors. 'Will you have some tea and bread and butter?' she asked them.

'No thank you Ma'am, we cannot sit, we are on duty and obliged to do our duty. We cannot take tea but thank you all the same,' the officer said. Both officers kept their red-topped peaked caps on. They stood awkwardly filling the small space between the door and the table. The officer, in a jerking voice, asked a few questions.

'Yes,' Clever, on the far side of the table, stood up. 'Yes,' she said, 'Yes, I saw them fall. Yes, I showed them, the soldiers, where the hidey place was. Yes, I was playing too.' Her voice was high pitched with her new boarding-school accents of honesty. 'Yes, I saw my sister with him. Yes, she had no knickers on. Yess he had them. Yess.' She was changing, answering in Ronnie's way, like when the mountain was falling.

'Yess, Yess and Yess. I saw them.'

The father, white faced like Mrs Hughes, looked across the table at her. And he looked across to Pretty too.

'Oh Sir what shall I do?' Mrs Hughes whispered, 'Oh Sir, what can I do? I am so sorry, so sorry.' She began to cry.

'There's nothing anyone can do,' the officer was brutal

under his soft moustache. 'Come along!' he jerked his head, raising his chin as he did so at Ronnie. 'The quicker and quieter the better for all concerned,' he said.

Ronnie, hardly looking up from his plate of food said, 'I don't want to go away,' he glanced quickly at his mother and his blue eyes, like hers, filled with tears. The tears overflowed and ran down his red peeling cheeks.

'Oh Daffydtee!' Mrs Hughes stretched out her arms towards her son. But the officers were already one on either side of Ronnie, and half lifting and half dragging him they escorted him from the kitchen and into the passage. The scuffling of unwilling feet was all that could be heard before the outer door slammed.

'If the man dies it's all my fault.' Clever, shrill and honest, was proud. At last she could do it, like the girls at school – 'But Sammy! It's all my fault. Honestly. Sammy'.

'What man? What man?' Mrs Hughes interrupted her dream of Sammy. 'What man?' and Mrs Hughes, as if recalling suddenly her own good manner, said, 'Eat your tea now, there's a good girl, sit down and eat your tea,' her voice trembled, 'there's a good girl, eat your tea!'

'*Our Father which art in Heaven, Hallowed be Thy Name* –' The father was kneeling on the kitchen tiles and praying aloud for Ronnie and for Mrs Hughes and for all soldiers. Clever felt embarrassed that her father should kneel down in someone else's kitchen and pray out loud. Looking across at the little girl she saw that her head was bent forward over the bundled up baby and, with her eyes tightly shut, she was moving her lips as if following the words of the father's prayer. Devoutly, Clever did the same still feeling ashamed of her father.

The journey home later that night took longer than could ever have been expected. The excursion train returning with day trippers was kept standing several times in sidings. The long pauses for no apparent reason were exhausting. At the Junction the already crowded and messy train became even more packed as soldiers, their skin roughened and pink from the khaki great coats, piled in. Soldiers, uniforms, boots and kitbags, the roughness alternately pressed and rubbed. The train began to move again, slowly. Suddenly Clever was terribly sick.

'It's all right. It's all right,' the father said gently, 'perhaps it is something you ate. You will be better soon.' He, though he had a bad headache himself, accompanied her to the lavatory, and while she was being sick some more, he held her head. Trying not to think of the holiday house, he consoled her as well as he knew how.

At home Anti Mote, in spite of her age and in previous years being unable to balance on a bicycle, had climbed a ladder.

'The ramparts,' she said, 'I paint them black in order to disguise, then the enemy will no longer be able to capture and destroy,' she explained. The mother, who had not slept, sat sewing black curtains.

'To hide our night light,' Anti Mote said. Under the stairs she had a secret store, proudly she showed them, 'Iron Rations it is called,' she nodded wisely, 'for an enemy if he comes.'

On the next day, which was Sunday, they sat by the wireless and listened to the announcement.

'Why did we go away on a holiday', Clever asked her father, 'if there was a war coming?' She watched Anti Mote comb out and cut off Pretty's hair till there was only a tuft on top like a turnip.

'My Princess must have picked up something in the train.' Anti Mote, with bandages like streamers, bound up Pretty's little head with vinegar and paraffin.

'If there was a war coming why did we go away on the holiday?' Clever asked her question again.

'I kept hoping there wouldn't be a war,' the father replied. He too was looking at Pretty.

'Don't cry!' Clever wanted to say to him. 'Oh please don't cry!' but she did not know how to say it.

The Shed

Just outside the back door is a spongy patch of ground it sinks and rises whenever I step on and off it. There is something about it to be avoided, a place not to step on because of what might be underneath. Sometimes I think I'll get a spade and dig it up and then I think better not to in case there's something curled up there better left in peace. Perhaps it's something living or it might be something dead, buried there and the ground loose still under the matted surface roots of the grass. Of course there are bulbs in the ground, perhaps it is bulbs.

From down the slope below the vineyards and beyond my orchards comes the harsh voices of young cockatoos. Somewhere down there in the paperbarks and she-oaks there must be a nest. I never thought of black cockatoos as being young ever. To me they are always big birds full grown in screaming marauding flocks flying in masses arriving with their tremendous noise, unwelcome, staying only for what they want and then moving on. I never thought about the childhood of a cockatoo. Of course they have to come from somewhere. I never thought of them pausing in their destruction to make a nest and to lay eggs.

I've just walked all the way up from the crossroads where I went to the store for onions and potatoes. There was a letter for me at the post office. I've fetched the letter too. I had to walk because there's something wrong with the mare and last week I had to leave the truck at the garage. It's stuck there down at the crossroads waiting for the delivery of a new battery.

'An old woman like you can't walk all that way in this heat,' Edgar said, he would have driven me back here but he couldn't leave the garage and I couldn't wait there all afternoon till he could close up.

I'll keep my letter for later. I'm looking forward to it. It's from England. My son's over there. I hope it's from my son. When you're all alone in the bush you're not lonely really till you get a letter and then you want to read it straight away. You're hungry to read a letter it's nearly as good as having someone visit you. Writing a letter is good too, it's like being able to talk to someone, it's like talking to your son. It's my son I'd like to talk to most, I'd like to have him talk to me too. I'd like to hear his voice.

Five miles only to the crossroads, it's nothing in the truck and not bad on horseback except that Nellie's lame and I can't ride a lame horse. I keep putting on poultices and dosing her but I'm afraid she's suffering from old age. I was up all night walking her up and down, that's the only thing for a horse with colic even if her legs are bad. It's good for human beings too. 'Never lie still with colic,' my husband used to say. 'Keep moving about and shift the wind.' He was right.

Five miles is a long way to walk with potatoes but I had the letter to look forward to. The letter feels very thick so it must be long. The address is typed. I hope it's from my son. He's been in England a long time now. He's in a university teaching mathematics. The England he knows is not the same place it was years ago. Everything changes all the time for worse and for better. We're all part of a slowly changing world. Even my stream, across the bottom of my place, is slowly changing course. In every flood the clay bank is carved out deeper on the far side or washed flatter on my side so that my pears are flooded. It's supposed to be good for pear trees to have their feet in water now and then. In a hundred years that creek will have altered course altogether.

I want to build a shed. I've had this shed in mind for years. I want a warm dry shed with space for tools and a trestle.

I want it somewhere at the side of the house but not where it will block out the view from any one of the little windows. We built this weatherboard cottage years ago and made the windows so that we could look out on all sides of the place, into the bush or down over the crops and orchards to the mud flats of the creek. If anyone is approaching from any direction I can look out and see who is there. That's why I can't make up my mind exactly where to put the shed. I've got the timber. I've had it for years. I have to keep shifting it for if you leave wood standing too long in one place in this country, white ants get at it and reduce it to a kind of corrugated dirty cardboard. You can't build a shed with dust and earth.

Every one of my little windows looks into some thing. The little windows on both sides of the fireplace are green, filled with honeysuckle, and the bedroom looks right into the scrub of blackboys and prickly moses. Every morning I can see the first light of the sun coming down through the bush lighting up the pale smooth trunks of the white gums. I spend a lot of time considering the position of the shed. At the back would be useful but I like to be able to sit in the kitchen and look out at the ground sloping up outside the kitchen window. The sun shines on the yellow stubble out there and I've got an upturned pail which shows wet spots so that I can tell at once when the rain is starting.

The letter must be from my boy, there's no one else to write to me from England. I'd like to open it at once but I'll keep it on the mantelpiece and open it a bit later on. I'll look forward to opening it. It's a long time since I had any news. He's not much of a letter writer. I suppose sums aren't like words. I've written to him. At one time I wrote every week telling him about the farm; I used to copy out the football from the paper for him and the jokes and the text for the day but his time was so taken up with his work he never wrote back. Since his marriage his wife writes at Christmas. I've got grown up grandchildren; they used to write at Christmas too but they've never seen me. I suppose I never seemed real to them.

Somewhere in the house I've got photographs of them all

dressed up in coats and leggings going out to pick black-
berries, and there's another with them all in party dresses sitting by their Christmas tree. I've stared at these photographs
trying to see as much of them and their house as I can, trying
to picture their lives. His wife, Kathryn, teaches in the university too, she always leans towards him in the photographs.
It's a kind of possessive lean. She leans with her head a bit
on one side, facing the camera and smiling and her body
bent as if to say he belongs to her. Country women stand
square beside their men as if planted and growing of themselves.

'My sweet corn don't look too healthy,' I said to him once
when he was a boy back home from school. Because of the
long distance he had to be a boarder.

'Nothing's healthy round here,' I remember his voice disagreeable with the misery he felt cooped up on the farm.
When he was a little boy he had his pet hens, he liked listening to their beaks pecking in the tin where he put the wheat
for them, he built chicken houses and pens and he made
paths but when he grew older it wasn't enough for him. As
he hacked at a log I tried to find words to comfort him but
it was so hot and there was nothing for him to do. He'd been
ill and it really was a long hot summer, we hadn't even had
a thunder storm and our usual summer rain. I could see he
was lonely too. I promised him then I'd send him to England
to his Father's people as soon as he was through school and
I kept that promise. I thought he would come back but he
never did. It suited him there, he studied hard and has made
his own way and I'm grateful for this.

Tonight when I'm resting I'll read the letter. Just now I'll
think about the shed. I'll have a window on one side and
double doors facing the west to catch the evening sun. A
shed's nice to work in when the sun's coming in. I'll have
round poles along the centre and the rafters reaching down
low on both sides so that there's an overhang, useful to have
covered places both sides of the shed. I'll have a plank floor
like a proper shearing shed though I don't go in for sheep.
There's no money in wool these days. You can't get a dollar

for a sheep and there's no sale for fat lambs even if cheap and yet a man can get seven years for stealing one.

I don't want to put the shed too far from the house. There's a kind of harmony about farm buildings, they have to be in a group which has shape and meaning. If I try to pace out the floor space and mark it off as a start here on the left of the house I see at once that the bamboo will need to be cleared out. The bamboo is a good screen and a wind-break. There's a reassurance about it too, for where there's a patch of it you know the water's not too far away. Under the earth, under this bamboo fresh clear water is running over the rock face down to replenish my stream. I like to think of this good cold water running.

On the lower slopes the sweet corn talks and whispers as it grows. The white stems thickened early and put out their fleshy green leaves. It's like a miracle every year when the cobs come pushing out from the stalks, and I want to sing, '*All good gifts around us are sent from heaven above*'. I do sing my thankfulness and my voice bruises the quiet.

All round my place the thieving goats are trying to get in. The top paddock is where they come and I've got my goat-watching chair up there. One night I fell asleep while waiting for the goats. When I woke up in the moonlight it seemed as if the trees had snow on them but it was the marri trees in flower, the creamy white clusters of flowers were tossed all over these great trees. It seemed as if my valley was dripping with honey and for days I could smell the honey.

Before I went down to the crossroads I tried to plough a bit above and below the cottage, but it's too dry and dusty. I wanted to get ahead of the season with the broad beans but I'll have to wait for the rain.

I'll go indoors. I'll leave the shed for the time being. It's no use worrying about things when you can't do much about them. Not knowing where to put the shed is like not being able to remember a verse of a hymn. I'm always trying to sing, '*Sometimes a light surprises the Christian when he sings.*' I'd like to sing this as I used to but not remembering the words stops me.

I'll go indoors and open the letter. It'll be like having my
son home for a while. I want to read his letter, I want to
know everything about him as I once did.

It's a typed letter. It's duplicated, copied by a machine.
Someone has written 'Grandma' in ink next to the duplicated 'dear'. The letter is long, it starts as if it's from a lot of
people:

'Dear Grandma once again it's time to catch the
Christmas mail. We send you our warmest greetings and our
best wishes for a happy Christmas and a good new year. The
year has been a busy and eventful one for all of us. The twins
recovered from measles and had their tonsils out and joyfully
entered secondary school. It has been a successful year for
them, both gaining the highest marks in the class. Their
taste in music is classical rather than pop and they read non-
fiction for pleasure.

'Half way through the year our new home was finally com-
pleted and we moved and settled in, all of us coping with
the necessary changes in our routine. As we are only six
houses away from the shops Kathryn can shop daily and
John can have the car without argument. The suburb is very
attractive with Tudor houses and a large fifteenth-century
church.

'Shortly before moving Edwina announced her engage-
ment and after graduating with honours she was quietly married and the buffet reception was held at a nearby hotel –'

Ah well, I suppose I'll have to read the rest of this, though
there's nothing of him, no sound of his voice and no touch
of his hand in it. It's all examination marks, interior decorating, food prices, holidays in the Alps with mushrooms
included in the breakfasts, art galleries and picture galleries,
museums and concerts. At the end his name is there with
hers and the children's but the signatures are machine copies. It's like the noise of the cockatoos screeching their news.
All these pages of successful academic activities, I keep seeing these dead words and no words for me, nothing I can
get a hold of and see and feel. It's a wonder they've had time
to build a house and lay their eggs. The last bit is all about
the election over there. I heard the result on the wireless but

this was written before that. I'm coming to the end of the letter – I'll read it to the end:

'At the moment we are facing another election with no party really knowing how to solve the serious economic problems arising from increased oil prices, particularly in view of increasing militancy and the tendency still to demand more despite a reduced national income.'

It's a big sentence, it's too big for the kitchen. I'll go up to the old chair in the top paddock for a bit and watch for them thieving goats. Starving goats can get through any kind of fence. I'll fix 'em tonight. Knowing the damage they do I'm surprised at anyone keeping goats. I'll fill 'em with pepper shot.

I can hear the cockatoos all the time. They've never stopped their screeching, a raucous gravelly noise like long big words that never stop. The parent birds must get to hate their young and yet continue to listen to them because there is no other way. How can a parent disregard the noise from the nest.

Perhaps the shed should be right outside the back door. Perhaps I should build it over that spongy patch of ground. I could start tomorrow to level it off. If it's bulbs there I won't know till the rains come. If there's something there to grow I'll see then whatever it is. Perhaps I'd better wait for the rains before I start to put up the shed and that gives me more time to think about it.

The Last Crop

In home science I had to unpick my darts as Hot Legs said they were all wrong and then I scorched the collar of my dress because I had the iron too hot.

'It's the right side too!' Hot Legs kept moaning over the sink as she tried to wash out the scorch. And then the sewing-machine needle broke and there wasn't a spare, that made her really wild and Peril Page cut all the notches off her pattern by mistake and that finished everything.

'I'm not ever going back there.' I took some bread and spread the butter thick, Mother never minded how much butter we had even when we were short of things. Mother was sitting at the kitchen table when I got home, she was wondering what to get my brother for his tea and she didn't say anything, so I said again, 'I'm finished with that place I'm not going back.' So that was the two of us, my brother and me both leaving school before we should have, and he kept leaving jobs, one after the other, sometimes not even waiting for his pay.

'Well I s'pose they would have asked you to leave before the exam,' was all she said, which was what my brother said once on another occasion and, at the time, she had nearly killed him for saying what he said about the school not wanting expected failures to stay on.

'Whatever shall I get for him?' she said.

'What about a bit of lamb's fry and bacon,' I suggested and I spread more bread, leaving school so suddenly had made me hungry. She brightened up then and, as she was

leaving to go up the terrace for her shopping, she said, 'You
can come with me tomorrow and help me to get through
quicker.'

So the next day I went to South Heights with her to clean
these very posh apartments. Luxury all the way through, one
place even has a fur-lined toilet. Mother doesn't like it as
it clogs up the vacuum cleaner.

'Let's weigh ourselves,' I said when mother had had a
quick look to see how much washing up there was.

'Just look at the mess,' she said. 'I really must get into the
stove and the fridge today somehow I've been slipping
lately.' She preferred them to eat out, which they did mostly.

'It's bringing the girls in that makes the mess,' she
complained. 'Hair everywhere and panty hose dripping all
over and grease on the stove. Why they want to cook beats
me!'

'Let's weigh ourselves,' I got on the little pink scales.

'I'm bursting,' Mother said.

'Well weigh yourself before and after.'

'Whatever for!'

'Just for the interest,' I said and when I got off the scales
I banged my head on the edge of the bathroom cupboard
which is made all of looking glass.

'Really these expensive places!' Mother rubbed my head.
'All inconvenience not even a back door! Mind you, if there
was a back door you'd step out and fall twenty-four floors
to your death. And another thing, the washing machines
drain into the baths. For all the money these places cost you
can smell rubbish as soon as you enter the building and all
day you can hear all the toilets flushing.'

Funnily enough her weight was no different after she'd
been to the toilet and we worked like mad as Mother had
some people coming into number eleven for a few hours.

'I want to get it nice for them,' she gave me the key to
go down ahead of her. 'I'll be finished here directly and I'll
come down.' As I left she called me, 'Put some sheets in the
freezer, the black ones, and see the bathroom's all nice and
lay those photography magazines and the scent spray out on
the bedside table.' She felt people had a better time in cold

sheets. 'There's nothing worse than being all boiled up in bed,' she said.

Mother's idea came to her first when she was in gaol the second time, it was after she had borrowed Mrs Lady's car to take my brother on a little holiday for his health. It was in the gaol, she told me afterwards, she had been struck forcibly by the fact that people had terrible dull lives with nothing to look forward to and no tastes of the pleasures she felt sure we were on this earth to enjoy.

'They don't ever get no pleasure,' she said to me. 'Perhaps the Pictures now and then but that's only looking at other people's lives.' So she made it her business to get places in South Heights and quite soon she was cleaning several of the luxury apartments there.

She had her own keys and came and went as her work demanded and as she pleased.

'It's really gas in there,' she used one of my words to try and describe the place. And then bit by bit she began to let people from down our street, and other people too as the word spread, taste the pleasures rich people took for granted in their way of living. While the apartments were empty, you know, I mean while the people who lived there were away to their offices or to the hairdressers or to golf or horse riding or on business trips and the things rich people are busy with, she let other people in.

First, it was the old man who lived on the back verandah of our corner grocery store and then the shop keeper himself.

'They've been very deprived,' Mother said. She let them into Mr Baker's ground floor flat for an hour once a week while she brushed and folded Mr Baker's interesting clothes and washed his dishes. She admired Mr Baker though she had never seen him and she cherished his possessions for him. She once said she couldn't work for people if she didn't love them.

'How can you love anyone you never seen?' I asked.

'Oh I can see all about them all I need to know, even their shirt sizes and the colours of their socks tells you a lot,' she said. And then she said love meant a whole lot of things like noticing what people spent their money on and what efforts they made in their lives like buying bread and vegetables or books or records. All these things touched her she said. 'Even their pills are interesting,' she said. 'You can learn a lot about people just by looking in their bathroom cupboards.'

The first time I went with her I broke an ash tray, I felt terrible and showed her the pieces just when we were leaving. She wrote a note for Mr Baker, she enjoyed using his green biro and scrawled all over a piece of South Heights note paper.

'Very sorry about the ash tray, will try to find suitable replacement.' She put the broken pieces in an honest little heap by the note.

'Don't worry,' she said to me. 'Old Baldpate up in the penthouse has a whole cupboard of things she never uses, she's even got a twenty-four-piece dinner service; you don't see many of those these days. We'll find something there. Easy. She owes Mr Baker polish and an hour of his electric clothes drier so it'll all come straight. She was forever borrowing things from one person for another and then paying them back from one to the other all without any of them knowing a thing about it.

As I was saying the old men came in once a week and had coffee served them on a tray with a thimble of French brandy and they sat in the bedroom, which was papered all over with nude arms and legs and bodies, they sat in armchairs in there as this had the best view of the swimming pool and they could watch the girls. There were always a lot of pretty girls around at South Heights with nothing to do except lie around and sunbake.

One of Mother's troubles was her own liking for expensive things, she didn't know why she had expensive tastes. She often sat at our kitchen table with a white dinner napkin on her lap.

'Always remember, they are napkins, only common people call them serviettes,' she said and she would show me how to hold a knife with the palm of the hand over the handle. 'It's very important,' she said. Anyway there she sat, dinner napkin and all, and she would eat an avocado pear before bawling at me to go down the road to get our chips.

'I just hope they had a nice time,' Mother said when we cleaned up in number eleven that afternoon. 'It's terrible to be young and newly married living in her big family the way they have to. I'll bet they haven't got a bed to themselves in that house let alone a room. All that great family around them the whole time! A young couple need to be on their own. They'll have had a bit of peace and quiet in here.' Mother looked with approval at the carpeted secluded comfort of the apartment she'd let this young couple have for a morning.

'There's no need for young people to get babies now unless they really want to so I hope they've used their common sense and modern science,' Mother went on, she always talked a lot when she was working. She said when I wasn't with her she pulled faces at herself in all the mirrors and told herself off most of the time.

'Babies,' she said. 'Is all wind and wetting and crying for food and then sicking it up all over everything and no sooner does a baby grow up it's all wanting. Wanting and wanting this and that, hair and clothes and records and shoes and money and more money. And, after one baby there's always another and more wetting and sicking. Don't you ever tell me you haven't been warned!'

She washed out the black sheets and stuck them in the drier.

'Open the windows a bit,' she said to me. 'There's a smell of burned toast and scented groins in here. Young people always burn their toast, they forget about it with all that kissing. We'll get the place well aired before the Blacksons come home or they'll wonder what's been going on.'

On the way home Mother kept wondering whatever she could get for my brother's tea and she stood in the supermarket thinking and thinking and all she could come up with was fish fingers and a packet of jelly beans.

Somehow my brother looked so tall in the kitchen.

'You know I always chunder fish!' He was in a terrible mood. 'And I haven't eaten sweets in years!' He lit a cigarette and went out without any tea.

'If only he'd eat,' Mother sighed. She worried too much

about my brother, the door slamming after him upset her and she said she wasn't hungry.

'If only he'd eat and get a job and live,' she said. 'That's all I ask.'

Sometimes at the weekends I went with Mother to look at Grandpa's valley. It was quite a long bus ride, we had to get off at the twenty-nine-mile peg, cross the Medulla Brook and walk up a country road with scrub and bush on either side till we came to some cleared acres of pasture which was the beginning of her father's land. She struggled through the wire fence hating the mud and the raw country air. She cursed out loud the old man for hanging on to the land and she cursed the money that was buried in the sodden meadows of cape weed and stuck fast in the outcrops of granite high up on the slopes where dead trees held up their gaunt arms, pitiful as if begging for something from the sky, she cursed the place because nothing could grow among their exposed gnarled boots as the topsoil had washed away. She cursed the pig styes built so solidly years ago of corrugated iron and old railway sleepers of jarrah, useful for nothing now but so indestructible they could not be removed.

She couldn't sell the land because Grandpa was still alive in a Home for the Aged and he wanted to keep the farm though he couldn't do anything with it. Even sheep died there. They either starved or got drowned depending on the time of year. It was either drought or flood, never anything happily between the two extremes.

There was a house there, weatherboard, with a wide wooden verandah all round it high off the ground. It could have been pretty and nice.

'Why don't we live there?' I asked her once.

'How could any of us get to work,' Mother said. 'It's too far from anywhere.'

And my brother said to her, 'It's only you as has to get to work,' and I thought Mother would kill him, she called him a good for nothing lazy slob.

'You're just nothing but a son of a bitch!' she screamed. He turned his eyes up till just the white showed.

'Well Dear Lady,' he said making his voice all furry and thick as if he'd been drinking. 'Dear Lady,' he said, 'If I'm the son of a bitch then you must be a bitch!' and he looked so like an idiot standing there we had to see the funny side and we roared our heads off.

The house was falling apart. The tenants were feckless, Mother suspected the man was working at some other job really. The young woman was mottled all over from standing too close to the stove and her little boys were always in wetted pants. They, the whole family, all had eczema. When a calf was born there it could never get up; that was the kind of place it was.

Every weekend Mother almost wept with the vexation of the land which was not hers and she plodded round the fences hating the scrub and the rocks where they invaded.

When we went to see Grandpa he wanted to know about the farm as he called it, and Mother tried to think of things to tell him to please him. She didn't say that the fence posts were crumbling away and that the castor-oil plants had taken over the yard so you couldn't get through to the barn.

There was an old apricot tree in the middle of the meadow, it was as big as a house and a terrible burden to us to get the fruit at the right time.

'Don't take that branch!' Mother screamed. 'I want it for the Atkinsons.' Grandpa owed those people some money and it made Mother feel better to give them apricots as a present. She liked to take fruit to the hospital too so that Grandpa could keep up his pride and self respect a bit.

In the full heat of the day I had to pick with an apron tied round me, it had big deep pockets for the fruit. I grabbed at the green fruit when I thought Mother wasn't looking and pulled it off, whole branches whenever I could, so it wouldn't be there to be picked later.

'Not Them!' Mother screamed from the ground. 'Them's not ready yet. We'll have to come back tomorrow for them.'

I lost my temper and pulled off the apron full of fruit and hurled it down but it caught on a dumb branch and hung there laden and quite out of reach either from up the tree where I was or from the ground.

'Wait! Just you wait till I get hold of you!' Mother roared and pranced round the tree and I didn't come down till she had calmed down and by that time we had missed our bus and had to thumb a lift which is not so easy now as it used to be. On the edge of the little township the road seemed so long and desolate and seemed to lead nowhere and, when it got dark, all the dogs barked as if they were insane and a terrible loneliness came over me then.

'I wish we were home,' I said as cars went by without stopping.

Wait a minute,' Mother said and in the dark she stole a piece of rosemary off someone's hedge. 'This has such a lovely fragrance,' she crushed it in her rough fingers and gave it to me to smell. 'Someone'll pick us up soon, you'll see,' she comforted.

One Sunday in the winter it was very cold but Mother thought we should go all the same. I had such a cold and she said, 'The country air will do you good,' and then she said, 'If it don't kill you first.' The cuckoo was calling and calling.

'Listen!' Mother said. 'That bird really sings up the scale,' and she tried to whistle like the cuckoo but she kept laughing and of course you can't whistle if you're laughing.

We passed some sheep huddled in a natural fold of furze and long withered grass, all frost sparkled, the blackened trunk of a burnt and fallen tree made a kind of gateway to the sheep.

'Quick!' Mother said. 'We'll grab a sheep and take a bit of wool back to Grandpa.'

'But they're not our sheep.'

'Never mind!' And she was over the burnt tree in among the sheep before I could stop her. The noise was terrible. In all the commotion she managed to grab some wool.

'It's terrible dirty and shabby,' she complained, pulling at the shreds with her cold fingers. 'I don't think I've ever seen such miserable wool,' she said.

All that evening she was busy with the wool. She put it on the kitchen table.

'How will Modom have her hair done this week?' she

addressed it. She tried to wash and comb it to make it look better. She put it on the table again and kept walking round and talking to it and looking at it from all sides of the table. Talk about laugh, she had me in fits, I was laughing till I ached.

'Let me put it round one of your curlers,' she said at last.

But even after being on a roller all night it still didn't look anything at all.

'I'm really ashamed of the wool,' Mother said.

'But it isn't ours.'

'I know but I'm ashamed all the same,' she said.

So at Mr Baker's she went in the toilet and cut a tiny bit off the white carpet, from the back part where it wouldn't show. It was so soft and silky, she wrapped it carefully in a piece of foil and in the evening we went to visit Grandpa. He was sitting with his poor paralysed legs under his tartan rug and the draughts board was set up beside him, he always had the black ones, but the other old men in the room had fallen asleep so he had no one to play a game with.

'Here's a bit of the wool clip Dad,' Mother said bending over and giving him a kiss. His whole face lit up.

'That's nice of you to bring it, really nice,' and he took the little corner of nylon carpet out of its wrapping.

'It's very good, deep and soft,' his old fingers stroked the smooth silkiness, he smiled at Mother as she searched his face for traces of disapproval or disappointment.

'They do wonderful things with sheep these days Dad,' she said.

'They do indeed,' he said, and all the time his fingers were feeling the bit of carpet.

'Are you pleased Dad?' she asked him anxiously. 'You are pleased aren't you?'

'Oh yes I am,' he assured her.

I thought I saw a moment of disappointment in his eyes, but the eyes of old people often look full of tears.

Mother was so tired, she was half asleep by the bed but she played three games of draughts and let him win them all and I watched the telly in the dinette with the night nurse. And then we really had to go as Mother had a full day ahead of her at the Heights, not so much work but a lot of arrangements and she would need every bit of her wits about her she said as we hurried home.

On the steps I tripped and fell against her.

'Ugh! I felt your bones!' Really she was so thin it hurt to bang into her.

'Well what d'you expect me to be, a boneless wonder? However could I walk if I didn't have bones to hold me up!'

The situation was terrible, really it was. Mother had such a hard life, for one thing, she was a good quick worker and she could never refuse people and so had too many jobs to get through as well as the other things she did. And the place where we lived was so ugly and cramped and squalid. She longed for a nice home with better things and she longed, more than anything for my brother to get rid of what she called his deep unhappiness, she didn't know how he had got it but it was the reason for all his growling and his dislike of good food, she longed too for him to have some ambition or some aim in his life, she was always on about it to me.

Why wouldn't the old man agree to selling his land, it couldn't do him any good to keep it. His obstinacy really forced her to wishing he would die. She never said that to me but I could feel what she must be wishing because I found myself wishing him to die, every night I wished it, and whoever really wanted to wish someone to death!

It was only that it would sort things out a bit for us.

Next day we had to be really early as, though she had only one apartment to clean, she'd arranged a little wedding reception, with a caterer, in the penthouse. The lady who owned it, Baldpate Mother called her, had gone away on a trip for three months and during this time Mother had been able to make very good use of the place.

'They're a really splendid little set of rooms,' Mother said every time we went there. Once she tried on one of Baldpate's wigs it was one of those blue grey really piled-up styles and she looked awful. She kept making faces at herself in the mirror.

'I'm just a big hairy eagle in this,' she said. And when she put on a bathing cap later, you know, one of those meant to look like the petals of a flower she looked so mad I nearly died!

Baldpate was so rich she'd had a special lift put up the side of the building to have a swimming pool made after the South Heights had been built. Right up there on top of everything she had her own swimming pool.

'It makes me dizzy up here,' Mother said. 'Is my back hair all right?' I said it was, she was always asking about her back hair, it was awful but I never said so because what good would it have done. She never had time for her hair.

'Some day I'm going to write a book,' Mother said. 'We were setting out the glasses and silver forks carefully on the table by the window. Far below was the blue river and the main road with cars, like little coloured beetles, aimlessly crawling to and fro.

'Yes, I'm going to write this book,' she said. 'I want it brought out in paperjacks.'

'Paperbacks you mean.'

'Yes, like I said, paperjacks, with a picture on the front of a girl with her dress ripped off and her tied to a post in the desert and all the stories will have expensive wines in them and countries in Europe and the names of famous pictures and buildings and there will be wealthy people with expensive clothes and lovely jewels very elegant you know but doing and saying terrible things, the public will snap it up. I'll have scenes with people eating and making love at the same time. Maybe they'll want to make a film of it, it's what people want. It's called supply and demand.'

'That's a good title.'

She thought a moment. 'I hadn't thought of a title.' She had to interrupt her dream as the caterer arrived with his wooden trays of curried eggs and meat balls, and the guests who had got away quickly from the wedding were beginning to come in. Mother scattered frangipani blossoms made of plastic all over the rooms and, as soon as the bridal couple and their folks came in, we began serving.

'People really eat on these occasions,' Mother whispered to me. She really liked to see them enjoying themselves. 'Where else could they have such a pretty reception in such a nice place for the price.' She had even put out Baldpate's thick towels and she sent a quiet word round that any guest who would like to avail themselves of the facilities was welcome to have a shower, they were welcome to really enjoy the bathroom and there was unlimited hot water.

'Show them how to work those posh taps,' she whispered to me. 'They probably have never ever seen a bathroom like this one.' And smiling all over her face, she was a wonderful hostess everyone said so, she went on handing drinks and food to the happy guests.

In the middle of it all when Mother was whispering to me, 'It takes all the cheapness out of their lives to have an occasion like this and it's not hurting anybody at all. Even sordid things are all right if you have the right surroundings and don't hurt anyone –' she was interrupted by the doorbell ringing and ringing.

'Oh my Gawd!' Mother's one fear, the fear of being discovered gripped. 'Open the balcony!' she pushed me to the double doors. 'This way to see the lovely view,' her voice rose over the noise of talking and laughing and eating. 'Bring your ice-cream and jelly out here and see the world.' She flung her arm towards the sky and came back in and hustled them all out onto the narrow space around the penthouse pool.

'No diving in,' she joked. 'Not in your clothes, anyhow.' She left me with the bewildered wedding and dashed to the door. I strained to listen trying to look unconcerned but I was that nervous. Baldpate could have come home sooner than she was expected and however would we explain about all these people in her penthouse. I couldn't hear a thing and my heart was thumping so I thought I would drop dead in front of everyone.

In a little while though Mother was back.

'A surprise guest brings luck to a wedding feast!' she announced and she drew all the people back inside for the champagne.

The surprise guest enjoyed herself very much. Mother had quite forgotten that she had told old Mrs Myer from down the bottom of our street that she could come any time to soak her feet and do her washing in the penthouse and she had chosen this day for both these things. One or two of the guests washed a few of their clothes as well to try out the machines.

'There's nothing so nice as clean clothes,' Mother said and then she proposed a special toast.

'Absent friend!' She was thinking lovingly of Baldpate she said to me. 'Absent friend!' And soon all the champagne was gone.

'Is my nose red?' she whispered to me anxiously during the speeches. Her nose was always red and got more so after wine of any sort or if she was shouting at my brother. She would really go for him and then ask him if her nose was red as if he cared. We could never see why she bothered so much.

'No,' I said.

'Oh! That's such a relief!' she said.

We were ages clearing up. Mother was terribly tired but so pleased with the success of the day. She seemed to fly round the penthouse singing and talking.

'Get this straight,' she said to me, 'One human being can't make another human being do anything. But if you are a mother this is the one thing you've got to do. Babies eat and sick and wet and sit up and crawl and walk and talk but after that you just got to make your children do the things they have to do in this world and that's why I got to keep shouting the way I do and, believe me, it's really hard!'

'Yes,' I said to her and then for some reason I began to cry. I really howled out loud. I knew I sounded awful bawling like that but I couldn't help it.

'Oh! I've made you work too hard!' Mother was so kind she made me sit down on the couch and she switched on the telly and made us both a cup of cocoa before we went home.

Grandpa was an old man and though his death was expected it was unexpected really and of course everything was suddenly changed. Death is like that. Mother said it just seemed like in five minutes, all at once, she had eighty-seven acres to sell. And there was the house too. Mother had a lot to do, she didn't want to let down the people at the South

Heights so she turned up for work as usual and we raced through the apartments.

As it was winter there wasn't anything for old Fred and the Grocer to watch at the pool so Mother put on Mr Baker's record player for them and she let them wear the headphones. Luckily there were two sets, and you know how it is when you have these headphones on you really feel you are singing with the music, it's like your head is in beautiful cushions of voices and the music is right in your brain.

'Come and listen to them, the old crabs!' Mother beckoned to me, we nearly died of laughing hearing them bleating and moaning thinking they were really with those songs, they sounded like two old lost sheep.

'They're enjoying themselves, just listen!' I thought Mother would burst out crying she laughed herself silly behind the lounge room door.

'I'm so glad I thought of it,' she said. 'Whatever you do don't let them see you laughing like that!'

Mother decided she would sell the property by herself as she didn't want any agent to get his greasy hands on any percent of that land. There was a man interested to buy it, Mother had kept him up her sleeve for years. I think he was an eye surgeon, Oscar Harvey, Mother said he should have a dance band with a name like that. Well Doctor Harvey wanted the valley he had said so ages ago and Mother was giving him first refusal.

We all three, Mother and myself and my brother, went out at the weekend to tidy things up a bit and to make sure those tenants didn't go off with things which had been Grandpa's and were now Mother's.

I don't think I ever noticed the country as being so lovely before, always I complained and wanted to go home as soon as I got there, but this time it was different. The birds were making a lot of noise.

'It's really like music,' Mother said. The magpies seemed to stroke the morning with their voices and we went slowly along the top end of the wet meadow.

'Summer land it's called,' Mother explained. And then suddenly we heard this strange noise behind us. And there

was my brother running and running higher up on the slope,
running like he was mad! And he was shouting and that was
the noise we had heard. We didn't recognize his voice, it was
like a man's, this voice shouting filling the valley. We hadn't
ever seen him run like that before either, his thin arms and
legs were flying in all directions and his voice lifted up in
the wind.

'I do believe he's laughing!' Mother stood still sinking into
the mud without noticing it. Tears suddenly came out of
her eyes as she watched him. 'I think he's happy!' she said.
'He's happy!' she couldn't believe it. And I don't think I've
ever seen her look so happy in her life before. We walked
on up to the house. The tenant was at the side of the shed
and he had just got the big tractor going and it had only
crawled to the doorway, like a sick animal, and there it had
stopped and he was supposed to get a fire break made before
the sale could go through.

My brother was nowhere to be seen but then I saw his thin
white fingers poking through the castor oil plants in the
yard.

'Halp!' and his fingers clutched the leaves and the air and
then disappeared again. 'Halp! Halp!'

'He's stuck!' Mother was laughing, she pushed through
the overgrown yard and my brother kept partly appearing
and disappearing pretending he was really caught and she
pulled at him and lost her balance and fell, both of them
laughing like idiots. Funny I tell you it was a scream and
for once I didn't feel cold there.

Mother and I started at once on the house sweeping and
cleaning. They had repaired a few things and it was not as
bad as she expected, there were three small rooms and quite
a big kitchen. Grandpa had never lived there, he had only
been able to buy the land late in life and had gone there
weekends. He had always longed for the country.

'He was always on about a farm,' Mother said, she
explained how he wanted to live here and was putting it all
in order bit by bit when he had the stroke and after that
of course he couldn't be there as it needed three people to
move him around and whatever could he do out there

paralysed like he was and then all those sad years in the hospital.

'It's not bad in here,' Mother said. 'It's nice whichever way you look out from these little windows and that verandah all round is really something! We'll sit there a bit later when we've finished.'

My brother came in, he was really keen about getting new fencing posts and wire and paint, he kept asking her, 'How about I paint the house?'

'Oh the new owner can do that,' Mother said, her head in the wood stove, she was trying to figure out the flues and how to clean them.

'Well, what if I paint the sheds then?' He seemed really interested. As she was busy she took no notice so he went off outside again.

Then we heard the tractor start up rattling and scraping over the rocks as it started up the slope to get into the scrub part which needed clearing to keep in with the regulations. Mother went out on to the verandah to shake the mats.

'Come and look!' she called me. And there was my brother driving the tractor looking proud and as if he knew exactly what to do.

'He's like a prince on that machine!' Mother was pleased. Of course he clowned a bit as he turned, pretending to fall off, once he stopped and got off as if he had to push the great thing. He hit the rocks and made a terrible noise and the tenant just stood there staring at him.

'It's been years since the tractor got up there,' he said to Mother.

We really had a wonderful day and, on the bus going back, my brother fell asleep he was so unused to the fresh air his nose and ears were bright red and Mother kept looking at him and she was very quiet and I knew she was thinking and thinking.

Next day my brother went out there by himself to try to get all the firebreaks finished, the agreement couldn't be signed till they were done also the fencing posts. Before he left he told Mother what to order and have sent out there, he suddenly seemed to know all about everything. The change in him was like a miracle, he was even quite nice to me.

As well as seeing to the sale there was Grandpa's funeral and Mother said he had to have a headstone and she came up with an inscription at the stone mason's.

'It is in vain that ye rise thus early and eat the bread of care; for He giveth his Beloved Sleep.'

I stared at her.

'I didn't know you knew the Bible.'

'I don't,' Mother said. 'It was in this morning's paper in that little square "text for today" or something like it and I think it's really beautiful and it's so suitable. I wouldn't mind having it for myself but as I'm still after the bread of care and not as yet the "Beloved" I'm putting it for Grandpa.'

There was no trouble about the price of the property. This Dr Harvey really wanted it, he had asked about the valley years ago, once when we were there, stopping his car just too late to prevent it from getting bogged at the bottom end of the track, and Mother had to say it wasn't for sale though, at the time, she said she would have given her right arm to be able to sell it but she promised him she'd let him know at once if she could ever put it on the market. We had to leave then for our bus and so were not able to help him get his car out of the mud. As he wasn't there by the next weekend we knew he must have got himself out somehow.

'You might as well come with me,' Mother said to me on the day the papers had to be signed. 'It won't do you any harm to learn how business is carried out, the best way to understand these things is to see for yourself.'

My brother had already gone by the early bus to the valley. Now that the property was ours in the true sense it seemed he couldn't be there enough even though it was about to belong to someone else. Mother watched him run off down our mean little street and she looked so thoughtful.

The weatherboard house at the top of the sunlit meadow kept coming into my mind too and I found I was comparing it all the time with the terrible back landing where our room and kitchen was. Having looked out of the windows of the cottage I realized how we had nothing to look at at home except the dustbins and people going by talking and shouting and coughing and spitting and hurrying all the time, having the same rushed hard life Mother had. Of course the money from the sale would make all the difference to Mother's life so I said nothing, she didn't say much except she seemed to argue with herself.

'Course the place means nothing, none of us ever came from there or lived there even.' I could hear her muttering as we walked.

No one can do anything with property, it doesn't matter how many acres it is, if you haven't any money, of course Mother needed the money so I didn't say out loud, 'Wouldn't it be lovely to live out there for a bit'. I guessed my brother was feeling the same though he never said anything but I saw him reading a bit of an old poultry magazine he must have picked up at the Barber's place. As a little boy he never played much, Mother always said he stopped playing too soon. But he would often bring in a stray cat and beg to keep it and play with it and stroke it with a fondness we never saw him show any other way and he would walk several streets to a place where a woman had some fowls in her backyard and he would stand ages looking at them through a broken fence picket, perhaps some of Grandpa's farming blood was in him. I wondered if Mother was thinking the same things as I was but the next thing was we were in the Lawyer's office. The Doctor was there too, very nicely dressed. I could see Mother look at his well-laundered shirt with approval. The room was brown and warm and comfortable, all polished wood and leather and a window high up in the wall let in the sunshine so it came in a kind of dust-dancing spotlight on to the corner of the great big desk.

I feel I will never forget that room for what happened there changed our lives in a way I could never even have dreamed of.

Well, we all sat down and I tried to listen as the Lawyer spoke and read. It all sounded foreign to me. Acres I knew and roods and perches that was Hot Legs all over again, same with the hundreds and thousands of dollars, it was a bit like school and I began to think of clothes I would like and how I would have my hair. The lawyer was sorting pages. I gave up trying to follow things like 'searching the title', 'encumbered and unencumbered land', instead I thought about some kneeboots and a black coat with white lapels, fur I thought it was, and there was a little white round hat to go with it.

They were writing their names in turn on different papers, all of them busy writing.

'Here,' said the Lawyer, Mr Rusk his name was, 'And here,' he pointed with his white finger for Mother to know where to put her name.

Mother suddenly leaned forward, 'I'm a little bit faint,' she said. Oh I was scared! I nudged her.

'Don't you faint here in front of them!' I was that embarrassed.

Mr Rusk asked the secretary to fetch a glass of water.

'Thank you my dear,' Mother sipped the water. I was a bit afraid I can tell you as I don't think ever in my life had I seen Mother drink cold water straight like that.

'All right now?' Dr Harvey, the owner of so much money and now the owner of the lovely valley, looked at Mother gently. He really was a gentleman and a kind one too, I could see that.

'You see,' Mother said suddenly and her nose flushed up very red the way it does when she is full of wine or angry with my brother or, as it turned out in this case, when she had an idea. 'You see,' she said to the Doctor, 'Dad longed to live in that house and to be in the valley. All his life he wished for nothing but having his farm, it was something in his blood and it meant everything to him and as it so happened he was never able to have his wish. Having waited so long for the valley yourself,' she went on to the Doctor, 'You will understand and, loving the land as you do, you will understand how I feel now. I feel,' she said, 'I feel if I could be in the valley and live in the house and plant one crop there and just be there till it matures I feel Dad, your Grandpa,' she turned to me, 'I feel he would rest easier in his last resting place.' They looked at Mother and she looked back at them.

The Doctor smiled kindly. 'Well,' he said, oh he was a generous man all right, he had just paid the whole price Mother asked. 'I don't see any harm in that.'

'It's not in the agreement,' Mr Rusk was quite annoyed but the Doctor waved his hand to quieten old Rusk's indignation.

'It's a gentlemen's agreement,' and he came over and shook hands with Mother.

'That's the best sort,' Mother smiled up at him under her shabby brown hat.

Then the lawyer and the doctor had a bit of an argument and in the end the lawyer agreed to add in writing for them to sign that we could live in the house and be in the valley till the maturity of just one last crop.

'I wish your crop well,' the Doctor came round the desk and shook hands with Mother again.

'Thank you,' Mother said.

'It's all settled and signed,' Mother told my brother in the evening. The few days of working in the country seemed to have changed him, he looked strong and sun tanned and, for once, his eyes had a bit of expression in them, usually he never revealed anything of himself by a look or a word except to be disagreeable. Mother always excused him saying the world wasn't the right place for him and his terrible mood was because he couldn't explain this to himself or to anyone and because he couldn't explain it he didn't know what to do about it. I thought he looked sad in his eyes even though we had had a bit of a spend for our tea we had ham off the bone and vanilla slices.

She told him how we could be there for one last crop.

'I'll paint the house then.'

'Good idea!' Mother said. 'We'll get the paint but we needn't rush, we can take our time getting things. We'll need a vehicle of some kind.'

'You haven't got your licence,' I said to my brother. Any

other time he would have knocked me into next week for
saying that.

'I'll get my test,' he said quietly.

'There's no rush,' Mother said.

'But one crop isn't very long.'

'It's long enough,' Mother said, she spent the evening
studying catalogues she had picked up on the way home and
she wrote a letter which she took out to post herself.

Mother was sorry to let down the people at the South
Heights so badly but after the gentlemen's agreement everything seemed to happen differently and it was a bit of a rush
for her. Already in her mind she was planning.

'We'll have the whole street out to a barbecue once the
weather changes,' she said. 'They can come out on the eleven
o'clock bus and walk up through the bottom paddocks. It'll
be a little taste of pleasure, a bit different, there's nothing
like a change for people even for one day, it's as good as a
holiday.'

The first night at the cottage seemed very quiet.

'I expect we'll get used to it,' Mother said. I meant to
wake up and see the place as the sun came through the bush
but I slept in and missed the lot.

Bit by bit Mother got things, oh it was lovely going out
to spend choosing new things like a teapot and some little
wooden chairs which Mother wanted because they were so
simple.

And then her crop came. The carter set down the boxes,
they were like baskets only made of wood with wooden
handles, he set them down along the edge of the verandah.
They were all sewn up in sacking and every one was labelled
with our name, and inside these boxes were a whole lot of
tiny little seedlings, hundreds of them. When the carter had
gone my brother lifted out one of the little plastic con-
tainers; I had never seen him doing anything so gently.

'What are they?'

'They're our crop. The last crop.'

'Yes I know but what are they?'

'Them? Oh they're a Jarrah forest,' Mother said.

We looked at her.

'But that will take years and years to mature,' my brother said.

'I know,' she seemed unconcerned but the way her nose was going red I knew she was as excited about the little tiny seedling trees as we were. She of course had the idea already, it had to come upon us, the surprise of it I mean and we had to get over it.

'But what about Dr Harvey?' Somehow I could picture him pale and patient beside his car out on the lonely road which went through his valley looking longingly at his house and his meadows and his paddocks and at his slopes of scrub and bush.

'Well there's nothing in the gentlemen's agreement to say he can't come on his land whenever he wants to and have a look at us,' Mother said. 'We'll start planting tomorrow,' she said. 'We'll pick the best places and then clear the scrub and the dead stuff away as we go along. I've got full instructions as to how it's done.' She looked at her new watch. 'It's getting a bit late, I'll go for chips,' she said. 'I suppose I'll have to go miles for them from here.' She followed us into the cottage to get her purse. 'You'll be able to do your schooling by correspondence,' she said. 'I might even take a course myself!' It was getting dark quickly. 'Get a good fire going,' she said.

We heard her drive down the track and, as she turned onto the road, we heard her crash the gears. My brother winced, he couldn't bear machinery to be abused but he agreed with me that she probably couldn't help it as it's been quite a while since she had anything to drive.

FOR THE BEST IN PAPERBACKS, LOOK FOR THE

In every corner of the world, on every subject under the sun, Penguin represents quality and variety – the very best in publishing today.

For complete information about books available from Penguin – including Pelicans, Puffins, Peregrines and Penguin Classics – and how to order them, write to us at the appropriate address below. Please note that for copyright reasons the selection of books varies from country to country.

In the United Kingdom: For a complete list of books available from Penguin in the U.K., please write to *Dept E.P., Penguin Books Ltd, Harmondsworth, Middlesex, UB7 0DA*

In the United States: For a complete list of books available from Penguin in the U.S., please write to *Dept BA, Penguin, 299 Murray Hill Parkway, East Rutherford, New Jersey 07073*

In Canada: For a complete list of books available from Penguin in Canada, please write to *Penguin Books Canada Ltd, 2801 John Street, Markham, Ontario L3R 1B4*

In Australia: For a complete list of books available from Penguin in Australia, please write to the *Marketing Department, Penguin Books Australia Ltd, P.O. Box 257, Ringwood, Victoria 3134*

In New Zealand: For a complete list of books available from Penguin in New Zealand, please write to the *Marketing Department, Penguin Books (NZ) Ltd, Private Bag, Takapuna, Auckland 9*

In India: For a complete list of books available from Penguin, please write to *Penguin Overseas Ltd, 706 Eros Apartments, 56 Nehru Place, New Delhi, 110019*

In Holland: For a complete list of books available from Penguin in Holland, please write to *Penguin Books Nederland B.V., Postbus 195, NL–1380AD Weesp, Netherlands*

In Germany: For a complete list of books available from Penguin, please write to *Penguin Books Ltd, Friedrichstrasse 10 – 12, D–6000 Frankfurt Main 1, Federal Republic of Germany*

In Spain: For a complete list of books available from Penguin in Spain, please write to *Longman Penguin España, Calle San Nicolas 15, E–28013 Madrid, Spain*

Also by Elizabeth Jolley

Mr Scobie's Riddle

Mr Scobie's arrival at the nursing home of St Christopher and St Jude – and into the clutches of Matron Hyacinth Price – is accidental. Self-educated and still preserving the gift of idyllic memory and wish, Mr Scobie stands apart from the others. For long-term resident and eccentric, Miss Hailey, he represents a kindred spirit; for Matron Price – a lady of questionable practices – the latest victim . . .

But unwittingly Mr Scobie has some recourse – his very simple riddle. Its answer – an ancient commonplace – jolts Matron Price.

Yet it is Mr Scobie's nephew, Hartley, and the group of nocturnal poker players, who ultimately change Matron Price's establishment.